A GRAVESIDE GALLERY: TALES OF GHOSTS AND DARK MATTERS

Fiction Written by Eric J. Guignard

Doorways to the Deadeye (JournalStone, 2019)

A Graveside Gallery: Tales of Ghosts and Dark Matters (Cemetery Dance Publications, 2025)

Last Case at a Baggage Auction (Harper Day Books, 2020)

That Which Grows Wild: 16 Tales of Dark Fiction (Cemetery Dance Publications, 2018)

Anthologies Edited by Eric J. Guignard

After Death... (Dark Moon Books, 2013)

Dark Tales of Lost Civilizations (Dark Moon Books, 2012)

Fantasmagoriana Deluxe (with Leslie S. Klinger) (Dark Moon Books, 2023)

The Five Senses of Horror (Dark Moon Books, 2018)

+Horror Library+ Volume 6 (Cutting Block Books/ Dark Moon Books, 2017)

+Horror Library+ Volume 7 (Dark Moon Books, 2022)

+Horror Library+ Volume 8 (Dark Moon Books, 2023)

+Horror Library+ Volume 9 (Dark Moon Books, 2026)

Pop the Clutch: Thrilling Tales of Rockabilly, Monsters, and Hot Rod Horror (Dark Moon Books, 2019)

Professor Charlatan Bardot's Travel Anthology to the Most (Fictional) Haunted Buildings in the Weird, Wild World (Dark Moon Books, 2021)

Scaring and Daring (HarperCollins, 2025)

A World of Horror (Dark Moon Books, 2018)

Exploring Dark Short Fiction (A Primer Series) Created by Eric J. Guignard

#1: A Primer to Steve Rasnic Tem (Dark Moon Books, 2017)

#2: A Primer to Kaaron Warren (Dark Moon Books, 2018)

#3: A Primer to Nisi Shawl (Dark Moon Books, 2018)

#4: A Primer to Jeffrey Ford (Dark Moon Books, 2019)

#5: A Primer to Han Song (Dark Moon Books, 2020)

#6: A Primer to Ramsey Campbell (Dark Moon Books, 2021)

#7: A Primer to Gemma Files (Dark Moon Books, 2025)

**The Horror Writers Association Presents: Haunted Library of Horror Classics
Edited by Eric J. Guignard and Leslie S. Klinger**

Vol. I: The Phantom of the Opera by Gaston Leroux (Sourcebooks, 2020)

Vol. II: The Beetle by Richard Marsh (Sourcebooks, 2020)

Vol. III: Vathek by William Beckford (Sourcebooks, 2020)

Vol. IV: The House on the Borderland by William Hope Hodgson (Sourcebooks, 2020)

Vol. V: Of One Blood: or, The Hidden Self by Pauline Hopkins (Sourcebooks, 2021)

Vol. VI: The Parasite and Other Tales of Terror by Arthur Conan Doyle (Sourcebooks, 2021)

Vol. VII: The King in Yellow by Robert W. Chambers (Sourcebooks, 2021)

Vol. VIII: Ghost Stories of an Antiquary by M.R. James (Sourcebooks, 2021)

Vol. IX: Gothic Classics: The Castle of Otranto by Horace Walpole (Sourcebooks, 2022)

Vol. X: The Mummy! by Jane Webb (Sourcebooks, 2022)

A GRAVESIDE GALLERY: TALES OF GHOSTS AND DARK MATTERS

Eric J. Guignard

Cemetery Dance Publications
Forest Hill, MD
2025

A Graveside Gallery: Tales of Ghosts and Dark Matters

Interior design by Eric J. Guignard
Cover design by Eric J. Guignard
www.ericjguignard.com

Cover art by Alexander Nazolkin: *Porcelain* (2022)
www.deviantart.com/nazolkin

First edition published by
Cemetery Dance Publications in April, 2025
ISBN-13: 978-1-964780-17-7 (e-book)
ISBN-13: 978-1-964780-16-0 (trade paperback)

First Harper Day Books edition
published in April, 2025
ISBN-13: 978-1-949491-61-6 (hardback)

Library of Congress Cataloging-in-Publication Data
A graveside gallery: tales of ghosts and dark matters / Eric J. Guignard.
Library of Congress Control Number: 2024952840

Cemetery Dance Publications
132-B Industry Lane, Unit #7
Forest Hill, MD 21050
www.cemeterydance.com

10 9 8 7 6 5 4 3 2 1

(V033125)

Dedicated in memory of Weston Ochse (1965–2023):
Author, Adventurer, Mentor, and Friend.

CONTENTS

PENNY'S DINER

UP here in North Dakota, the highways at night look like they run on forever, way each turns a hypnotic line that wavers, shimmers, sucks you in once the sun has died out. Highway 81 or 29, Route 220 or 18, they all appear the same in the dark, in the snow, cut-outs of prairie land glistening under a frost-white moon.

From Pembina to Grand Forks to Grandin, Harper's been driving three hours straight, and it suits him just fine. He likes the long stretches, the sense of communion with the road. Watching the occasional cars shoot past the other way, the approach from nothing but a twin-halo of headlamps transforming into a shotgun-racked pickup or a family-filled jalopy, a flash-glimpse as he looks down on the driver's face, of another life as they cross lanes. Harper's good at that, catching the glimpse of someone, just that slash of a second when the windows are at the right angle, holding the view in his head . . . of course tonight, the trick is all screwed up, the perspective changed.

He feels the road dipping, and his hand drops to downshift by instinct; with ice on the highway, it's a real danger. Only there's no gear shifter, and Harper has to remind himself he's not driving his 50,000-lb. rig, but a little V-6 sedan automatic instead. The turns are easier, the acceleration faster, the view like he's belly-down sliding on the asphalt. It's hard to reconcile the difference, going from an 18-wheel tractor-trailer he's driven twenty years to this little kid's toy of a rental. It's hard to reconcile too, what happened earlier, and that's the shitter of it all. Life and its effects, and why Harper hangs onto those flash-glimpses of faces sometimes, imagining what it'd be like to be someone else, somewhere else. Imagining anyone else but the pale woman . . .

Three hours, and Harper has to piss. He's hungry, and cold too. Heaters in these little imports ain't much stronger than to keep himself barely thawed. A turn-off could do some good. Coffee and a steak, maybe a sweet pie to cap it off, just the right amount of sugar and caffeine afterward to wire him up another two hours 'til he gets home.

A weather-faded sign rises from the road, splashed by his headlights: *Turnoff 22 Next Right: Food. Gas.* Harper prepares for deceleration, calculating his stopping distance, his foot searching to double-clutch and slide in, spine anticipating the drop in RPMs, that shudder of the diesel, until he remembers—again—the fucking mess of the day that took away his rig and put him in this Budget-Rental sedan.

He accelerates instead, just to do something different, until he feels the tires start to lose traction on an icy skid, and he taps the brakes to take back control.

Cars whiz past, markers, more traffic signs, and Harper hits the turnoff, swings out onto the county's double-lane and carries on for another quarter mile until a crossroad slices through like a knife. There's a set of buildings at one corner there, a rural stop-over. The buildings though are mostly dark: a general store—cracked signage reading *Dry Goods, Grain, Soda.* A second sign, smaller: *Closed.* There's the gas station, with warped plywood boards nailed over the windows, and a hand-painted notice reading "No Fuel, Thanks Carter." A commercial depot, all stained aluminum walls and padlocks, giving nothing away as to its purpose. Above it, like a sentient eye, a water tower looms upward, scarred by buckshot, bird shit, and a four-foot-high company logo of a rose.

One sole building in the lot's midst appears open, and it is fortuitously a narrow caboose of a diner. It's stream-lined silver with some 50s-era accoutrements, a smiling waitress made of fluorescent bulbs that probably hasn't glowed for two decades, some dinner specials written in soap on the windows, and a long parking area with no cars. But the lights are on inside, and there's a drift of smoke flitting up from a roof vent.

Harper turns there, parks in the middle, and crunches through a crust of brittle snow to the entrance, rubbing his hands together, watching his breath whoosh out into skittish clouds. The diner is called Penny's, and there's a sign telling him it's open. Fact is, there's all kinds of signs at Penny's, signs about hours and rules, and cute country-quotes, like the one branded on the welcome board, reading: *In For a Penny, In For a Pound . . . of Chuck Beef!*

A bell chimes real gently when he enters. The diner looks empty, but he smells all he needs to know otherwise: a rich, heady aroma of coffee; the sweet tang of grilled onions; beef slow-simmering in cloves and butter. His stomach rumbles. His skin warms to the heat. The floor is checkered black and white, the counter red Formica and fronted by a line of vinyl stools every few feet. He sits at one, remembering eating at places like this as a boy with his parents, these streetcar-styled greasy spoons. His father always wanted more, some ritzy French house where you had to wear ties to dine, and everyone talked about the vintage of sauvignons or some shit. But for Harper, places like this were salt of the earth.

He looks around, sniffles. "Hello?"

A door swings open at a short hall off the diner's rear side, and a woman's head prairie-dogs out. "Heya, be there in a jiff."

Another sign on the wall with a stick figure clacking its heels together exclaims, *Eureka, Restrooms!*

"No rush." Harper paws at a coffee mug-ringed section of newspaper stacked under a napkin dispenser. The counter's worn, smeared. Some crumbs are nestled in the cracks. It bothers him somehow, things that shouldn't be there.

A young, dark-skinned man appears, passing into the kitchen. His hair is in a net, his mustache faint and trim, and he's wearing a grease-stained apron over striped pants and jersey. In another life, he could've been a movie star or a mag model, this cook. He does a double-take at Harper, follows with a nod. "Say, evening."

Harper gives a lazy two-finger salute. "Howdy."

"Snow comin' down out there?"

"A little, you know. Not bad, some flakes, just enough cold to bite."

The man interlocks his fingers, gives a big stretch, a yawn. "Gonna pick up later."

"I heard. Hoping to get home before it starts."

"Far to go?"

"About a hundred miles."

"You should make it."

Harper nods, slides out the sports section. Sees Bud Grant led the Vikings to another victory over Green Bay, two touchdowns thrown by Tommy Kramer, and he isn't surprised, but he isn't in much of a mood to read, either. He killed a woman today, he killed a woman, he killed a woman, and he can't stop thinkin' it, and it wasn't his fault, but he killed a woman, a pale woman with blond bobbed hair, and he can't get over the whole fucked-up world—

"What'll it be, hon?"

The waitress is facing him, eyes as blithe as they are searching, and it startles Harper. She's on the downslope to middle age, auburn hair bobby-pinned back, some crow's feet forming around her eyes, but the kind that come from laughing. She's got a plaid jacket on over her buttercup-yellow uniform; the jacket's unbuttoned, and Harper sees the name tag reads Janice.

"Coffee to start, a glass of water too, please."

She gets it for him. Harper takes the coffee black.

"Have anything else in mind, or you want me to run through our specials?" She directs his attention to a menu board of food items and prices. He notices next to it, and then beyond, a line of framed signs, filling the diner's walls and even slung off the side of the brass cash register. More of those cute country-quotes, hand-lettered in chalk and acrylic, riffing on the diner's name:

When Asked a 'PENNY For Your Thoughts?', Let 'em Know it's the Veal Cutlet!

Don't Be a Penny-Pincher When It Comes to Dessert—Put the à la Mode on that Apple Pie!

What Gets Cooked Here is Worth Every 'Penny'!

"What's on the stove right now?" Harper asks.

"Beau's grillin' up some Salisbury steak. Comes with mashed potatoes and string beans."

"I could do with that."

"All right." She relays the order to the cook.

"I got one," Harper tells her.

Janice turns to him. "What's that, mister?"

"The jingles posted around here, the signs. One came to me you could use: 'Be penny-wise and pound-cake-foolish.' Get it?"

She gives a laugh, the kind responsible for those crow's feet coming in around her eyes, and waves a nub of a pencil in Harper's direction. "More like, 'A bad penny always turns up'."

He stares at her incredulously, suddenly unmoving. *Was that a crack at him, a bad penny showing up? What the hell did that mean?*

She catches on quick, pats his hand. "Oh, honey, not you. It's the diner I'm talking about, some old superstition."

"Oh, right. Sorry, just edgy is all."

She laughs again, a sound warmer than any furnace. "Driving late at night out here'll do that."

"I'm used to it."

"You night-drive much?"

"Me and my rig have been at it over twenty years," he says proudly.

Janice strains her neck looking out the front plate glass window, at the view of a dark parking lot and a sedan, of frost-topped pasture lands beyond, and the stretching finger of Highway 81 pointing far off, wearing a sprinkling of lights like ornaments.

She waves the pencil nub again. "That yours, the car? Kinda small for a rig."

It's Harper's turn to laugh, only his is a bitter, broken sound. Hollow as the gravel throat of Highway 32 breaking off to Walhalla. "I was in an accident today, went off the road. Front axle bent, threw a rod. Repair service is working on her, but it'll be a week or so. Insurance company sent me home in a loaner."

"Oh, hell. You okay?"

"Yeah, I . . . it's not me, I mean." Harper's voice cracks. "I killed a woman, though. I killed her. She jumped right in front of me, a suicide, cops said. This woman, she just . . . just jumped into the road, and laid down, like she was gonna sleep . . . I tried to stop, to swerve, but with a twenty-ton load, there wasn't a chance, y'know? I ran her over, and went off the highway, went into a ditch, this woman's guts dragging under my locked brakes like goddamned streamers . . . There was a shoe left behind, on the road, nothing but a red smear and a blue loafer, the type with a bow on it, and the woman's face . . . her face . . . I do this thing where I glimpse driver's faces, people I see on the road, and I hold that view in my mind, like a photograph, so to make up shit about who they might be, their life, and I did it for her, oh God, I did it for this lady, right before she laid down and I ran her over, and now she's stuck in my head, this pale face with a crooked nose, blond bobbed hair, eyes like a fog rolling in, and I killed her . . . "

For a moment, the diner seems frozen, even the smells, the steam coming off the grill is hung on itself, a trick of time with just the hitching of Harper's voice to reset it.

Janice purses her lips, one hand going to her breast. She takes Harper's hand with the other. "I am so sorry, honey. Lord, you don't deserve it. No one deserves to go through that."

The cook knocks over something metal that clangs to the tile floor. "Blue loafer with a bow on it?"

"I'm sorry," Harper sobs, "sorry to unload on you like that . . . It just came out, what I've been holding in, it . . . I couldn't stop it."

Janice makes a face at the cook and squeezes Harper's hand tighter. "What you went through, it's not your fault. Remember that. And I know your heart hurts, but pains like those find a way to work themselves out."

Harper gets up suddenly, flustered, embarrassed, rubbing his eyes, wanting to flee the moment. He mumbles, "I gotta use the john."

"Over there," she points.

Beau the cook shakes his head, whispering in awe. "God damn, just like you called it, the bad penny."

Harper crosses the diner to the entrance of a short hall, where the sign with the stick figure reads, *Eureka, Restrooms!* The woman rises up in Harper's mind, the pale face, the blond bobbed hair, the dead eyes . . . the red smear afterward. The last sign he'd read had been: WINNIPEG, 70 MILES. And then *her*, the woman who'd ran and dropped in front of him. Harper can still feel the cab bumping up over her body, then coming down, while he slammed the brakes, spun the wheel . . . His eyes blur with tears now, and he wants to punch something suddenly, kick over a table, shriek. Bathroom signs, diner signs, highway signs everywhere telling him what to do, how to behave. A lifetime of following signs, reading signs, doing what the signs said. Signs needed to provide identity, to give warning, to evoke a laugh, to make a sale, to make a threat . . . But there wasn't any sign for what he went through today, was there? No "Beware Suicide" forewarning him, advising him how to act.

He walks on. Inside the hall are two restroom doors, one marked GENTS and one LADIES. On the wall across from the doors is hung a big framed photograph with a black ribbon wrapped around the edge. His heart stops: It's a picture of the woman he killed—pale face, crooked nose, blond bobbed hair. A gold-foil name plate reads: *In Memoriam to the Founder of Penny's Diner: Penny Turner, March 18, 1907–December 3, 1959. R.I.P.*

Death date, twenty years ago.

Harper turns real slow, wanting to demand what the hell is going on, but then he sees the two of them, Janice and Beau, standing there by the counter, shaking their heads sorrowfully, oh so sorrowfully.

And there's another person, too, moving steadily toward him in her blue loafers, the types with a little bow over each tongue, and instead of trying to run down that hall with no exit, he thinks absurdly that the bad penny wasn't him or the diner at all.

A KINGDOM OF SUGAR SKULLS AND MARIGOLDS

HEY pachuco,

You ever seen the lights go green in a lady's eyes when she takes the hand of a man made of bones? He's dressed like the finest of charros with his greca suit of black and gold that twinkles as stars in a moonless night, and the buckle of his piteado belt is carved from sacred jade. He could be the mariachi of dreams, though for all the voice of his song he don't play no music, he just dances.

He's a badass *chingón* too; even if just a thing of bones, you wouldn't mess with him. He wears this big top hat instead of a sombrero, and it's tall as an eagle can fly, all shiny black with a silk band around its crown covered in roses and cockscomb and chrysanthemums, and it's crazy the hat never moves while he dances, and somehow you get this feeling you don't want it to move either, because if it did, it'd be bad, even though it's a skull already wearing this hat, just a skull with carnival paint and sweet candy hearts, but what's under the hat is still worse . . .

And he don't stop dancing for nothing.

With *her*.

The lady whose eyes go green, whose face turns a cobweb of stitches, a slash of crosshatch lips in the shape of a heart, an empty cutout of eyes surrounded by whorls of orange, surrounded by azure, surrounded by crimson, all curled-up squiggles, like a wind washing long hair down a pale-faced chasm, and they dance until she's gone.

That's how death takes you, okay?

And that lady, pachuco, she could be a man, too. She could be anyone, even you.

Órale . . .

I KNOW you'd ask, wouldn't you? How I woke in the morning to realize I'd fucked up twice?

No *madre* around, I know you'd ask that too, if I kiss her with this mouth, but the *puta* ran off when I was three, left me and Papá and my sisters for some *wheto* bandleader . . . I wonder what'll happen when she dies; she won't be mourned here. Where do the lonely souls go, the sad girls?

So when I wake, it's just me in the kitchen, and my aching head is lying on the table feeling like a punching bag that's overstuffed, 'cause maybe I drank too much last night . . . maybe I passed out thinking of Santi.

And like I said, I'm alone, but also there's this voice speaking in my ear.

"Hey, vato," the voice says. "Hey, sleepyhead, wake up."

I crack open my eyes, and light in the kitchen burns like the sun has a grudge, and all I can do is squint. The kitchen is turned sideways too, the mezcal bottle looking knocked over, it should be pouring into my face.

"You going to sleep the day away?" It talks fast, this voice, but it's quiet too, like whispering some urgent secret.

I groan and suck in the drool that's puddled by the crack of my mouth. Inside my mouth it's dry as sand, like all the spit worked its way out and stuck the side of my face to the tabletop, you know?

"Pachuco, you won't like if I have to wake you."

I lift my head real slow, and the kitchen turns how it should. I blink, and the light gets less bright, just a yellow bulb and some rays slipping through messy curtains. Okay, better, so I look around, but there's no one else, maybe I'm imagining things. Besides the drool I left on the table are the skull, the bottle, the switchblade, and the book.

"*Cojeme*," I mutter. You don't get hung over with mezcal like you do tequila, but you still feel like a couple rocks go grating in your head.

I could blame Yoli I'm like this, since she left the mezcal open on the counter like a gift not just to Papá but to me as well. But then again, maybe it's my own fault . . . Maybe I should finally grow up and shit. Yoli's mezcal knocks your ass out like a Kid Gavilan bolo punch, and I knew it would.

"There you are."

The voice again, and no one's around. It's stupid, but all I can say is, "Who's talking?"

"*¡Órale!*" the skull on the table answers, all excited like a dog you reward for doing a good trick.

I startled, and you'd think I should have reacted more, but my brain just doesn't get it. "How?"

"Don't you know, vato? You're the one made me."

That's true, I guess, out of sugar and water and meringue powder. Some paint, some icing . . . But I didn't make it to talk. "Who are you?"

"Read my name, pachuco."

Though my eyes are all bleary, I look what I'd written on its eggshell brow. The letters are carved between frosted vines, Cupid hearts, playing card spades.

"Santi?"

"You need go back to school," the sugar skull answers. "Learn your letters."

I rub my eyes twice, each lid feeling made of cement. Focus. The skull is life-sized, I'd inked some crazy work on it: red scar stitching that pulled its rictus grin up razor-sharp cheekbones, and a classy butterfly spread-winged across the cavity that would have been a nose. Above the green swirls and flames of orange are the letters I carved last night, but something's wrong with them: they don't spell what they're supposed to. My breath hisses out, "*Ay wey.*"

I'd switched two letters . . . instead of *SANTI,* I'd carved the name, *SAINT*. Which is how I fucked up the second time. And I haven't even said anything yet about the *first* time.

I turn my head away from the skull. "No, you ain't real."

"Don't disrespect me. You think I'm a dream, open your eyes."

I do. I turn back. Nothing changes.

"Happy?" Saint asks.

"No."

On my way to the faucet to dunk my head, it all comes back, revving, rushing in my mind, flashbacks of making sugar skulls with my sisters, Yoli and Li'l Chica.

See, Yoli turned the back porch into an art studio couple years ago. She's got all the marionettes and ceramic animals with stars for eyes and shit, the masks that laugh through one mouth and cry through another. You never seen skill like hers, weaving dried peppers into moon faces, painting pictures of Mayan gods and these warriors fighting under night-sky pyramids, and they don't wear no protection but for bird feathers, it's crazy.

She got us to make our own skulls for Dia de los Muertos this year instead of buying from the old ladies in market stalls on every corner in the 'hood. You just mix the ingredients in a mold and let dry, and yesterday they were ready. So we decorated while listening to AM radio, where Miguel Aceves Mejía sang his heart out in "Tú Solo Tú," and no one could sound better, 'cept maybe that cowboy yodeler, Bill Haley, who came on next with "Rocket 88" that was *chinga* cranked.

Yoli made her skull for Papá, and Chica made her skull for Abuelita, and I made mine for Santi . . .

I hack and spit into the sink, rinse my mouth, run water through my hair, until my head feels a little better. I turn back, admitting, "I don't know what I was thinking last night."

"Not strange for you, pachuco," Saint says, "and that's a problem."

"Yoli said maybe the spirits could visit, you call them right, being Day of the Dead, you know?"

"Maybe they do. Maybe there are other ways to save them."

I grab the bottle of mezcal off the table and take a gulp straight from its lip. "Who needs saving?"

"Besides you? You tried calling someone else, I think."

I did.

It's Yoli who also inherited this big ass book of black magick, *Brujería Magia Negra* . . .

The autumn heat had cooled to ice when the sky broke yesterday, and Yoli started messin' around with that book, reading things, lighting candles, and her novio, Dante, came over, and we opened up the mezcal that was supposed to be a gift to Papá's altar, and Dante smoked out the room with joints of hash and ground-up peyote. Yoli spoke about calling back spirits, if you carve their name into the sugar skull and read this certain passage, and I started seeing things, I was fucked-up, but that was it.

I didn't read none of her book, I didn't say none of the chants, I don't mess around with that shit . . .

Until they left, and I was alone, everyone else partying on the streets for the festival. I could have gone too, but I couldn't, if that makes sense . . . I mean, me and Santi used to roll together every year since we were little, and me doing it without him just made me fuckin' cry.

I couldn't do nothing but sit at the kitchen table with the skull I made for him, and something in my chest grew all heavy, and I started drinkin' more, and I started talking to Santi, like why it had to go like that . . .

And somehow Yoli's book of black magick ended up in my hands and, like I said, I don't mess around with that shit, but maybe I spoke a few words . . . Maybe I read from some pages things I don't understand, but said them anyway, out loud, like a certain passage, while I carved Santi's name with a switchblade into the skull.

"Hey, you with me, or you back in la-la land?" Saint asks.

"So, what now?" My question is a shrug.

"Go say hello."

"To who?"

Sudden as Chivo's gunshot, there's a *clack-clack-clack* sound coming from the sitting room. I don't know what it is, and part of me doesn't want to find out. It's the kind of sound don't belong in a home, a sound like tap dancers moving on *American Bandstand*, their shoes making that sharp clatter on the wood floor when they step hard and fast.

"You got a visitor, vato."

I eye Saint wearily and flick open my switchblade. "Someone like you, or I gotta cut a fool?"

"Why don't you find out."

Again: *Clack-clack-clack.*

I push through the swinging saloon doors and would've screamed right there if my voice hadn't fled for my balls.

There's a skeleton in the room, walking around as if no problem, smoking one of Papá's cigarettes we left on his remembrance altar. It isn't a corpse, not like scarecrow-ragged or anything, no blood, no dirt, no worms crawling from its eyes, but it's clean, okay, like a cartoon skeleton, pale and scrubbed, every bone in place. It's dressed to the nines too, better than I could do, like it's going dancing at the Cocoanut Grove. The skull has a real thin mustache, like how Papá had, and it wears these big steel rings on its bone fingers like Papá used to wear—his *thumpers*, is what he called them—for street brawling.

It's looking at the altar, where a photo still shows Papá's face—no smile—behind a frame of glass, decked out in brimmed tando as wide as his shoulders, and the starched white collar of his satin shirt flares over a fingertip coat no one could wear so well. The R.I.P. in lipstick is Li'l Chica's, and the collection of votive candles is from Abuelita, one for each saint she brought from Juárez, which number more than the altar can hold. Abuelita's own mourning altar is across the room; she followed Papá three years later to the underworld of Mictlan.

Eight years ago, I was twelve, when Papá got beat in East L.A. by sailors with baseball bats and lead pipes. Papá got beat so bad, his head looked like a piñata busted open, and all the little candies pour out.

Those are the candies now painted over the face of this skeleton.

It turns to me, wearing those same clothes from the picture, and it says my name: *Clack-clack-clack.*

Saint's voice comes from the kitchen. "Family reunion, *ey*, vato?"

It's Papá who lifts up his big bony arms for a big Papá hug, and I don't want to touch him, but I ain't got a choice either; he's coming to me, and I have my switchblade in hand and could cut through a rib, but I'd never raise a hand to him, even if he's just a dead thing clacking my name over and over, and so we embrace.

And there's a fuckin' trickle of water coming down my eye, that's how it makes me feel, but I've been all kinds of somber emotions lately too.

"You going to leave me out?" Saint asks, like he's lonely.

When Papá lets go, he goes into the kitchen and brings the sugar skull back, held in the clattering crook of an elbow that looks like a yo-yo, the way it swings loose back and forth.

"This is all kinds of nuthouse," I tell them, shaking my head from one to the other. "I don't even know."

"This ain't nothing. You wanna see some shit? Let's roll, paint the town, get some skull *heinas*."

Clack-clack-clack.

They don't glance back, Papá and Saint just fling open the front door and walk outside.

I follow, and the door frame creaks when I grab it for support, because my legs go to soup at what I see. I almost turn away, though it's no more crazy than talking to a skull made of sugar or of dead Papá carrying it around.

Jet-black and electric blue: that's the night sky, shimmering and buzzing like lights of an all-night diner, while agate-dusted shades zoom by, darting through alleys of a crowded universe. My eyes fight to adjust, to make sense, because the crescent moon is this sideways grin of teeth, clamping a cigar that blows puffs of firecracker flares, which drip shadows onto the hands I shoot up in reflex. The stars pulse too, like you've never seen. They're glitter pinwheels and pink hearts and lemon snow cone twirls, and the pin-striping of a Chevy hardtop runs across it all in zigzag waves like stitchwork that if you undid, everything would fall apart . . .

Your head would spin dizzy, you tried looking too long.

All I could stutter is, "What . . . " and, "How . . . " and, "Where's the daylight . . . ?"

"It's midnight, vato."

"It's only morning, like ten."

"It's Dia de los Muertos, pachuco. It's always midnight."

I nod, *okay*, and I know this is crazy, but I kinda felt I belonged too, as much as you *can* belong walking into the page of some dime-store comic.

"*¡Órale!*" Saint exclaims at my lowrider. "Your bomba is slick. Shotgun!"

I don't even recognize my Impala, parked curbside, it's been changed. The trunk is popped open like a casket of red silk, but instead of a corpse it overflows with wild marigolds, bright in every hue of gold;

my wheels are nothing but tribal suns, dark blue as tattoo ink, surrounded by whirling flames; and the car's paint job is of skulls, I mean every skull you could want, funny skulls with winking eyes, vicious skulls with fangs for teeth, even *mamacita* skulls lookin' sexy with emerald smoke simmering from empty sockets, and all these skulls got teeth that are clattering.

Papá gets in back right behind the driver's seat and places Saint so he'll sit next to me.

"Rev it up," the sugar skull says.

"Where we going?"

"Where you think?"

Clack-clack-clack.

And I guess I knew all along where I'm supposed to go . . .

Santi.

So we cruise, and it reminds me of the last time I was with him . . . Fuckin' everything reminds me of Santi: the touch of his long fingers that were always crazy warm; the way his voice would drop when he whispered some shit no one else should know; even the smell of his hair, he'd mix olive oil into the pomade, and it'd just glow like you've never seen.

We'd grown up on the same block and would ride our bicycles together up Whittier Boulevard the way older cholos drove their rides low and slow. When I was nine, he took me out shooting the first time, and we'd capped glass bottles in the concrete channels of the L.A. River. He handled my business when I got fucked with too; others disrespected me 'cause I'm a little thinner, a little smaller than most in the varrio, maybe I talk a little shit, too, but Santi always had my back . . . Even when I got older, and I wanted to be hard and roll with the Eastside White Fence gang, it was Santi set me straight.

Now he was gone, like everyone else I'd loved, like Papá, like Abuelita—

"Wait, I just thought of something," I say.

"You can think?" Saint asks, like a smartass.

"I made your skull, and you're here, and Yoli made Papá's skull, and *he's* here. But Abuelita... Li'l Chica made her. How come she's not around?"

"It takes longer coming up here from Juárez."

Oh. I nod, like I should know.

Clack-clack-clack. Papá wants to reminisce about Abuelita the way I'd been on Santi.

Clack-clack-clack, he says again, as I turn a steering wheel that's made of peppermint through our varrio, down 4th to Lorena, past Fresno St., past Concord.

Clack-clack-clack, he goes on, and there's all kinds of people out tonight, people who don't belong, ghosts of people. I can see through them, like the stories always tell, these ghosts that are half-mist, half-solid, only their faces are all painted slick for Day of the Dead, and their eyes glow green as molten jade.

There's other things too, skeletons like Papá, and there's headless conquistadors on steeds of papier-mâché, there's a marching band of big brass instruments, like I mean, it's the instruments themselves marching, with little key feet, just blowing crazy tunes. There's banners that fly like Arabic carpets, there's wolves made of agave, even dogs and cats saunter around on two legs like they own the streets, and their eyes are huge and round as shiny gold wheels.

Clack-clack-clack, Papá says, and Saint nods along, a sort of roll back and forth on the seat, since he's without a neck.

"Your abuelita don't like the life you're leading," Saint adds, like he's all concerned. "You need to make something of yourself, go to school or some shit."

I blow air, shrug him off. "The fuck you know?"

Papá's hand is quick when he slaps the back of my head. *Clack-clack-clack.*

"*¡Chingados!*" That hurt; a skeleton whack, especially when it's wearing thumpers, leaves a mark.

"Abuelita and I go back, vato," Saint says, all nonchalant. "Maybe she came up through a different school, but I've been hangin' with our people of the sun since the Mexica fled to Tenochtitlán."

I don't even sweat him to explain, I don't need to. That big ass book of black magick Yoli inherited—*Brujería Magia Negra*—was Abuelita's, and don't ask where she got it. Abuelita sacrificed so we could have a better life.

Abuelita was a witch doctor in Mexico, conjure, maybe you call hoodoo. She'd go off on these spiritual journeys to Mictlan and do some shit. Abuelita was the only person ever scared Papá.

She died five years ago, only when Dia de los Muertos came around a few months later, she thought maybe she'd come back. The next morning, they found the sailors accused of beating Papá to death. Those sailors looked like red candy apples after you take a big bite, and their heads were skulls with black holes for eyes, each plugged by a marigold that spun on pinwheel stems.

All I know is, you don't fuck with Abuelita.

Meanwhile, Saint is still talking. "Abuelita says, you don't change your ways, you're gonna dance soon with Mictlantecuhtli, the top hat man. His dance, vato, it takes only a bullet to do. You'll see soon, like your friend. And he was the smart one."

"What you know about Santi?"

"More than you think. Like I said, I've been around. He's down there in Mictlan, kingdom of the underworld. There it's sugar skulls and marigolds forever. And not in a good way."

I shake my head. "What'd you come here for? To lecture me from Abuelita or cut me with Santi?"

"I didn't come here for your sparkling conversation, that's for sure. I help people. Give them what they need."

"You do?"

"Don't you know? You called me."

"I didn't call you."

"What's my name, pachuco?"

Again, that misspelling. I nod, okay.

"So think. What you need?"

I know what it is when we arrive at Evergreen cemetery. It's how I fucked up the first time... Only what do I call it now: Closure? Atonement? Forgiveness?

It's Santi, and I don't deserve nothing from him but his hatred.

Truth is, I'm not a fighter, I'm not tough, I ain't shit, and Santi always saw through my bluffs, my doubts. He *knew* me like brothers do, knew more about me than even myself, and he accepted it all.

It's hard to repeat what took place, to even admit . . . But listen, okay, it happened I wasn't thinking. Two months ago . . .

We were back in the concrete channels of L.A., laying low in the shade of ducts that crisscross the dry river, just chillin' from late summer heat. I was downin' a bottle of Four Roses whiskey, and I didn't even care.

"*Carnal*, you need to kick back some," Santi said. "You're going to drink yourself to a grave young."

"Who the fuck cares," I said, and I meant it.

"I do, *carnal*."

I blew out air, shrugged him off.

"You don't believe?" And out of nowhere, he turns to me like he's going to say something else, and there's this fire in his eyes as he leans in, like now it's one of those secrets he's got to say, only there's no one around, so why's he need to whisper, and then his lips were on mine . . .

I froze, there's this warmth I never felt before. His chest pressed lightly to my own, his hands circled my wrists, pulling me closer, and I dropped the whiskey bottle.

The explosion of glass, it was loud, okay, especially in those channels, it echoed. It made me jerk back, I yanked my arms free, but my mouth hesitated, like it acted on its own, didn't want to give up.

Then we were apart.

"Fuck was that?" Santi asked, like I was the one did it to him.

And I flushed, got all hot under the collar he was calling me a queer in my mind. My heart was confused, it was excited, it was scared, angry, embarrassed . . .

"I didn't do shit," was all I could say, this flat denial.

But now I think back, what Santi really said was, "Fuck was that?" in a voice that's only joyful, like a weight had lifted off . . . it was me took his words the wrong way.

And there wasn't nothing more than what happened anyway, just a kiss. My homie kissed me, is all.

But, turned out, we weren't alone. Chivo was passing through on the embankment above us with some of his White Fence cholos. The whiskey bottle exploding, it must have drawn his attention. He *saw* us, if even for a moment.

And they were at us like that, running down the cement slope, all kinds of curses and shouts. I knew it was trouble when I heard the words, "Fuckin' *hotos*!"

Nobody does that here, what Santi and me did, nobody who doesn't want to get jumped by every dude looking to make a name about how badass they are, how *vigilant*, protecting the streets from cock-sucking homos.

So I knew what was going down: someone tries putting a gay jacket on you, and you don't deny it with fists, you'll be wearing that jacket the rest of your life, no matter what else.

"Butt bandit *pendejos*!" It was a blur of faces, my head rocked left, knocked right, I saw stars fly overhead. I swung back, connecting with I don't know who or what, I just hit and ducked at the same time, shouting that I didn't do nothing.

"*¡Hotos!*" I heard again, and I couldn't believe I once wanted to run with those guys.

But by then I'd already said it, I'd thought it, I believed it: When I broke free from the fight, tumbling away, I swore it wasn't my fault. I turned and pointed at Santi. "He's the fag, not me!"

Like I said, it's hard to admit . . . There's Santi, blood leaking from his mouth, an eye all swelled, and I called him out like that. I was dazed, afraid, there was no time to think; I just didn't want to have been seen doing that . . . I was thinking my family would hate on me, though now I find out no one could hate on me more than myself.

And it didn't matter anyway what I said, the White Fence crew was just lookin' to brawl, to hurt anyone for any reason, 'cause that's how they earn fuckin' street cred.

They advanced on me, I remembered the switchblade I carry around, and I pulled it out.

Chivo paused, then from his own pocket he pulled this zip gun, handmade from piping and a block of wood, the firing pin nothing more than a rubber band, but it puts a .22 hole in your head all the same. He'd used it on a rival from the Maravilla street gang the month before.

"You want to play, *puto*?" he asked.

I trembled, my switchblade went away. I raised my hands. Santi launched himself at Chivo, hit him dead-on, and he said, "Run, *carnal*!"

And I did.

Behind me came the crack of Chivo's gunshot, louder than anything . . .

And now here we are.

I lead Saint and Papá through the cemetery, its bright colors nothing like a cemetery should look, with lawns of rose petals and vaults of starburst. We pass gravestones of sweetbread emblazoned with crossbones on the crust, each topped by La Madonna candles that flicker flames of red, of pink, of blue.

Saint says, "The flames are made of sugar, vato. You know that?"

I shake my head slow while a sweet scent of clay and icing skims across the wind.

Green-eyed ghosts are everywhere too, prosperous or poor, old or young, boxers, brides, priests, and monsters, they've all had that last dance, all had their faces painted. They ignore us, smoking cigarettes with loved ones, toasting shots to old times upon their burial mounds of flowers and fruit, and we ignore them in turn.

My heart's for only one grave. And I could get there with my eyes closed, I've been here almost every day.

"Over the next rise," I say, my chin pointing the way up while my hands wring at each other.

We pass a crypt decked in lucky charms and flaming heart tattoos, and only then I see too late, a clique of gang members—seven of them—from the La Purissima Crowd, Eastside Varrio White Fence.

It's crazy twisted they're here too, but I guess even cholos got loved ones to visit.

I recognize them all: Big Shadow, Spider, Puppet, Javi, Huero, Scrappy, and their leader, fuckin' Chivo, passing a bottle with dead homies.

My heart goes cold with hatred.

Puppet sees me, elbows Javi. They point, throw their *W.F.* signs. The others stare me down, and Chivo sticks a finger in and out of his mouth, I know what it's supposed to mean. I step quicker. They got better shit to do at least, they return to their own affairs, though their laughs echo.

"Fuck those punks," Saint says.

"Yeah," I reply, hoping they don't hear.

We crest that last rise and follow a slope down. Around us *señoritas* dance, and musicians play, and even little boy and girl ghosts go chasing each other with hoops and sticks.

And then we're at Santi's grave. It looks fresh, the dirt turned over, moist. Here, whorling wet vines slink across, and tall-stemmed cherries fan out like swirls of smoke. The flower wreaths I laid for him are still in bloom of precious scents, even if they're two months old.

A figure is sitting on the headstone, looking down at the earth, looking all solemn too, nobody's here to mourn him.

"Santi?"

He glances up, and the faintest of smiles pulls at the stitching of his lips. I could think he's wearing makeup, only no makeup can cause eyes to glow green like this. Besides the smoldering light and the cobwebbed forehead, the corkscrew brows, the crucifix chin and carved spade nose, Santi might appear as I seen him last.

"What's up, *carnal*," he says.

"I—I . . . " and it's all stutters from me.

"You need a moment alone?" Saint asks.

I shrug, and he knows that's a *yes*. Papá carries the sugar skull away, I see them last turning behind a mausoleum. And by "last" I mean I don't see nothing else for a minute after, because my eyes are a well of tears, everything's a blur.

I break down, "I'm sorry, man, I'm so damned sorry—"

"It's okay, *carnal*, I shouldn't have done that."

Which makes me feel worse, him apologizing, when it's me done all the wrong. That moment between us, what we did, I didn't expect it, but it felt like it's supposed to, and I can't think of nothing else, except how I left him, and here's Santi taking the blame.

"No . . . " I want to tell him more, but it's hard to get the words out.

I reach to touch him, and my hand passes through.

"It's too late for me, *carnal*. The top hat man already came, we did the dance."

"It should've been me, Santi, I shouldn't have left you. I'd have fucked those bitches up for what they did."

A voice snaps from behind. "What'd you say about us, *ese*?"

The world freezes, everything silent but for that voice . . . When I turn, there's Chivo and his White Fence crew.

Big Shadow taunts, "You come here tonight to suck some ghost chorizo, *hoto*?"

They laugh while spreading in a circle around me, I think of a hangman's noose set to tighten.

I look to Santi for help, his eyes meet mine then fall. His head is a sad shake when he says, "I'm only a ghost, *carnal*, I haven't been called forth. The name on the skull, you know it's not mine. I can't step through."

The old defense rears up as their noose constricts. "I didn't do anything!"

"Then why're you here?" Chivo asks. "And why'd you run from us, *puto*? That was guilt."

I go to my second defense, flick out the switchblade from my pocket.

"You got stones to use it now, *hoto*?" Spider says, and the White Fencers move in even closer.

I slash at the air, but it's no good, the effect like a child throwing his rubber ball at a pack of wolves, and my heart's pounding enough to break ribs. I know what's next, they start whistling, shadow-punching the air around me, taking warm-up swings with crude weapons.

"You're gonna wish you stayed last time," Javi promises.

I close my eyes: all I want is to be a child again, me and Santi riding our bicycles up Whittier Boulevard together, only I know it's too late, and now I just want this over . . .

A clatter erupts, a sound like tap dancers moving on the wood floor of *American Bandstand*, and I open my eyes to Papá! He doesn't give warning, just launches himself at the nearest White Fencer with a deafening *clack-clack-clack!*

Papá hits the dude with his thumpers; it takes a couple moments for me to recognize it's Scrappy he hit, because Scrappy's face goes sliding to the left, while a couple teeth go flying to the right.

Now it's on . . .

I lash out with my blade fast at Chivo, but he dances backward, I miss by inches. My arm's extended when I slice at him, and Big Shadow has a big baseball bat . . . He swings down, and my forearm cracks. The knife goes flying, and I scream in pain and anger, and all else while I trip to my knees.

I was never a fighter like Papá—even if just his skeleton—who goes after Huero next. At least my screams don't sound like Huero's, once Papá hooks a frightening punch to the cholo's kidney and follows with a cross that caves in Huero's nose.

I'm not even a threat anymore, holding my arm and groaning, but Chivo makes sure I feel the kick of his steel-toe across the side of my face. I go from kneeling to sprawling while he laughs.

Papá roars, *Clack-clack-clack!*

Javi goes down next under Papá's thumpers, I think Javi's face will be scarred as Frankenstein once he's out of the hospital.

And all the time, Saint is shouting from the ground where Papá dropped him, "Kick 'em in the huevos, gouge out their eyes!"

It's three down, but then Big Shadow uses that bat to the back of Papá's skull, and Papá stumbles. And Spider has a lead pipe, and Puppet has iron link chains wrapped around each fist . . . They take turns pounding at Papá, one after the other, and with each blow, pieces of bone break away in dust and splinters, cometing across the night sky.

There's just too many of them, and it's like Papá getting beat to death all over, only I'm here to witness it; his skeleton arms snap away, his spine comes apart, his bones fall to pieces, like Tinkertoys you toss across the floor. There's nothing but pegs and rods, connectors and slots.

Saint's not a smartass anymore, when he says, "Oh, damn."

And all the while, Chivo's still laughing.

Santi's ghost says to him, "Haven't you done enough, asshole? Just get out, leave us alone!"

"You're the one talking about assholes, you must like them so much, huh?" Chivo mock-thrusts his hips with grunts.

"Always a punk, only tough with a gun and a gang. I'll see you in Mictlan, you'll be sorry."

"If that's where *hotos* go, you won't see me ever." But Chivo stops laughing.

He scans his crew, realizing half of them are out. Suddenly he pulls that zip gun, points it at me, his dark eyes glinting flames.

"Look what happened to Scrappy and Huero," he says like it's my fault. His voice drops, it's even worse than his shouts, his taunts, when he speaks real quiet to the others. "Get him."

I'm curled up in a protective ball until they grab me, pulling each of my arms and legs so I'm spread-eagle, face-down, straining. I can barely cry out 'cause I can barely breathe.

And I don't see what's going to happen, but I feel it: Chivo's gun pushing deep in my ass, and all this because of a kiss . . .

"You like it going in, don't you?" Chivo asks.

"He didn't do nothing, it was me!" I hear Santi's voice. I want to scream, *It's not true*, but neither will it matter.

"You should thank me," Chivo answers. "I'm sending him to you, you can pork each other in Hell."

More laughs. More jeers.

A thud sounds like a dump truck smacking into a wall, and my right arm is freed. I look up to see Puppet sailing twenty feet through the air. He shatters two headstones when he lands, and he don't get back up that night.

The others let me go, I roll over. There's a new skeleton standing beside Papá's bones, a short, squat skeleton wearing a handmade Campeche dress trimmed with lace and mourning crepe. Its skull is draped by a black mantilla veil, held in place by a tortoiseshell peineta I recognize as having been passed down from its own grandmother's grandmother.

Abuelita has arrived from Juárez, and her hair is of marigolds.

She's holding that book of black magick, *Brujería Magia Negra*. She says, *Clack-clack-clack*.

Spider's head is knocked sideways like a crowbar tried to pry it off his body. He spins a full circle from the blow and lands in a heap.

Big Shadow gapes, and his eyes fill with the fright of your last dance, when she says again, *Clack-clack-clack*.

And something sorta collapses under his T-shirt when he gets hit, I don't know how many ribs it is, only his feet fly up while his head goes down, and then he's curled in a ball, like I was, gasping for breath with sobs I never heard before.

"Fuckin' *puta* witch!" Chivo shouts, turning the gun from me to her, that gun he thinks makes him so tough.

He fires, and the shot is thunderous; there's a gasp when the bullet hits Abuelita's head, only I half-realize the gasp is from me.

The tortoiseshell peineta that had been her grandmother's falls away, smashed to bits by the bullet. There's a smoking hole in the front of her skull too, but a spray of marigolds blossoms instantly from it. I don't think she cares about the bullet hole anyway; it's the tortoiseshell peineta—since that was a family heirloom and all—that's going to be the thing to set her off.

And I won't joke, at this moment I almost feel bad for the *cabron*. He don't even know what he's done . . .

Like I said before, you don't fuck with Abuelita.

Her skull eyes seem to widen, or maybe it's the barbed wire thorns that circle them causing the effect of those sockets to stretch and spin, and she raises both her arms like she's holding up the night sky, and when the sleeves of her dress slide down, I can see the ink still there, tattooed runes along thin bone arms.

Clack-clack-clack, she says.

Clack-clack-clack,

Clack-clack-clack!

The air in the cemetery just goes still, like it's been sucked out, and this red light glows around Chivo, and then he fuckin' explodes.

There's no other way to put it, but it's like he had a stick of dynamite inside; Chivo is dead as dinosaurs.

I gulp, wiping splatter off my face. Blink a couple times.

And Chivo returns . . .

He rises from the muck that was himself, this version that's half-mist, half-solid. His eyes are all cartoon-huge, like he can't believe it either. He pats himself over while we watch. There's no blood, no mud, nothing wrong, his khakis still got their tight crease.

He glares at us one-by-one, last at me. "I'm gonna make you pay, *hoto*."

"No, vato, you forget," Saint tells him. "It's time for your last dance."

And maybe Chivo was half-mist already, he looked so pale, but now any color left in his face goes to milk.

There's a sorta swirl like a whirlwind of fog and leaves, and the big whooshing sound of a waterfall, and this painted skeleton of a giant steps from the air as if coming through an invisible doorway.

He's larger than anyone and dressed sharp in *charro regalia*, with a greca suit sparkling to the sheen of ten thousand gems, and if you don't know already who he is, the top hat on his skull is tall as an eagle can fly . . .

It's King Mictlantecuhtli, the top hat man, and when his great gold teeth clatter, the ground shakes.

The king of Mictlan glances to each of us with a smile you could drive a car through, and he makes a grand bow, and that top hat brushes along the ground, and everywhere it touches, marigolds sprout.

He turns to Chivo and holds out a long bone hand, inviting the dance to begin, and I see the appliqués at his jacket cuff are webs of crystal.

Chivo don't accept the hand.

The leader of the White Fence gang looks to piss himself, if ghosts could do such a thing, and he turns and bolts like his shoes are on fire.

Only there's no running from the underworld.

Chivo's run turns into a twirl, and he spins and spins backward to the King's hand, and with each spin, Chivo's face has a bit more marking to it, a dab of violet, a swirl of orange, a dash of teal.

Mictlantecuhtli clicks his boots together and circles Chivo, their fingers touching so dainty, one foot skimming forward, while the other slides back, then a reverse, and the toe and heel click together in this hop and stomp style I recognize from *ballet folklórico*, the kind of folk dancing I seen Abuelita do when I was a little boy.

And the mariachi ghosts of the graveyard emerge around us playing from their shadows, a roar of trumpeters and guitarists, a sweet racket of violins, a jangle of spurs and bells, and there's even a bass guitarrón that's almost as big as Mictlantecuhtli himself.

The King does a triple-step turn, and his knees are flexed just right, so he leaps and lands so silent, you could hear his shadow applaud.

I move back to Saint and Abuelita who are whistling along.

Chivo screams as brilliant rosebuds stipple his brow, he flails his arms while curlicue stitches cross his cheeks, his foot skips forward, crosses behind the left, and he whirls graceful as a ballerina while his eyes spill green fumes. Mictlantecuhtli dips him, leaning in close to the cholo's face.

Chivo screams again, curses some string of insults, then swings a wild haymaker punch. Mictlantecuhtli was lifting Chivo back up while leaning to the music, and in such a way Chivo's punch knocked off the tall top hat.

That top hat, you know, you don't want to see what's beneath . . .

It isn't no crown of a skull under there, no inside of a bleached bone cranium or nothin'; it's a door, this crumbling hole in an ageless wall, and we glimpsed through to Mictlan itself—Mictlan, where the skulls and marigolds don't ever dance; Mictlan, where the flames are made of sugar . . .

Chivo's screams dry up, I think right there he just quits. Mictlantecuhtli is done with him anyway. The King lifts Chivo in that big bone hand and lobs him like an underhand baseball through the opening in his skull.

Then the top hat goes back on, and Mictlantecuhtli makes a final bow to us before spiraling away in a cloud of fog and leaves.

And I stop holding my breath.

Abuelita makes a *clack-clack-clack* sound like she don't care no more, and Papá's shattered bones knit back together, and he stands up.

Papá clacks back to her, his eye sockets cast down, all sheepish and shit.

Abuelita clacks to Saint next. He winks and tells me, "Adios, vato, it's been swell, but the swelling's gone down."

Then he's gone, the sugar skull fallen still.

Abuelita last shakes a single bony finger at me. *Clack-clack-clack.*

And I'm like Papá, my eyes cast to the ground. "Yes, ma'am," and, "I'll be good, ma'am."

She gives one more *clack-clack-clack*, it's almost affectionate, and hands me the book of black magick.

Abuelita looks around, throws some gang sign of the underworld, and she and Papá vanish. Around me, other ghosts start fading too, and the moon above is normal again, I know there's not much time.

I turn to Santi, he's already growing dim, but I haven't made my peace . . .

"Wait!" I say, only he just shakes his head all sad like I failed a test, and he dissolves.

I stare at his headstone, a slab of cold marble stabbing up from dark earth. There's only the echo of my name drifting on a breeze along with a sound could be clacking to remind why I'm here . . .

"Wait for me, wait for me," I start praying. I didn't go through all this just to lose him again.

I find my switchblade lying on the ground, and though my arm's still throbbing, I first scratch out the name of Saint so that it's gone from the sugar skull.

Maybe it's no good, maybe nothing happens. Maybe it's too late, the magick breaks at dawn, or all this ain't worth it, but I have to try, what I got brought here for. I don't want to start a new day all alone but for a mold of sugar inside a cemetery.

And even if it *does* work, I don't know how long he can stay, how strong Abuelita's witchcraft is, but I hope it's a lifetime. I hope he can hear me say every day what I should've told him for so long . . .

I open the *Brujería Magia Negra* to a certain passage, and I read out loud while carving a new name into the skull's brow, and this time I make sure to get every letter right.

IF I DRIVE BEFORE I WAKE

THE salesman had told him—and not just "informed," but passionately and breathtakingly extolled the wonders of—what awaited him in his new driving immersion with the SADA 5.0. That was another thing, it wasn't just a driving experience anymore, was it? Not like lolling down the road on a warm Sunday afternoon, watching little blackbirds flitting over fruit stands . . . no, it was an *immersion* now, another vocabulary transition as seemingly indispensable to include in the negotiations as was a sunroof, or heated seats, upselling the jargon options package on the latest model trim.

And here he was now, *immersed.* And one thing about the salesman, that vaguely ferret-looking twentysomething with an upturned nose like he was born to look down on the rest of the world, and with eyes the color of tombstone granite that hasn't felt sunlight since being sunk into the wary earth . . . that salesman, that overly-tanned fast-talker had been right on: SADA 5.0 was the single greatest innovation and wonder in Danny Linden's life.

Self-driving cars.

Gone were the days of his right knee locking up from pushing down so much on the gas pedal, then the brake, gas, brake, gas, brake, stop and go—over years of driving on the monstrous Los Angeles freeways; over time, his right leg had actually gained an additional two inches of musculature in circumference over his left . . . Fifty years old, and now his legs would match again. And gone were the days of screaming in rage at the assholes who commuted around him, actually shrieking so loud sometimes his voice would go raw. Gone were the days of feeling so weary on the hours-long slog home that he'd have to take uppers to stay awake; it was not a singular occurrence he'd rear-ended some rubber-necker while his eyes slipped closed for just one sweet second of somnolence.

Now he loved driving or, more accurately, he loved letting SADA 5.0 drive for him, he thought, as the car turned left on Winchester Blvd., a motion as smooth as a devoted lover's caress. Thanks to short-term radar, there was no deceleration in the kinetic motion. Thanks to the electric battery, there was no sound. The office buildings outside swung by in a slideshow, almost surreal in their skyline symmetry. Other SADA 5.0s traversed on the road, all equidistant apart, all moving the same speed. Danny didn't have to do a thing but relax. He could play apps on his phone or eat a bowl of soup. He could take a nap, and he planned to do so. SADA 5.0 did it all and, truthfully, did it better. Wasn't that another selling point in the salesman's spiel? *Ninety-nine percent of road accidents are caused by human error.* So why not eliminate that factor? Let autonomous cars take over and regulate themselves, like workstations on a network. *You don't see workstations crashing into each other, do you, Mr. Linden?* Danny had laughed at that little joke, while inside still disbelieving he was buying into the shit that weaselly kid was shoveling onto him. But it had all been true, all true . . .

"SADA, take me home," Danny ordered.

"Yes, Danny. I will drive you home."

Damn right. No chauffeur was ever so attentive.

"SADA, what's for dinner?"

SADA's recitation of restaurants they'd be driving past was numbing in its tranquility. SADA's voice sounded androgynous and gentle. No accent, no inflection. In the old days, people paid a fortune for their kids to master that level of elocution at preparatory school.

"SADA, raise the temperature one degree."

"Yes, Danny. The temperature is rising one degree. It will be seventy-four Fahrenheit."

SADA 5.0 turned right on 32nd, then merged into a faster lane. Driving in this thing brought back memories of childhood, dreams really, of flying, flying on his bed while he lay there late at night, before the vestiges of slumber overtook him. Amazing how life does change: back then he hated nothing more than sleeping, of wasting away hours that he could otherwise have been exploring the world, running, playing, and now, as an adult, when the world had finally opened its ways to him, had basically turned the cosmic stoplight to unblinking green for him to travel any direction, do anything he wished, now he found himself too tired for it, just exhausted, consigned to commute the same daily route, the same pattern, and not only with his crappy insurance job, but in all of life's cruel ways, the circling hamster wheel of adulthood. But back then, back as a child, on his bed, flying, flying to the stars, to the terrene counters of his reality, unencumbered, unrestrained, feeling nothing more than the sensation of dulcet passage, and isn't that the truest lift-off to dreams?

He'd awaken in that bed of his childhood, as he awakens now in SADA 5.0—

Only there's been some unexpected thump, something that's knocked him aside, and when he looks up, it's dark outside. Bleak. He blinks away afterimages of other SADAs, silhouette people within pounding at windows to get out.

Dream dust . . . the wrong kind. Danny rubs his eyes, there are no other cars around.

He realizes how dry his mouth is, when he asks, "SADA, where are we?"

There's no response.

He repeats the question. Still nothing.

Outside, what before had been office buildings are now tall concrete rises, the side-slopes leading away to on-ramps, to off-ramps. There's graffiti, tons of it, English, Spanish, Armenian, but the mess of the letters, the slang, the juxtaposition of Z for S and exclamation marks for vowels leave him at a loss to their meaning. It's night, but there's no moon. No stars. Then again, this is L.A. There's nothing for shit to see past the smog, the city lights refracting through haze and gloom. SADA drives through it all.

He punches a button on the computer console. "SADA, SADA, wake-up."

Oh, the irony is rich there. And still, nothing. He curses. Is there a defect already? A short in the circuitry, or one of the hard drives . . . ? It should be that SADA tells him anything. He could ask SADA, "What's the dot over a lower case "i" called?" and SADA would reply in its inflectionless, emotionless voice, "The answer is *tittle*."

He could *tittle* now, or scream. SADA 5.0 had cost two years' salary. Plus financing, interest accrual. And problems already? He punches another button on the console. The onboard navigation powers on, a pleasant fluorescent glow of pink and blue.

That at least still works, *Thank God.*

But Danny takes a closer look, sees the vaguely holographic image that is his car on the G.P.S. system, glowing over the screen as it navigates the labyrinth of cityscapes, but there's the problem: there's no labyrinth or city at all, there's no layers of maps, only one straight parallel set of lines bracketing the car as it blinks over a matte black screen. Danny taps another button, then another, nothing helpful, and he fights the urge to just slam his fist into the whole damn thing.

"SADA, SADA, can you hear me? SADA, pull over."

Nothing.

Or, if anything, the car seems to accelerate. Without noticing, they've also entered another freeway, an unfamiliar expanse bordered on both sides by those concrete sound barriers, section by section of upright brick and stone. There's a vague impression of the graffiti fading away until the walls are uninterruptible. He can't see past them either, wouldn't know if it's still L.A. or China on the other side. He strains his eyes looking for any overhead traffic signs, but they do not appear. Only arrows pointing ahead, lanes splitting, merging. The painted, broken divider lines are hypnotic, the way they race toward him, then disappear.

There's no steering wheel in a self-driving car, no pedals. No chance to take control, override the artificial intelligence. That salesman's voice again: *You don't see workstations with steering wheels or pedals, do you, Mr. Linden? No, you just turn them on, tell them what to do, and they comply. That's SADA 5.0 . . .*

That same bastard who'd also told him, *Ninety-nine percent of road accidents are caused by human error. So why not eliminate that factor?*

Danny had been so astounded with the car, so worried about the bill, about nickel-and-diming the add-ons, calculating in his mind what he could *really* afford, maybe if he cut back on a few non-necessities, ate out less, took shorter showers—although he'd immediately begin to save money on gas . . . "Fuel efficiency," that salesman had said, that cocksure weasel. *You'll save hundreds right away with an electric, autonomous car.*

And all that had gotten in the way, hadn't it, had muddled his brain, had rerouted the most obvious fucking question of all: *What about the other one percent?*

SADA 5.0 crests a rise, then another. Danny feels himself being pulled back against his seat, the soft hand of gravity exalting in its dominance over his guts. They're rising upward.

He can jump from the car, just throw open the door, make a dive out, be sure to roll. Like in the movies. He doubts he can go through with it, knows it's going to hurt like hell. So he yells at himself, "C'mon, do it! There's no other way, get out, before this gets worse!"

He tries the doors. They're locked. Was there really any doubt?

A sense of terror begins to grip Danny, an actual nausea creep-creeping up his gullet, and he has to calm himself, has to close his eyes, take long, slow breaths, counting to eight for each exhale. Vomiting is never a pleasant sensation; vomiting in the closed confines of a moving car from which you cannot escape would be intolerable.

What good is technology if he can't say, "SADA, clean that up."

The response comes to him, immediately, not from out loud, not from this terror-box of a vehicle, but from his own imagination: *There's more where that came from, sir.*

His imagination . . . it picked the worst moments to peek out from whatever depths it had long ago sunk. His imagination, once the backdoor of escape from unloving parents, from bullies, from school, from boredom, from depression, anxiety, fear, the miasma of childhood doubt and bewilderment . . . imagination, where he could fly in clouds, could dance through rain, could hold exquisite talks with antelope, could swim the oceans that plummet to other realms of optical elasticity where all he saw that should not have existed were but pebbles to claim and toss away.

And still he's ascending, and he cannot imagine what freeway in southern California gains this much elevation, unless they were headed over the Tejon Pass, south of Bakersfield, but that's four hours away.

"Time, time is the thing, isn't it?" The voice that is not SADA 5.0

whispers. "What does it do, when you're not watching it, how does it nick you, unobserved, the death of ten thousand little cuts? How do you lose, that which you once dreamt?"

Danny longs to hear SADA's real voice. Anyone's voice. What good would it do to scream through the soundproof windows for help?

Freeway lights, they come and go overhead, spawning flashes of pooling iridescence that dim to murk, only to flash again, as bright as lightning strikes.

One flash, he's alone. The next flash, the salesman is sitting beside him in the passenger seat, buckled up nice and tidy. He's patting the glovebox, as one might pat a beloved dog.

"What's happening?" Danny asks him.

"How's the SADA 5.0 working out for you, Mr. Linden?" the salesman asks. "We can still add on an extended warranty."

The next flash, Danny realizes he is bleeding profusely. His hands are sliced up, something is wrong with his chest, his vision wavers, there's blood spreading down his shirt, blood on the console, on the windshield, it's dark, viscous. Danny coughs, and a fresh spatter adds to the gore. "I'm dying," he says at the realization. "I'm dying."

"Looks like it's time for an upgrade, then." The salesman's tan has paled, there isn't sunlight from where he comes. His upturned nose is a snout, of swine. His smile remains, bright, reflective, a mirror.

"I can't afford any more," Danny moans, his voice dropping. "I spent two years' salary on this."

"Oh, Mr. Linden. You only paid for the car. Didn't you read the fine print? There's an additional cost for the driver."

The next flash, Danny is alone, but the blood remains.

"SADA, we crashed, didn't we?" he asks. "How bad . . . was it?"

Real baaad . . . imagination retorts.

The console is cracked, a spiderweb of glass and plastic shards. And blood. But there's a soft whirring now from within, the winding of a spool, the powering-on of a machine. Something crackles. Buzzes back to life. Danny hears a series of clicks, then a ding.

The car has finally reached the top of its freeway ascent, it's levelled out, and the concrete barriers drop away. The view becomes panoramic, elegant roadside awe from Mulholland Drive, winding through lush switchbacks to overlook the marquee shine of Los Angeles in all its glory, its façade of skylights and top hats. This is a memory. He'd been happy once, in awe of his surrounds.

SADA speaks suddenly, breaking the moment. Its voice remains unaffected, pleasant when it says, "There has been an accident."

"No shit . . . "

"You have thirty-nine severe wounds. Rerouting to County Hospital."

The car turns, and Los Angeles falls away as if it were settled on a tabletop that's collapsed. In its stead, a universe unravels, planets like aerial lights blinking red, white, azure, gold. Blinking like eyes, watching him. Blinking like hands beckoning, open, close, open, close, gas, brake, blinking like emergency lights nearing . . . The epiphany of spacefaring spectrums, undulating, challenging emission nebulas to the draw, to the flights of what could have been, what once was, the expanse of infinity.

Danny feels no pain, only wonder. SADA 5.0 turns again. The universe coalesces to a street view of office buildings, of wreckage. A cinderblock wall is blackened. A walkway destroyed. A hover truck is sheared off at the roof, its cab firmly impaled through the front display window of a coffee shop. An older model SADA 5.0—a SADA 4.0, perhaps—is overturned, some mechanism from its undercarriage bouncing back and forth in the air like a petulant spring.

People are running, screaming soundlessly into smartphones. A tire blossoms flame from the sidewalk. Those blinking emergency lights advance closer. Danny looks again at himself, at the blood pooling in his lap. Even within the sealed interior and its five-star carbon filter system, he smells the reek of smoke.

"*Rerouting to hospital. Rerouting to hospital. Rerouting to hospital.*" SADA spits at him. The car shudders, jerks erratically, he's thrown forward, backward, forward, as it struggles to limp down the street, like a mule crawling desperately with two broken hind legs.

And then SADA 5.0 turns again, very smoothly, but sharp, circular almost, spiraling down a drain, and he's back on the freeway.

"*Rerouting to hospital. Rerouting to hospital—*"

And this is where Danny sees a new city, looming before him from far, far away, glowing green, as if made of mythical emeralds like in *The Wizard of Oz*, though he somehow knows that this city's glow is not due to any light source bending through the facet of gemstones to influence fabricated brilliance, but rather the glow comes from within, from itself, the glow of a mirage, the glow of a rainbow, the glow of himself, once upon a time when he had hope, when he was a child in his flying bed . . . Before him is the city of cloud flights, antelope talks, oceans that plummet to other realms, the city of his dreams. He has at last found it.

"*Rerouting to hospital. Rerouting to hospital—*"

Freeway signs dance into view, warning of route divisions branching soon. Los Angeles Medical Center rises up by way of stalwart pylons wrought from curved glass and complex steel, those miracles of modern architecture. A freeway off-ramp leads to it, one-quarter mile away and closing in.

SADA 5.0 begins to turn again, veering into the slower lanes, preparing to make the exit.

"*Rerouting to hospital. Rerouting to hospital—*"

And if not for that off-ramp, the rest of the freeway is a straightaway leading nowhere else but to that glowing, growing emerald city, which maybe isn't a dream after all.

He shudders, his skin feeling cold, knowing it is blood loss, while his heart strains to keep pumping just a little more . . . a little more . . .

And there Danny closes his eyes, yet still seeing that final green city, wondering when did his bed stop flying, and he hopes with all that remains for it to take flight just one more time.

"SADA," he says. "Change destination. Take me home."

BUMMIN' TO THE BEAT OF THE ROAD

THE day I went bummin' down the road was the day Marilyn Monroe died. That really says somethin', don't it? Ms. Glamour herself, drugged out on sleeping pills. That was all the fifties, big show and forced smiles, everything's okay 'cause the picture box in your house tells you so: eat your corn flakes, drink your Ovaltine, wear tweed, the bigger your Buick is the bigger your dong. I'm not being harsh or nothing, just find it fitting; the country was still sleeping then, dreaming of General Motors and Hollywood, and their darling—that czarina of tabloids and red carpets—finally fell to the deepest sleep there is. When the Blonde Bombshell died, it was the end of that era.

And that was the day I wore tread off my shoes. It wasn't because of her I left, but it's that kind of sign you look back on, says you made the right decision. See, I'd read Kerouac, and I'd read Salinger and Steinbeck, Herbert Huncke, and even some Joseph Conrad. I knew what they meant, when they said things like, "Nothing behind me, and everything ahead of me," and, "The land is so much more than its analysis." I wanted to see things, feel 'em, not just read about 'em in the *Gallup Eagle*, or hear Carl yammer in the diner, where I used to bus dishes, about the she-wolves and bikers and rock-and-rollers tempting proper American folks to all manner of sin and damnation.

I already had sin and damnation enough, and boy, I couldn't believe there was more waitin' for me somewhere else.

I owned one of those battered suitcases with a wood frame and canvas sides, all wrapped in cracked leather and brass locks that was a real piece of work. I didn't think I'd be carrying it much, just tossin' it in the back seat of the first jalopy that came rumbling by, but the case filled pretty fast with books and shirts and a picture of me and my younger brother who died three years ago when I was in school. I sure didn't put much thought into packing; the case was heavy as hell. I'd forgotten my mother had once kept a picnic set in there, since it'd been so sturdy.

I thought about heading to San Francisco or maybe New Orleans, what Nelson Algren called, "Downtown Gomorrah." I'd really heard the calling, can you believe? A great ruckus that charged me to leave—maybe the same voice that told Marilyn Monroe to sleep was telling me to wake. The world was changing around us, stirring, *the beat, man*, you could feel it in the air if you opened your mind, an energy sizzling, that for most would burn your hands to the bone, but I could catch it, and I took its ride.

Well, the sun was barely up when I started, just this paint drop dappled behind the thin line between earth and sky; there were no cars around, no people, no dogs barking, no birds yelling. Just me and my suitcase that was once used to picnic.

I left behind my childhood, and I left behind my three-room brick house on Hollister Drive where the hedges were trimmed weekly to exactly four feet high, and I left behind my parents lying in their bed in their old-timey night robes with knives sticking from their chests. I loved them, if you can believe it, but they were already dead to the world, so I just buried 'em with the rest of the fifties. They always hated a mess though, and the way I left them, I know they'd be sorry about that.

I walked the main drag that leads to Route 40, my feet making a swish-clack sound as the sole hit the concrete first, and then the heel came down. *Swish-clack*, *swish-clack*, and I was breathing hard, too, carrying that big suitcase. I'm in no great shape, mind you.

But I made the crossing, and the first car I came upon was this rattletrap of loose bolts waiting, it seemed, just for me.

The driver must've turned a hundred years old before I was born; he had gleaming buck denture teeth and one of those derby hats you'd think an Englishman wears while playing polo. He said he was leaving town and nodded at my case. "Looks as you are, too, *boyo*."

"I'm ready to see the world, sir."

And he smiled, and it made his buck dentures look even bigger—*buckier*, if that's a word—but I was raised not to laugh at such things, so I didn't.

My life lay spread out before me then, like a blank sheet of paper, and I had the pen to draw in all the lines of a map, wherever I wanted them to go. So we scrammed out, taking flat stretches awhile that went nowhere special, and we small-talked, he with a funny, clipped voice that sounded like each word was the beginning of a new sentence.

"The country's changing, *boyo*, don't y'know?"

"Yes, sir, and I'm gonna be a part of it."

"Can't be a part if you're just watching."

"That's not me, sir. You won't find me sitting forty hours on the couch staring at the boob tube."

"That's the spirit. Only live once, and all."

Naturally, just as we were gettin' steam, the rattletrap blew a hose in front of a sign for Grants. The driver—his name was Fergie—smiled through those buck teeth and said he'd get another, if I cared to wait.

Really, I didn't want to wait for anything, but sometimes there ain't much of a choice, you do things you don't want. It was already hot as hell, and the thought of thumbing from the side of the blacktop with that suitcase in hand was dreary. I'd have told Fergie my goodbyes if a cab came along, just so I could keep moving, but none did, so I ran my tongue over the gap where my tooth is missing, and I stayed.

Across the road was this diner, a real red onion of a place with no other name than *DINER*, in these big block letters twenty feet high over the roof, so it couldn't be mistaken for anything else. I went inside, thinking about a coffee and pie, but the ditzy waitress said they were out of both, can you believe it? A diner with no coffee, some sort of mix-up on delivery she tells me, though her excuse doesn't mean anything to my grumbling stomach. Coffee and pie is what I wanted, and she offers milk and cake instead. Boy, ain't that all of life sometimes?

Anyway, I wasn't going to settle, and was about to tell her so, but the entrance door chimes open with one of those bells that jingles every time someone comes in or out, and there's Fergie, his derby hat cocked upon his head in a way nothing else but the word "jaunty" could describe. Says he's got the new one, and just waitin' for me.

"Ready to sally forth, *boyo*?"

I paused, my mind not able to make sense of that, like an algebra problem from Ms. Cranston's class you recite over and over, but everything about it seems wrong; I'd only been in the diner five minutes. "How'd you get a new hose already?"

Fergie laughed, a crazy jazz bop of clattering teeth and splutter. "Hose, *boyo*? I got us another *car*."

Maybe my face said the words I couldn't voice, since Fergie stopped laughing. "You want a ride, or you'd prefer squattin' here with the dust and flies?"

And maybe it's Allen Ginsberg who nudged me forward, saying, "I wake to see the world go wild . . . "

So I nodded okay, and Fergie smiled again, and we left, and in front of the diner is this Ford Thunderbird convertible that's *everything plus*. The top is down, and the silver paint shines like a blade, and it's got long fins in the back, and a trunk big enough to fit a second car.

Fergie took my picnic-suitcase and threw it behind the front seat, and like some old butler he came around and opened the passenger door for me.

"After you, *boyo*."

I'm about to sit, when I noticed a smear of blood on the seat, and I won't lie, I kinda gawk and hesitate, though it's something I should be used to.

But Fergie, still like a butler, just slid a kerchief from his pocket and polished it away. Real polite, this Fergie.

"Bit of a slip there," he acknowledged.

I don't ask what happened, and he doesn't tell, and like that we drove away.

Now, maybe here I should stop and tell you about my brother, since I mentioned him already, but it's probably not enough for you to know he's the reason I went bummin' to the road in the first place, and why I'm here and everything else.

My brother—Dennis was his name—died from cancer. Took him a year to die, the worst year of my life, I'm sure you can imagine. There wasn't anyone like Dennis, we did everything together, and happy too, both of us, and all the time, not like now.

When it started, my parents took him to the hospital, and doctors gave him radiation, said radiation was the wave of the future, just like it killed all those Japanese, it'd kill the cells of cancer. *Radiation Bomb*: they actually used those words.

Only my brother got sicker, and doctors said that was a *good sign*, the radiation was working, killing the cancer . . . but there's Dennis, his skin turning yellow, then turning pale until it's almost translucent, you might see inside if you tried hard enough. He had beautiful blond hair, and it fell out in patches. He had perfect white teeth, and they dropped out of his bleeding gums one-by-one, and he thinned, except for his eyes, which seemed to grow larger as the rest of him shrunk away.

And all the while these doctors are thumpin' each other on the back about how good they are, how smart and crafty they are, until Dennis died, looking like a hairless, toothless old man, at the end too weak to even stand and pee, we had to hold a bedpan for him while he lay, staring at us.

The lousy doctors wouldn't even talk to us after that. My parents said everyone had done their best, but I railed about it and got sent to a goddamned headshrinker who told me I shouldn't have expected my brother to survive, and I'd only "heard what I wanted to hear" all along in hoping the radiation would heal him. The doctors never *promised* he'd survive: this shrink really said that, like I was a moron for thinkin' you go to a doctor to get healed, and I'd filled myself with false hope, and what'd I expect?

So that's a lot I'm layin' on you, and anyway Fergie was silent a long time too as if pondering his own things, when he suddenly says real corny, "A boy's eyes shine when he's thinking too hard."

I ran my tongue over the gap of my missing tooth, and didn't want to talk about Dennis, so I lied. "Just kickin' around destinations, sir. Thinking of maybe going to Paris, maybe South America, I can't decide."

"There's no destination but the grave, *boyo*. Life's a journey, and when you stop movin', you're passed by. Remember that." And he smiled the smile again that made his teeth look *buckier*.

It's funny, but I noticed then, up close, none of the teeth in Fergie's dentures seemed to belong together. They're sorta uneven, each a different hue, one big, the next small, another angled to the left, like a fang knocked sideways. Fergie's teeth looked like a lamp you'd break into a million pieces and try to glue back together; the lamp still works, but you can spot the damage afterward, the gaps and chips and zigzag seams.

I almost made a crack about it too, but thought better, as like I said before, I was raised not to laugh at such things.

Fergie must have noticed my stare anyway, since his eyes flicked to mine.

"My teeth went bad long ago," he admitted, and clacked those buck dentures together for emphasis.

"Sorry," I said, though more for politeness than actually feeling remorse or anything. I just hoped that ended the subject; I felt crummy thinking about Dennis and didn't want to talk anymore.

Fergie was drivin' faster then, like we were in a rush to go nowhere, so I just strolled in my thoughts while looking out at the scenery. There were twisted chaparral trees along the highway whose identities I once learned in the Boy Scouts, and we passed a landmark telling about some Indian Reservation, one of those bronze markers that turns shale-green in the desert rain; it had buckshot dents scattered across. A jack rabbit tore by, fleet as wind, and everywhere bloomed sprays of tiny yellow flowers that looked like lemon candies melted over the gravel and grime. As soon as I saw each thing, it was whisked by, swept into the rearview mirror, as thoughts, misshapen like nightmares . . .

And, boy, talk about nightmares after Dennis's death, always of me lyin' in his place, me rotting away in front of everyone, me dying slow and not able to do a thing about it. My teeth fell out in my nightmares too, but I know that's common in everyone's dreams sometime or another. In my dreams, they just got worse, and I kept trying to put the teeth back into my mouth, only they won't fit no more, 'cause the rest of me is shrinking away so much . . .

One morning I woke, a tooth really *had* fallen out, no reason. My parents said I thrashed around in bed at night so much, I probably struck myself. Ain't that a gas? Me punching myself, I'm so miserable, and I don't even know it?

I thought their explanation was dopey, so I noodled on it awhile, 'til I figured instead it was one of those self-fulfilling prophesies where you cause something to happen by your own fears, or what's called a sympathy pain, or whatever else; I'd obsessed so much about rotting and dying, my body just started to agree with my brain, and had surrendered to wither and fade . . .

Lucky thing I was reading Joanne Kyger then, who pointed out, "What is this self I think I will lose, if I leave what I know?"

I was rotting because of the past, see, it was the old generation I was dying from, or I was dying *with*, their flat ways, their musty ghosts, pecking at my life like a filthy rat nipping at cheese; each day I did the same old stuff, and each day I inched closer to oblivion . . . But I didn't want to go out like that, not like Dennis lying there, watching the world go by, not like my parents, sleepin' in front of the idiot box to escape the pain . . . I had to get out and change the world, help shape a *new* generation . . .

And that's when Fergie crashed my thoughts again, speaking real casually like asking a grocer about the price of plums. "Y'know, I used to sell people's teeth."

I couldn't help it, my lip curled. "Teeth for sale?"

"Aye, teeth of the dead."

Next my brow furrowed; I'm sure my expression looked ugly.

He smiled, a sigh of reminiscence. "Nothing wrong with an honest livin', *boyo*."

"No offense, sir, taking teeth from the dead doesn't sound much honest, nor swell."

"Selling teeth was big business, once upon a time." Fergie clacked his teeth again, as if that were all the proof I needed. "Course, lads like yourself, delicate souls don't like the sound of a name, we'd call 'em Waterloo Teeth instead."

He reached over one-handed, since his other hand was gripping the wheel, and patted the side of my mouth real soft, with a little linger, a little caress. I pulled away with a grimace. The skin of Fergie's hand was a wrinkled sponge like the underbelly of a rotting fish; it sure gave me the willies.

"Back in the days of Waterloo," he went on, "this is Napoleon, mind you—dead soldiers got to numbering in the hundreds of thousands. Young, healthy men these were, all butchered in heaps on the field, and the bodies start to rot, the human scavengers taking their clothes, vermin scavengers taking their flesh. But what's left is teeth . . . You ever seen a corpse, *boyo*, there's always the teeth left behind."

I've seen plenty of corpses, but they're always fresh enough I never thought about the teeth one way or the other.

"Teeth don't rot," Fergie said. "After death. Since the bacteria in your mouth perishes with the body. Teeth're better off after you die, in a way *transformed*, made stronger, immune to decay."

I didn't want to seem like a moron, so I agreed.

"I came to America," he added, "importing teeth by the barrel, sold to dentists and dandies alike. Rivet the teeth to animal ivory, and you've got pearly whites strong as a bear trap."

"People buy those?"

"Used to, *boyo*. Practice died in the fifties—last century that is. Folks prefer porcelain now, same as a toilet's made. Might as well be shittin' in your own mouth, you ask me."

I nodded, I couldn't think of any other response.

"But I still got the teeth." He winked a long sideways wink. "Teeth don't rot."

Fergie was gettin' corny on the subject, I wanted him to drop it. He'd worked himself into a lather blabbing about teeth, and he floored the accelerator even more. We flew like mad, and I clenched the seat tight, feeling like the wind could lift me right out.

It's a funny thing hearing wind, it gets stuck in your ears sometimes, it can sound like anything you want, like a voice or a fire alarm to get away, or maybe just applause if you're on the right path, since I was.

You ever read the poetess, Joanna McClure, she really knows her groceries; it's her advice I took in Gallup when she said, "Reach out and catch a resonance . . . "

Once I'd read that, I swore to do all I could in life, feel every experience, and why the hell not? I went out to the old hotel by the depot that once was real fancy, and I found this goat-milker of a broad,

Ruby Jane, and we *did it*, and she only charged half price since it was my first time, said it made her feel special, and that made me feel special too. She was a real sweetheart.

She sold me a bag of uppers, and I did those too . . . I wasn't asleep then to the world, no way.

And the night after that, I slashed two tires of a highway patrol car, and night after that, I burned down a phony's church, and night after that I did more, and more, my brain turning on, *man,* I was feelin' it, this beat growing around us, and I was greedy from bein' starved so long. Each new feat was like steps up a ladder . . .

And then I'd bumped into the goddamned headshrinker, the one my parents made me visit after Dennis's death. The shrink was shopping, his arms full of packages in every shape; it impressed me very much he could balance them all while walking.

I had my Boy Scout knife in my pocket, and I followed him down the street, and when no one was looking, I slipped it across the inside of his thigh from behind. They teach you that in the Boy Scouts, about the femoral artery, how it's easy to sever in an accident, and the proper First Aid skill to bind it and apply pressure and all. They don't teach you how to cut it or anything, but I figured it wasn't that hard, and I was right. So the goddamned shrink gasped as a big spurt of blood came out, and all those packages in every shape went sailing through the air like a montage of product commercials; *Buy!* Pucci Handbags, *Look!* Almond Oil Soap, *Want!* Kotex hats that are a mile tall, and the shrink had even bought lousy furniture for his pets, I still can't get over it.

I'd wanted to tell him his psychoanalysis was crap, but instead I acted very cool and just walked away, and no one saw me.

And onward I went, until I found myself bummin' to the road in a Thunderbird convertible with this old Englishman who's crazy for teeth . . .

And there Fergie pawed my cheek again, accelerating the car further. "Lend me your ear, *boyo*, and I shall confide sagacity."

I flinched, I wanted to break those fingers of his.

"You've never thrown a tooth away, have you?" he asked.

"Pardon?" I was honestly perplexed.

"No one does," he went on. "There's something instinctual in that. Teeth are bits of the spirit, y'know. When children's teeth fall out, they're saved by parents, placed on shelves, in curio boxes, taped into scrap books, until they vanish, and you don't know where. You and your kin have never discarded a tooth, yet if you ask back, those old teeth aren't around anymore. They're *missing*, and where'd they go?" He tapped his dentures. "Think on it."

I didn't want to, but I did.

"Teeth fall out in your nightmares," Fergie said. "It's the fear of losing self. Your teeth fall out, *boyo*, it's a sign of aging, of dying."

The sky winked blue at me through streaks of sunshine that glittered like a pinwheel always moving, it's mesmerizing. I shrugged. "I guess so, sir."

I hoped Fergie wouldn't get any nuttier, but of course that's when he really got to raving . . .

"And I'll bet you don't believe there's some men come from teeth, do you, *boyo*? Sprouted, you might say, from the sown teeth of dragons, the way trees sprout from seeds."

I figured he was bein' a real phony then, sayin' stuff to get my goat, but even if my face showed incredulity, he kept on.

"They're special teeth, the teeth of men who can kill, murderers at heart, and if even if they hadn't killed already, they would have, given the chance. Men, women like that, *boyo,* it's ingrained in their genes, the *potential*, the *intent*, it's how we stay pure-blooded."

"You don't say . . . "

"Someone's got to keep the world moving forward, *boyo,* someone's got to fill in the gaps. Someone's got to kill off the old, make way for the new." His tongue looked to be lolling around in his mouth while he spoke, like he was moving something besides words.

My mind is tuned sharp, you can bet I understand things. Dennis used to say I had X-ray eyes, I was so smart, but here I was lost as Earhart, and I was startin' to regret takin' a ride with this old loon. Sure, it was a grand new experience bummin' with a certified kook, but even me, I gotta draw the line.

"See, every tooth has a story to it, a memory . . . The teeth, why, they've still got *life* in 'em. They've got the experiences we need to stay fresh. It's how you keep movin', *boyo.* You want the magic of life, it's in the teeth."

"Mister," I interrupted, "can you drop the subject?"

That long sideways wink came again, and Fergie reached into his mouth.

"Fella from Peoria," he said, pulling out this tooth I realize he'd been sucking on like a piece of hard candy. "Drove a streetcar, married with a lass on the side, three children, one a bastard. Once he saved a neighbor's dog from drowning. Once he raped an idiot boy. Once he raped the dog that he saved. His dreams I taste as blackberry chiffon, his failures as salted gin . . . He was a dragon through and through."

Fergie flicked the tooth out the car as we bounced and flew along.

He opened up his suit jacket one-armed, and inside the lining were all these little pockets, hundreds of them, maybe more, tiny stitched flaps, like a cabinet of drawers made from cloth. His hand ran up and down each pocket, brushing them with his fingers, real erotic about it too, until selecting one to reach inside.

"There're all sorts of teeth, *boyo.*"

He flashed a lonesome yellow molar between thumb and forefinger, then popped it into his mouth, normal as anything. "This one—an aged widow, Donia's her name—hails from Portugal, though came to Brooklyn as a babe. She loved to dance, did Donia. Danced with death in fact, killed herself once she killed five spouses, all with arsenic. A dragon, if ever there was one."

Honest, Fergie was givin' me the creeps.

"It's a new era, *boyo,* either you move with it, or you flounder and you die."

"Mister, why don't you let me out here, and we'll call it square."

"You said you were ready to see the world, be a part of her experiences . . . You'd rather sit on the couch, brainwashed by the boob tube, 'til you're droolin' like a babe, the cancer eatin' your brain from its inside out?"

"What's that got to do with this business about teeth?"

"Perhaps this'll help you catch on," Fergie said, reaching over to again snatch a stroke of my cheek. “I’ve got just the tooth for you. Comes from your brother, young Dennis, was it?”

And right there, I went cold. I hadn’t told him a word about my brother, not a word about what he suffered.

“You don’t look too enthused,” Fergie added after a moment’s silence.

“What the hell you trying to pull, mister? My dead brother? You don’t know what I’m capable of, someone tries pushin’ me.”

“Oh, I know plenty, *boyo.*” Fergie’s eye sort of twinkled like some old star that’s dyin’ out in the sky. “It’s why you’re comin’ along, ’less you’d be sleepin’ the grand sleep like your kin.”

I didn’t think I could get any colder, but I did, even how hot it was that I felt my forehead turnin’ redder than roses in that convertible.

“Open up,” Fergie ordered, his voice flat as roadkill, a new tooth in his hand . . . Dennis’s tooth.

My subconscious screamed at me, *don’t do it*, but the rest of me was clay, unmoving but for how Fergie chose to mold me, like my nightmares, me dyin’ slow and not able to do a thing about it.

Fergie’s hand went into my mouth, pushing Dennis’s tooth root-first into the empty socket where my own tooth had gone lost, and it fit fine, though it hurt like hell, him ramming this tooth into my gum that had healed over some time ago.

“Goddamn you, mister,” I spat out, once I could.

“Your brother’s a part of you again,” Fergie said, “He’ll live on, share your experiences.”

Only Fergie’s words seemed to drift away, if that makes sense, and other thoughts, feelings and emotions that didn’t seem to belong, warmed my head like takin’ a deep whiff of gasoline fumes . . .

KILLFUCKKILLFUCKKILLFUCKKILL

Fergie just smiled as if reading my mind. “Your brother wasn’t who you thought he was, eh, *boyo*?”

Dennis’s life flashed before me, highlights, like those abridged books by Reader’s Digest: There Dennis was pointing a finger gun at the back of my head when I wasn’t looking; then taking a whiz in my Coca-Cola bottle; poisoning the neighbor’s cats, one after the other;

putting glass shards in trick-or-treat candy. There he was, only thirteen, and doin' it with the goat-milker, Ruby Jane, already, atop a grave . . . *KILLFUCKKILLFUCKKILLFUCKKILL* . . .

The warm gasoline fumes cleared away, and boy, did I steam. "My brother never did anything like that his whole life!"

"It's who he *would* have become. People change, the lucky ones to dragons. You and him were a lot alike, both seekers, *eh*? It's new experiences, what keeps the mind sharp. It's how we know we're not sleepin' like the rest of the country . . . He just discovered it earlier, which was still too late for *him* . . . but not for his *teeth* . . . "

And Fergie started laughing like a damned maniac.

So, you can guess, I started planning to kill him; I've got my Boy Scout knife, only it's wrapped in a pair of socks in my suitcase that's behind his seat. I think, *Hell with that*, I'll just take the entire big, heavy picnic basket and smash Fergie over the head with it, again and again and again.

But Christ though, he was driving so fast, I couldn't figure how that wouldn't end bad, and I knew I'd have to get him to slow or stop . . .

Meanwhile Fergie just kept laughing, and in some dental sleight-of-hand, he suddenly held more teeth, which he tossed into the air, out the car like throwing confetti at a Macy's Parade.

It made me think of school, hearing about the missionary, Johnny Appleseed, tossing seeds along his journey to grow fruit trees across the land.

And there's Fergie growing his own warriors from the teeth of dragons.

"We're sowin' a new generation, *boyo*."

And still we're drivin' faster and faster, I couldn't imagine a race car going this speed, and my heart's beating faster and faster too, it coulda busted from my ribcage, and I started thinkin' of myself as a tooth inside Fergie's mouth, as much a part of him as he's of me, until he tosses me to the side of the road, the seed of a dragon to be reborn, a warrior charged to shape this new generation . . .

And as I thought of that, and I thought of Johnny Appleseed, and I thought of my brother, and I thought of that goddamned shrink, I saw something sprouting in the rearview mirror, real distant as we zoom along, but—no kidding—the sprouts, they look human, even from far away, tall with arms and legs, blurry too, but they're people for sure, forming wherever Fergie's teeth had landed, forming to cleanse this country, to push it forward . . .

NOW here's what's funny about it all: This bright chime sounds, one of those bells that jingles every time someone comes in or out of a door, and I blink, and I'm still standing in that red onion of a diner with the big block letters over the roof.

Pretty wild, huh?

See, the ditzy waitress had just told me how there's no coffee and pie, so I really did give her a piece of my mind. She won't ever run out of coffee and pie again, since my Boy Scout knife is jammed down her fucking throat . . .

I turned to the chiming door and there's old Fergie standing there, only he doesn't say anything. He's just staring at me with this look that says clear as day he's never seen anything so horrible in his life; his jaw's hanging wide open, I could peer down his throat to his stomach, if I wanted. But it's his teeth I'm eyeballin' . . . Those buck dentures are all perfectly white and flush and normal as hell. They ain't dragon teeth!

So, I pulled the knife from that ditzy waitress's throat, and she bled all over the floor that's checkered like a game board, and I pointed at Fergie. "What the hell you tryin' to pull on me, mister?"

"Wh—what's this, *boyo*?" he asked, real phony.

I took a step at him. "Where're the dragons, mister? The teeth from the car?"

"C—car?" he stuttered, his dentures clattering like there's a cold wind only he can feel. "The blown hose . . . I just came to join you for some c—coffee . . . "

I ran my tongue over the gap in my teeth, only there's no gap anymore since a tooth was there, and my brother's voice was part of me, like I'm a part of Fergie's voice, the *real* Fergie. "Is this what the road does to you? Is this how we become warriors? Is this how the country changes?"

He took a step back, and his ass bumped against the glass door, real comical too.

"Tell me!" I demanded, though by then I knew he couldn't tell me the name of his mother, he'd gotten so flustered.

"Just take it easy," is what he might have said, only another voice overpowered him, that great hipster, the murdering hedonist, Lucien Carr, who reminded me, "To be reborn, you have to first die . . . "

I nodded that I got it, and even a grin came to my face that had forgotten how to grin. Fergie turned and went running out the diner, and I chased after him, since that's now my charge and all. No kidding, it felt good.

A new tooth is in my mouth, and a wide-open road lies ahead, and I sure believe how the country's changing, and, boy, now I'm a part of it!

THE TELEPHONE GAME

IT was six o'clock in the morning when her phone rang. Janice had been sleeping, of course, lost in the comfortable unconsciousness of darkness and dreams and a sensation of floating untethered o'er vales and starshine rays. The ringing sensation was jarring, pulling her from that nether realm, like an arm yanking at someone unexpectedly from a crowd. Her thoughts were sudden, jolting, confused.

The ringtone on her phone at full volume let loose an electronic medley of blaring staccato notes that imitated some old-timey Germanic composer. She hated the ringtone but hadn't yet bothered to scroll through her settings and figure out how to change it.

She fumbled for the phone to answer it, felt its vibration. She'd fallen asleep with it at her side, scrolling memes or media the night before. Normally the phone would be on the cradle across the room, charging. Normally, the volume of the ringtone would be lowered, too, and she'd ignore it, let the call go to voicemail. But now that it had begun to ring its incessant screaming clatter, and she'd begun the process of answering it, she felt the obligation to finish such task.

Her husband Tom had left early for work, so it likely could be him, caught in an emergency, or perhaps just asking to meet for breakfast later. She rolled over, took the phone with two hands, saw with bleary eyes that the number was blocked, unlocked the screen, and mumbled, "Huh?"

"Janice? Janice?" the voice repeated quickly until Janice admitted, "Yes."

"Janice, something terrible is happening, I need to talk to you."

The voice sounded familiar, a woman's, but slightly garbled as if the phone was on speaker mode, a touch of static at the end of each word. Cellular service in her neighborhood was maddeningly spotty; she lived among hills, and although phone companies promised unobstructed connectivity, it never happened. Janice's mind was numb, too, still full of cobwebs and dream dust, and she sat up, trying to will her brain to turn on faster, as if perhaps that alone might make the voice on the other end become clearer.

"Someone's been calling me," the woman said. "Over and over, someone sick, tormenting me!"

"Who?" Janice asked, and she almost added, *is this?* She cut short that second part though because the caller was plainly distressed, and Janice felt like she *should* know her, that the recognizability of the woman was just a moment away from occurring, and this odd situation would be aggravated should she demand the caller to identify herself.

The woman gave a long sob. "I don't know who it is!" Her voice turned loud and high and choking. "It's someone claiming to be your father."

Janice's mind roared awake then, a sheer tsunami wave of anger and indignation. "My father's been dead for over two decades! Who the hell is saying they're him?" Her hand clenched the phone so hard, she felt tendons cracking between each finger. A memory roared past like a fireball, scorching her in its wake, the thought of her father crushed and mangled in the rig he'd driven into a center divider one day while hauling a 53-foot trailer of tractor parts.

"That's what I'm telling you," the woman went on. "It's some man, he keeps calling non-stop. Says his dead brother is calling him, and he's worried he's losing his mind, like I could do anything about that! And this man says he's your father and that he's going to come over here, come home."

"You need to call 911," Janice said immediately. "Whoever this person is, he's a lunatic, stalking you, threatening to go to your house."

"Oh, okay, yes, you're right, that's what I'll do. Thank you, Janice, you always know what's best." The woman's voice lightened with a sigh, and she went on. "It's such a relief to talk to you first. I just didn't know if I should waste the police's time over something like a crank call, as awful as it is though. But I'm going to call them right now."

Janice almost dropped the phone in shock. The moment seemed to freeze, hung on itself, and she felt immediately numb. Her skin prickled, her chest hitched . . .

She recognized the voice.

That martyr-like lexicon, long-suffering and helpless: *her mother.* Janice hadn't heard the voice in over eight years, since her mother had died leaking cancer out of every pore of her desiccated body.

Janice's anger and indignation should have doubled, mounted an uncharted magnitude, but instead lost its ferocity, its inflexion, its tone, when she asked, "Who is this?"

"What?" the woman said. "What kind of a question is that, Janice?"

"No," Janice said flatly. She needed to be firm here, not appear rattled. "Who are you? What do you want?"

"It's me, your mother. Don't scare me anymore."

"My mother's deceased. And I think you know that, calling to say you're being contacted by a dead husband, and bringing up his dead brother before that. This is some sick game, trying to get me to reveal personal information, ask for a loan or to send money."

"What a way to speak to me!"

"You ever call here again, I'm contacting the authorities, filing a case of identity theft, intimidation, harassment, you name it!"

"Janice—!"

She ended the call and started shaking. It was an unfamiliar sensation, actually trembling from the barrage of emotions, something she'd only read about previously in ghastly books. It was chilling, and she blew out a long, deep breath.

Then the call came again, that same horribly loud series of staccato Germanic chimes. She just stared at the phone, let it go to voicemail, and then turned off the ringer. But she watched it, and sure enough, the screen lit up, the now-silent, blocked number showing as calling. Again and again.

The shaking worsened. She started to feel nauseous. What a horrible, filthy ploy by con-artists preying on people they'd woken from sleep. That was the perfect time to swindle someone, wasn't it, easy marks, half-drugged from dreams and pacificity?

But the calls kept coming. And then her voicemail began showing notifications.

She timed it between calls, and dialed out, silently pleading for Tom to pick up.

He did. "Hello?"

"Tom," she said breathlessly at the sound of his voice. "Tom, I hate to do this, but can you come home? Someone's calling me, pretending to be my mother. Something's happening, and I don't say this lightly, but I'm scared."

There was a pause, and Janice thought the connection had dropped. She almost cursed in hysterics, almost ended the call herself in order to redial.

Then Tom spoke. "Who is this?"

"It's me, Janice. Can't you hear me?"

And his response came then as no greater shock, but rather a sudden keen and gnawing awareness of what it all meant.

"You've got some damn nerve calling me like this, lady," he said. "My wife Janice died years ago."

THE TALE OF SAMUEL WHISKERS CONTINUED; OR, A LONDON DIGRESSION

(in homage to *The Tale of Samuel Whiskers or The Roly-Poly Pudding* by Beatrix Potter)

POOR Tom Kitten grew to fear the very thing he was raised to expunge, that assuredly diabolical creature known as the common rat.

But this tale is not about Tom, the only son of frazzled Mrs. Tabitha Twitchit. Thomas, as we know, was a disobedient puss, so perhaps his resulting *Rattus* phobia was just recompense, as well as a firm moral lesson to other intractable kittens. Tom is mentioned here in fleet introduction only for indulgent reminiscence, so as to refresh the terror of that which nearly devoured him, and of which the following anecdote *is* about: Mr. Samuel Whiskers and his wife, Anna Maria.

The old rats are known to have escaped the Potter residence at Hill Top Farm in Cumbria and make final lodging in the barn of Farmer Potatoes, where they vexed the poor man through future generations of their children and grandchildren and great-grandchildren. But for a time, Samuel Whiskers and Anna Maria made journey farther, fleeing the reprisals of Mrs. Twitchit, Cousin Ribby, and the terrier, John Joiner, all who'd come to Tom Kitten's rescue and would have eaten the rats, in much the same way as the rats wished to have eaten the kitten.

"Anna Maria," Samuel Whiskers chattered with his big yellow teeth. "I expect London is the habitat best suited for our hiding."

"London?" she replied, pushing their little wheelbarrow as fast as she could manage, it filled with luggage, sundries, half a smoked ham, and mutton bones. "That's too far away. We'd be twice as old when arrived and with feet as flat as your wit."

"If you pushed more and fretted less, we'd be there in half the time."

"Fine for you to say," she squeaked indignantly. "I'm the one pushing the wheelbarrow!"

"I've oft wished for finer snuff than what the countryside affords anyhow," he replied, ignoring her protest.

And in this way, they scurried down thin lanes to dark crooked roads to a wide dirt highway upon which travelled splendid carriages pulled by towering palominos.

Samuel Whiskers was an enormous rat with jowls that fell over the stiff collar of his overcoat and a prosperous girth that seemed to test the resolve of buttons straining at his waistcoat. His ears were big as his hands, and his tail a pink serpentine thing blotched by coarse hair. His wife stood as tall as Samuel Whiskers, though she was as lean as he was portly. Anna Maria's countenance cast an array of gaunt angles: ears that peaked abruptly, eyes that cut deep, and tight lips that crinkled when she scolded. Her nose extended so acutely as to reach a point like that of a kettle spout.

"I have a plan, Anna Maria," Samuel Whiskers announced quite suddenly. "You must dart into the highway and frighten the passing carriage's horses. It's well known that palominos are dreadfully alarmed at the sight of rats."

"Goodness, I could be trampled upon," she said.

"It's a risk," he agreed.

"And what will you be doing?"

"I'll clamber aboard the carriage's side-spring and hide beneath its tail board, and there repose in amenity for the remainder of our journey to London."

"Then what of me?"

"You will join me aboard, of course!" Samuel Whiskers exhorted with fine generosity. "While the horses are rearing at sight of you, run around, collect the wheelbarrow upon your back, then climb after me up the carriage. I will ensure you have room once I am settled."

"Shouldn't you raise the barrow while I am frightening the ponies?"

"I fear we cannot deviate from the plan in order to guarantee its success," and he patted his considerable belly with much regret.

Anna Maria's ears turned back in reproach, but before she could utter a scold, Samuel Whiskers cried out, "There, now! A carriage approaches. You must hurry!"

His wife dropped their barrow and darted into the highway's center, raising up on tiny slippered feet and chittering irascibly through her daunting teeth.

A pair of tethered horses arrived and paused before her, craning their heads low to glare suspiciously at her behavior.

"If you're not convincingly frightening enough, they're like to proceed before you can join me on board!" Samuel Whiskers warned her as he leapt away, scrambling up the rear carriage wheel. "And mind you don't spoil your dress!"

Anna Maria raised a clawed fist to the palominos, then darted forward and sank her long fangs into the foreleg of one. The horse screeched in pain and reared back, shocked and enraged at her unexpected attack. While the carriage rider sought to console his wounded animal, the old rat wife found she did indeed have enough time—if barely—to run around, collect the wheelbarrow upon her back, then climb after her husband up the carriage.

"A fine plan indeed," Samuel Whiskers congratulated himself while taking a bit of snuff. "Dinner, I suppose, will be served in short?"

LONDON was arrived by following day.

Samuel Whiskers and Anna Maria had never been to *The City* before and, finding themselves in so foreign a locale, decided safety might be sought within its first available sewer vent. Upon seeing such, they dropped from the carriage and raced immediately down into a murky conduit filled with taint and muck and strange crimson roaches that even undiscerning rats could not find appetizing. The smell was dismal, like eggs they would steal from the hen house but lose down wall cracks, so that the dying embryo stewed inside its shelled case emitting toxic fumes of rot and regret.

Samuel Whiskers' waistcoat quickly turned from lemon yellow to dung brown. "I find myself yearning already for return upon the Potter residence."

"I find it unlikely we shall ever enjoy a welcome return there," Anna Maria replied, grimacing at the mottle besmearing her own dress; never again would that garment shimmer periwinkle blue.

"A shame and a grieving indeed, our displacement beget by a lost kitten. Should I ever encounter another, it will suffer my displeasure."

A splashing came from the sewage ahead, and the rats scurried along a stone edge to investigate. They discovered a small baby bird flailing desperately in the sticky water. It wore the frock and pleated skirt of a chick, and when it saw them, the chick's eyes grew large as marbles, and it thrashed more, chirping for help to come from anyone but the rats.

"Quite a difficulty you've met, lad," Samuel Whiskers said.

"Please sir, please ma'am," said the frightened bird. "I was practicing to fly, but a wind caught me, and I fell through the grating."

"Anna Maria, lower your tail to the poor dear," the old man rat said.

"I have little ledge to stand on, and I'm quite sure he should nip me with his beak."

"Dear lad," Samuel Whiskers said, "You wouldn't nip my beloved should we afford rescue from your current plight?"

"I will not," tweeted the little chick, "if you should promise not to eat me."

"I make no such vow," Samuel Whiskers squeaked, rather indignantly. "For that, I've a mind to let you drown and be off about my own considerable business."

The chick appeared decidedly worried, so the rat added, "Besides, I was in the mood for kitten, and you do not fit the bill."

The desperate bird nodded, and Anna Maria lowered her tail from the ledge, and helped pull it from the mire.

Once the chick was within their grasp, the two rats set upon it, slashing its breast open with claws as sharp as daggers. The chick squealed while Anna Maria bit into its neck, and Samuel Whiskers ripped at its feeble wings, each showering the other in bits of flesh and bones. The rats chewed at it until little remained thereof but bloodied feathers and a soggy frock, though at the last the crying bird did give a sharp nip to Anna Maria's unwary tail.

"The horrible brat!" she exclaimed.

"I would like to have cooked it in breadcrumbs, but I suppose *au naturel* must today suffice," Samuel Whiskers commented.

Afterward, they sighed contentedly and licked clean their whiskers and their paws, and then proceeded further through the strange ducts and pipes, Anna Maria balancing their wheelbarrow precariously along the slippery ledge.

"Mind not to tip it," Samuel Whiskers advised.

"This barrow is rather unwieldy," she said.

"Take that to lesson, as next time you steal one to ensure it's of agreeable proportion."

"I should take to lesson that my next *husband* shall be of agreeable proportion," she retorted, nodding to his considerable belly.

"That, Anna Maria," he said, "is unbecoming of a wife."

Soon, a tang of stale brine filled their little noses. Blue-gray light filtered through mortar cracks, and from the gaps in rusted steel grates high above they heard cries of harried distant gulls.

Samuel Whiskers said, "I suppose one of those is looking for its lost chick."

Anna Maria chortled, a sound that when coming from a rat is very akin to the squeaks of a coughing goblin.

The sewers led to a pool of seawater, trapped underground by seepage and smelling horribly of decaying crabs and sick fish. Here the walls seemed soggy with rot, and from an abundance of chasms the heads of other rats peered out, eyes glowing red as polished gems.

"Cripes, but you ever seen a couple so fancy?" one of the rats said in a high, raspy voice. It emerged in motion that was more slither than scrabble, matted fur barely concealing the washboard of its thin ribs.

"And that one's rotund as a wheelhouse," observed a second, pulling itself with great objection from a drain. One ear was a ragged flap, and half its face showed blistered in scars.

"Ee's wearin' more clothes than a pack rat!" A third rat tapped its claw ominously against a bolt cover. "And is that a bleedin' ascot?"

"Sewer rats," Samuel Whiskers whispered to Anna Maria. "I'm told they're quite cannibalistic."

More rats emerged, a dozen, a score, two score, each as bedraggled and muddy as its peer.

"I suggest here we decamp to the bright outdoors," Samuel Whiskers said, motioning to a crumbling shaft cut through the foul masonry. "As I've had my fill of the sewers."

"For once, I agree," his wife replied.

"I'll go first, so you may protect my backside," and without awaiting reply, he hastened to the shaft ahead of her, squeezing through . . .

Until his squeezing halted. Samuel Whiskers exclaimed, "I'm stuck, Anna Maria. Push!"

The old woman rat scrambled behind him and kicked vigorously at her husband's rump, not without slight measure of warranted satisfaction. Unfortunately, the approaching sewer rats detracted from any momentary felicity. She chattered, "Suck it in, husband!"

Samuel Whiskers made a terrible squealing noise as he tried to exhale every bit of breath from his chest, while wishing he did not gorge so strenuously upon his last meal. With a particularly robust kick from behind, and a resounding *pop*, the rat burst free into the shaft's wider aperture.

Anna Maria scurried after, dragging the wheelbarrow and their possessions behind her.

The sewer rats hissed in umbrage at the escaping couple and dashed hurriedly in pursuit, but entering the very same shaft found there was room for only one rodent at a time to advance through, and Anna Maria's retreating wheelbarrow blocked the reach of any rats attempting to clutch and pull her back to the depths of the seawater pool.

But still the rats tried, oh how they tried. The first rat in line was a vile beast with boils dotting his flanks and limbs long and stringy that very near could reach over the barrow, and behind him screeched and clacked his fellows, each trying to shove past another in their fury to catch the well-dressed and succulent-appearing Samuel Whiskers and his wife.

Samuel Whiskers huffed and puffed his way up the shaft with a pace seeming to undermine even the slowest of leisurely tortoises.

"I am trapped in a most unpleasant predicament behind you," Anna Maria complained to him.

The stringy rat following Anna Maria snapped its jaws and spit, scrabbling wildly to get at her. He clawed at the wheelbarrow and ripped at its tiny wood frame with crooked teeth, trying to chew through in ragged fits.

"Anna Maria, do not let them get my snuff box," Samuel Whiskers implored.

"Your snuff is certainly the very thing they're after, I'm sure!" she snapped.

The shaft turned to an outlet pipe, and Samuel Whiskers slipped and tumbled down, sliding through a long descent of green algae and bits of rubbish. A shrill cry assured that Anna Maria followed. The pipe opened to a steely colored sky, cluttered with masts and sails of great ships, and the two rats shot from its spout to plummet a distance twice their height, landing with noisy splash into the puddled sludge of a street gutter.

A booming voice roared above them, "Gods, look at the size of those filthy things!"

Samuel Whiskers gazed up the feet of a grizzled monstrous real live person. The man wore leather-wrapped boots and trousers thick as four walls and smelled terribly of cold fish stew.

"We are filthy only by circumstance," Samuel Whiskers replied irritably as he stepped from the puddle, brushing gobs of smut from his overcoat.

There was a sound of yelps and scraping claws, and the pursuing sewer rats began to pour also from the spout, landing in a pile beside Anna Maria who was busily setting the wheelbarrow to right and searching for spilled mutton bones.

"Gods," the grizzled man roared again, "it's a drove. Kill 'em!"

The man lifted one dreadful boot and brought it down in a sickening crunch, mashing the sewer rat with boils on its flanks. The beast shrieked, a sound cut markedly short, and then the sludge puddle filled with blood and rat entrails.

"Run away!" Anna Maria yipped quite curtly.

"As you say," Samuel Whiskers replied, "though I hope you did not lose many mutton bones from the fall."

"They'd not have spilled from the barrow if you had tied them better inside the counterpane."

"You're perfectly aware my fingers are not as nimble as yours, Anna Maria. Responsibility for knots lies entirely with you."

The grizzled man stomped hard upon another sewer rat, and more men joined him, bashing rats with heavy wood oars and long poles tipped by iron spikes. One club crashed perilously close to Samuel Whiskers.

"But we tarry," the old man rat decided and scurried from the massacre through a cobblestoned gutter, and the old woman rat followed, pushing their wheelbarrow at a steady clip.

The sun shone high above, burning off London's haze and, should they've had time to admire, the ocean presented a fine view of rippling sapphire waves. But Samuel Whiskers and Anna Maria ran, and they perspired beneath their clothes, wet and heavy with filth. The gutter ended in a street paved by bricks that was currently and heavily traversed by people, carriages, and even a motorized car with open top and buttoned bucket seats. The two rats ran willy-nilly through it all.

A girl in dainty pale gown saw them and pointed, letting loose a shriek so singularly resounding as to drown out the tolling of ships' bells. Her parents scooped the girl high into the air with immediate dispatch, and the mother exclaimed, "Disgusting!"

A prim man in straw hat shrieked next at sight of Samuel Whiskers, and his voice carried louder than the girl's. He leapt to the top of packing crates, causing quite a scuffle and chain reaction, whereas each successive person in the rats' path also squawked or screamed and dodged aside. Traffic halted, packages were dropped, curses proclaimed, and pigeons scattered from their roosts upon gay shop eaves.

A mustached policeman in tall helmet waved his truncheon, "Bloody rats!"

Two greyhound dogs looked down their long snouts in disdain of the rodents. Even a pig locked in his cramped cage—most apparently in transit to slaughter—emitted an oink of revulsion, as if declaring assuredly that he would never trade circumstances with the likes of them.

"It seems we're not wanted anywhere we go," Samuel Whiskers sadly exclaimed.

The couple continued pell-mell, upsetting fruit vendors and newspaper boys, and dapper men in bow tied-suits, and sniffy ladies in pulled-waist gowns boarding or debarking from vast luxury liners.

"I should like one of those gowns, once we are more settled," Anna Maria commented.

They came to shelter beneath a buggy and remained until forgot by the passersby, and Samuel Whiskers worked to catch his breath. He panted and groaned and held the stitch in his ample side.

"Now, this way!" His wife ordered and scampered away again.

"Anna Maria, I'm not sufficiently rested. Do not leave me behind!"

"Must I load you also into the wheelbarrow?" she snipped. "Or can you see fit to reach the entry ahead?"

A warehouse with open dock doors awaited beyond the curb of the street.

"I have my sincere doubts," he admitted.

But Samuel Whiskers gave it the old English effort and used his enormous tail to push himself along like a gentleman leaning on his cane. With increasingly louder gasps, he made his way inside the warehouse shortly after Anna Maria.

It was a long windowless building littered with straw on the plank floors and filled with shelves, loose timber, scaffolding, crates, corroded pipes, crumpled papers, bottles, and other rubbish. Also, there was a large steam boiler at one side with flue leading to a sooty chimney that raised above through rafters and steel arches into a lofty, shadowed ceiling. Workers wearing twill caps and shirts with sleeves rolled tight over thick muscles moved amongst it all, muttering and shouting orders at one another in haste.

"I trust you have a more proper destination in mind than remaining in center of this warehouse floor," Samuel Whiskers complained, wheezing.

"Yes, to the chimney."

Anna Maria led the way, and the old rat husband staggered quite exhausted at her heels.

The boiler had not been lit in some time, and the rats climbed up its cold fender and over combustion billows, through the vents of a fan and into the dark flue. By the time Samuel Whiskers fit inside and squeezed past a loose damper, he found himself alone.

Sounds of the warehouse workers had turned muffled, but a soft clanging now issued from the darkness overhead.

"Anna Maria?" he appealed quietly.

"Here," she squeaked from high above. "There is a hole in the chimney, and I've found space between two boards for us to nest."

"Up there?" he queried, squinting into the gloom. "You jest, Anna Maria. Further exertion would be the end of me."

She clicked her teeth, the sound magnified throughout all the chimney, and then a thin line of woven cobweb dropped upon Samuel Whiskers' head. "Tie yourself on, and don't allege clumsy fingers. I'll not carry you on my back like the wheelbarrow."

Samuel Whiskers tied himself securely to the cobweb, and Anna Maria lifted him up, and they collapsed with their luggage and sundries into the small stuffy room, filled with plaster and dust and mold.

"Ah, just like home," he said, stretching out plump legs in repose. After a heartbeat, Samuel Whiskers reached for his snuff box and added, "What I wouldn't give for a spot of pudding right now."

She made no reply.

"A bit of pie perhaps? Surely there's some fowl or a wood mouse you might ferret out, a cache of herbs and butter?"

A cricket chirped from faraway.

"Anna Maria, would you have me starve?"

Samuel Whiskers heard only a slight whistling sound and then a resounding thud.

WHEN he awoke, it was nighttime and the warehouse fallen silent.

"Anna Maria . . . whatever happened?"

"Your head seems to have taken a knocking," she replied, chattering her teeth with feigned worry.

The old man rat felt along his tender scalp and touched at the bloodied indent of a frying pan.

"I didn't realize you'd brought along your favorite skillet."

"It comes in handy when needed most."

"Perchance I'm not as hungry as I once thought," Samuel Whiskers suggested.

"That's pleasant to hear," she replied. "Particularly as we've no food remaining."

"But the smoked ham!" he protested.

"I'm afraid it's gone, most the like lost in transit, though conceivably it took leave with your senses."

Samuel Whiskers frowned at her snip, but decided the absence of retort might avoid another skillet blow. Nevertheless, he let it be known, "I haven't eaten since the chick."

The old woman rat kneaded her bony hands in exasperation. "If only you could dine upon your own grouse."

"Don't be intolerable, Anna Maria. What shall we do?"

"We're in a warehouse!" she cried out with a voice grown weary from scolding. "Surely there's a buffet of rubbish in every corner of the floor."

"Moldy meats in backroom stalls or rotten produce in the dustbin is all very well for sewer rats and you, but I should like something fresh to partake this evening."

His wife's eyes bulged the most frightful size Samuel Whiskers had ever seen. But before she could retort, he said suddenly, "*Shh*, Anna Maria. I hear a sound."

A strange muffled song had begun to rise up through the pipes, and the two old rats listened closely to its garish off-key tune.

"O Martin said to his man
Fie, man fie
O Martin said to his man
Who's the fool now?
Martin said to his man
Fill thou the cup and I the can
Thou hast well, drunken man
Who's the fool now?"

"What can that frightful racket mean?" Samuel Whiskers wondered aloud.

"Sounds like a pack of revelers has arrived. But why bring their whooperups here, to an old warehouse?"

"I suppose I've not heard song like that since young Pigling Bland got into the ale cart and tried squealing verse of *Lusty Young Smith*."

"That's certainly an adequate likeness."

"I saw a flea heave a tree
Fie, man fie
I saw a flea heave a tree
Who's the fool now?
I saw a flea heave a tree
Twenty miles out to sea.
Thou hast well, drunken man
Who's the fool now?"

"It must be aft midnight for such a hullabaloo," Anna Maria objected. "They sound toasted as a band of bishops."

"I concur, Anna Maria. But I suggest where there's drink, there's surely edibles!"

"My preference is to remain undisclosed. Humans tend to hurl shoes at us."

"Of course we must make stealth, but a chance presents itself to sneak some savory victuals. Perhaps they've brought peanuts or pork scratchings or a head of goat's cheese," he said and leapt up.

"Quite a second wind you've taken," the old rat wife snuffled as her husband led the way from their room.

Instead of descending back down the chimney, Samuel Whiskers turned across a rickety wood board and emerged through vast skeletal rafters. Each joist followed the width of timber scaffolding, crossing grimy bars and spliced beams thirty feet high in the warehouse's sharply sloped ceiling. He scuttled over the span until reaching a large platform of veneered plywood.

"A perfect view for observation," he announced.

The platform stored dusty crates, stuffed sacks, and cartons of faded ledgers and bylaws and catalogues, all shelved between diagonal braces and iron wall plates. Its existence proved long forgot by the rot and decay of packaging, much of it held together by no more than moldering threadbare rope.

The song yowled louder below and, incredibly, more discordant, like a cat whose tail is fed further and further into a buzzsaw.

A whiff of tobacco smoke spiraled upward, and Samuel Whiskers traced its path in reverse to the source. "There I spy a man with drink, pipe, and song."

"I saw the mouse chase the cat
Fie, man fie
I saw the mouse chase the cat
Who's the fool now?"

"A man?" Anna Maria asked. "But where's the rest?"

"I think there's no more than he."

"Truly? One man making all that stir?"

"I saw the mouse chase the cat
Saw the cheese eat the rat
Thou hast well, drunken man
Who's the fool now?"

"Cheese eat the rat?" Samuel Whiskers criticized. "I find this song not at all agreeable."

"He is getting upon my nerves," Anna Maria said.

"The man is quite stewed, in as much as he is bedraggled. The hair on his face is longer than our own. I would name that creature, a real live vagabond."

"It must be, he cares not for social norms."

"It must be," Samuel Whiskers agreed, rolling his chin hairs in a very dastardly manner. "Imagine a helpless chick the size of a man."

"Are you suggesting . . . ?"

"It would be quite a coup, Anna Maria."

She nodded thoughtfully. "He's certainly marinated enough."

"I have a plan," Samuel Whiskers announced quite suddenly. "Anna Maria, you will leap from the rafters and land on the man's hat. It's well known that people are dreadfully alarmed of rats. When he springs up to flee in terror, trip him with your tail."

"Goodness, I could miss and splatter on the ground," she said.

"It's a risk," he agreed.

"I've a better plan," she countered with glint in her black eyes. "Stand over here and do as you are best suited: Lean against this barrel and watch me work."

"I utterly fail to see what you have in mind."

But Samuel Whiskers complied and leaned against the barrel, which creaked anxiously at his weight. It was an old oak hogshead half-filled with the rods of leading used to weld panes of stained glass. The barrel sat on a case of brass nails and another crate of tiles below that, jammed against a weak wood railing, and tied back by complicated knots of frayed rope.

"I saw the man in the moon
Fie, man fie . . . "

Anna Maria ripped into the rope with the savagery of a rabid polecat, gnawing it apart by swift snaps of her fangs. In moments the line shredded and split at her attack.

"I saw the man in the moon
Who's the fool now?"

The crate of tiles slipped. The case of nails veered. Samuel Whiskers felt the barrel teeter under his enormous weight. As he shifted, it shifted too, and he leapt back just in time for the barrel to topple, smashing through the remnants of the railing and falling, falling, falling thirty feet . . .

"I saw the man in the moon
Clouting on St. Peter's shoon.
Thou hast well—"

The verse was cut plainly short by a resounding blast and the short, shocked yelp of a drunken warbler.

"That should do him proper," she said.

Samuel Whiskers rose upon his chunky, velvet-shoed feet and looked over the ledge of the platform. "That, my wife, was splendidly done."

They scampered back along the rafters, down the chimney and flue, through the fan and out the boiler to the plank floor, which amongst its other debris was now covered in rods of leading and old oak barrel shards.

Also on the floor was the bedraggled man laying prone inside a steadily widening pool of crimson. He wore a mismatched suit of tweed with corduroy patches at the elbows and knees, one boot of brown leather, the other of black, and a green bowler's hat of which part was shoved deep inside his mangled head. One eye seemed to have been knocked loose and bulged out staring at them unblinking, while the other eye glazed half-lidded under the brim of the smashed hat. A bottle of *Old Tom* gin lay shattered a foot away and its pungent fumes caused Samuel Whiskers' eyes to water.

"Again, I say splendidly done."

"If a rose by any other name would smell as sweet, the man here must surely be called Guano," Anna Maria quipped, sniffing the air.

The drunkard's half-lidded eye fluttered and rolled to look at them. A gasp choked first from his broken-toothed mouth, then a cry, then a shrill scream.

"What's the meaning of this?" Samuel Whiskers demanded, holding his paws to his big ears. "Why are you still living and clamoring?"

"Help me . . . help me . . . " the man grieved. "Somethin' terrible has 'appened."

"That is entirely true," Samuel Whiskers agreed. "There's not the slightest of dumplings to accompany you."

"Dumplins? Y—you're not goin' to eat me, are you?"

"I do not think we shall play tiddlywinks together."

"Help!" the man suddenly shrieked, and his head flopped as he trembled to rise.

"I trust you've packed twine, Anna Maria. The frump needs tying off, for it appears your plan was not successful after all."

"Better than me leaping thirty feet through the air," she replied sharply.

"Help! Help me!" The man shrieked again.

"Stop that!" Samuel Whiskers commanded. "Anna Maria, strike him."

Before she did, the drunkard gasped for breath, and a line of blood gushed from his sad mouth. "P—please . . . I can't move me limbs . . . "

"There you have it," Anna Maria squeaked. "No need for twine at all. Man's crushed as a mouse in a trap. Broke back, most like."

"How serendipitous. Now if only there were hope for even the slightest of roly-poly pudding to accompany our dining . . . "

"Unless you can spare some dough off your roly-poly belly, I'm afraid our supply is exhausted."

Samuel Whiskers looked stung. "My belly is not to be trifled with."

The drunkard turned considerably more frightened, listening to the two old rats discuss ways best to devour him. With a singular effort of cunning he offered, "I'd like to suggest . . . I—I'm not at all tempting or digestible . . . in absence of dumplings or pudding."

"Nonsense, but I suppose only again it must be *au naturel*," and Samuel Whiskers showed his big yellow teeth.

And the man screamed and screamed and screamed.

Anna Maria chided her husband. "You're being overwrought."

Samuel Whiskers paused in motion to bite, presenting her a questioning eye.

"We're not in the sewers after all," she continued, motioning to the large steam boiler. "Draw a fire and I'll grill him in his juice."

"I wouldn't the slightest notion how to get that enormous contraption running."

"Sometimes I wonder if your appetite did not consume your own brains," she admonished. "There's straw about the floor, loose wood, the man has tinder for his pipe. You need only build a cook fire inside the metal chamber."

"*Ahh*," Samuel Whiskers exclaimed in a long exhalation.

"Give a moment, and I'll retrieve my skillet," she said and darted away.

"P—please, have mercy . . . rat," the man beseeched.

"That's *mister* rat to the likes of you. Or Samuel Whiskers if you wish, should you desire to be formally met."

"Please, oh please, Mr. Rat—Samuel Whiskers—it hurts . . . " the man's voice cracked in a most despondent whimper. "Please don't eat me."

"I'd rather the taste of kitten, but you must suffice."

"I've a wife . . . children . . . " he sobbed.

"And here you are, carousing at all hours of the night? You, sir, are a cad."

"T'was me birthday . . . " The man's voice fell quiet as a deer mouse. "I just wanted a nip off by meself . . . "

"*Tsk, tsk*, gin, the 'Mother's Ruin'," Samuel Whiskers upbraided. "And yours too, apparently."

"Is there n—nothing I can say . . . can be done?"

Samuel Whiskers considered for the length of a finger waggle. "No."

Bright tears and long snot and thick blood mixed at the man's chin.

"On another matter," the old man rat interjected, jabbing his tail at the man's face. "That ballad, sir, was positively dreadful."

"Th—the what?"

"The song you despoiled, the ode that mocked our very ear drums. What's it about?"

The man gulped, coughed. "It's jest a drinkin' song, a jingle. Not meant to mock you at all, Mr. Rat—Samuel Whiskers, sir. I—I'm sorry if it did."

"Surely. The cheese ate the rat?"

"It's frivolous, a bit—a bit of hilarity to make up verses that rhyme with each round, 'tis all."

"I see. Perhaps I might sport a turn as I've just thought verse for you."

Samuel Whiskers cleared his throat and filled the warehouse with bright tenor (and his tone was surprisingly delightful):

"I saw a cad ate by rats
Fie, man fie
I saw a cad ate by rats
Who's the fool now?
I saw a cad ate by rats
Chewed his gristle, bones, and fats
Thou hast well, drunken man
Who's the fool now?"

"I'll think of more, perhaps," Samuel Whiskers added, "but you'll like not be around for its next verse."

The man heaved a great wracking sob.

"You don't care for it?" the rat inquired, frowning his peaked brow. "I'd have thought you more receptive."

"I'm dreaming, I'm dreaming..." the man mumbled. "A nightmare, a boozer . . . a bloody talkin' rat in silken suit. You're nothin' but rainbow rubbish . . . "

"Quite the fancy," Samuel Whiskers replied.

Anna Maria made enthusiastic return with her tiny frying pan and a small pouch. "Such providence, I discovered a cut of thyme dropped behind the piping support!"

And the drunkard began laughing, expelling hacks of blood and wafts of breath most fetid upon naughty Samuel Whiskers.

"Here I thought my waistcoat could become no fouler," the old rat husband complained.

"A dream, 'tis a dream indeed!" the man suddenly shrieked.

"What's so amusing?" Anna Maria asked in shrill voice.

"Your skillet is so small, naught but half a thimble!" The man laughed hysterically, and his bulging eye popped further from his head in expression, then retreated to a half-bulge, akin to some ghastly wink. "*Ha ha, oh ho!* How could I ever fit in there?"

"You will, sir. I assure that piece by piece, you will," and Samuel Whiskers again showed his big yellow teeth.

And the man's laughs returned to more screams.

THE following morning, when the warehouse's broad doors were pulled apart by sleepy-eyed workmen, beneath a dark sky filled with soot and filaments of early ruddy light, the corpse was discovered.

"Bugger me mum," one workman exclaimed without reservation.

The drunkard's remains lay herring-boned upon the floor, split and torn asunder in several bloody directions. Dainty incisions patterned up his bare midriff to a half-carved chest that appeared diced as if with thin carving knife, while glass and crimson and wood shards made halo around the body's severed neck. The space smelled of gin and dung and rot, a bevy of scents all curiously at odds with the more overwhelming aroma of fine braised mutton.

The smell, of course, wafted from the man's head, slow-roasting in a waning cook fire built within the chamber of the steam boiler.

"He's be' eaten," a man observed, then punctuated the remark by regurgitating his breakfast of mash and eggs.

"I'll never consume mutton again . . . " professed another.

"There's rats!" A man lifting his lantern pointed in horror.

Samuel Whiskers raised his head in alarm from behind the boiler's exhaust. A bit of juice dribbled from pudgy lips, and he'd finally succeeded in popping the buttons off his waistcoat. His belly had never been so extended.

"Call the bobbies!" a workman cried out.

"We are discovered, Anna Maria!" Samuel Whiskers fretted with much dismay.

"Yet my fillet is not concluded," she replied.

"I grieve to abandon such prime faire as well, but I fear we must depart the premises at once."

"A waste of thyme," she lamented. "Very well, but let us collect our property before retreat."

The old woman rat leapt across ducting, then led back through the boiler's vents and into its murky flue, Samuel Whiskers puffing terribly behind her all the way. They arrived at the chimney's ascent, Anna Maria at the first and waiting impatiently for him to catch up.

The old rat husband took pause to catch his breath for half a dozen huffs and puffs. He looked up to his wife and sighed with profound regret. "Why must we be loathed so, Anna Maria?"

She snuffled and turned a sharp eye to him. "A fine time for existential melancholy. We need climb the chimney, tie up the finger bones and smoked ears, pack our barrow, and make escape before the humans begin searching our whereabouts in earnest!"

"A fine time for drollery," Samuel Whiskers retorted, massaging his distended belly with tender care. "I've not a chance to make it up the chimney, even if you again lifted."

Her scowl shared equal parts resignation and displeasure. "Must I do everything?"

"As you wish," he sighed, and his mien held only the slightest degree of contrition.

As she glared, Samuel Whiskers cleared his throat and added, "Perhaps, Anna Maria, it is time we return to Cumbria. I begin to think London is not well-suited for us."

The old rat wife paused, twirling her little whiskers between long-clawed fingers. She considered for two beats of a scamp's heart, and nodded. "I do know of a splendid hay barn at Farmer Potatoes . . . "

And so, the story goes, that is exactly where their journey concluded.

DRINK, DRINK FROM THE FOUNTAIN OF DEATH

I WORKED over thirty years in purchasing for a company out of Manhattan that replicated antiques and heirlooms around the globe into home décor pieces and showroom designs, museum accessories, elegant toys, seasonal ornaments, and other high-end *objet d'arts*. To say I was well-travelled would be to say that a bird knew clouds. I was the Jacques Cousteau of back-alley bazaars, the Magellan among dealers of knickknacks. And over those years, throughout those travels, I was ever attuned to peculiar ideas, superstitions, fables and legends, tales of the grotesque or of the wonderful. My business, after all, was not just replicating antiquities, but of crafting the stories that went along with them.

Of all that I've been told, of all that I've seen or experienced, of all I've learned of the peoples of this planet, this following episode, occurring in my own country, is perhaps the most hideous and unbelievable.

It was late October, and rainy that year in 1987, when myself and a friend, Roy Prince, travelled along the southeastern seaboard of the United States on one of our famed buying expeditions. Already I'd procured botanical art and porcelain whimsy; stainless steel mobiles; art deco bowls; polished bronze sun dials; insects in Lucite; gold dinnerware; tea pots and mariner wheels; and more. More, more, yet always I wanted more. *We* wanted more.

We were driving a rental station wagon down Interstate 95, having left Jacksonville en route for St. Augustine, the oldest occupied city in the U.S. and a hotbed for Spanish colonial ornamentation. Roy had a giant map unfolded on the dashboard of the car, when he said, "Let's turn off here, Jim. It's a shortcut."

Famous last words.

We ended up on a winding, rough slit of road that seemed nearly to drown in the surrounding swamps, which Florida is so well known. After thirty minutes and the beginning of an argument as to whether we should turn back, inexplicably the road opened up from more than a single dirt path to something of a two-lane asphalt byway, for which I was entirely grateful. Old barns came into view, fruit stands, and possibly more rustic antique shops than I've ever seen grouped together in one locale.

"Dare I say, mother lode?" Roy grinned under the suspicion his shortcut would prove to be a great success.

At the time, I couldn't help but agree. "You're a divining rod for yokel treasure."

Our shared laugh was a comfortable moment, and from there we spent the remainder of the day ransacking and plundering as our credit cards would allow. Yet even among such riveting and endless novelties and heirlooms, I found myself growing apathetic to stuffed alligator luggage, cannon balls, and collectible cigarillo boxes.

"Is it just me," I asked, "or does this town seem like the lost graveyard of conquistador armor dupes?"

"If there's ever a run on those things, we'll know where to go."

It was getting to be obnoxious, pushing through shops overflowing with conquistador shields, helmets, swords, and all their knock-off ilk. Just how many antique-crazy shoppers came out this way with an inextinguishable compulsion for collecting Spanish-American exploration of the 1500s?

By the twelfth shop, a converted outbuilding named by a weathered oak sign as *San Giblets*, I added, "And paintings of Ponce de León. In every one, he looks to be suffering consumption."

"It's the statues of him that bother me more," Roy replied, as we descended into the shop's cavernous basement of maritime kitsch. "They're creepy, pointing a finger off into the unknown. I find myself turning to where he's looking, wondering what it is I'm not seeing."

Incredibly, what awaited us at the bottom of the stairs was the exact subject of Roy's distaste: a life-sized figure of the famed Spanish explorer, carved of wood and, admittedly, painted in remarkable detail, wearing a sleeved doublet of golden thread overlaid by a cuirass armored breastplate. Ponce de León stood aside two glass cases of intricate sailing ship models, one arm casually affixed above the hilt of his sheathed sword, while the other arm was raised, gloved hand pointing to a place directly behind us, which was nothing but laminate planking of the stairwell.

"Ha," I laughed, "it's a warning for visitors with little self-control of their wages to stay away from the overpriced merchants of this town—"

My voice dropped as the joke went flat, for I realized I didn't know what town we were even in, and then, further, I was interrupted by someone from behind who'd overheard us.

"There's been great debate over it," the person said quite seriously. Turning, I saw it was an unsmiling man, tall and lean, wearing a Panamanian-style white linen suit. The man continued, "Some people contend the pointing hand is symbolic of Ponce de León's discovery of this land, first sighting what he would later name La Florida from the bow of his ship *Santa María de la Consolación*."

"Illuminating," Roy said flatly.

"And the rebuttal of those debates?" I inquired.

The man gazed almost longingly into the painted eyes of Ponce de León. I followed his regard and felt nearly mesmerized by some trick of light or passing shadow into seeing a flickering within the statue's pupils.

"What others believe—" the man said, "what I believe—is that Ponce de León is pointing the way to the greatest fountain of all time, the Fountain of Youth."

"Indeed?" Roy was amused. He looked at me, while I felt only inexplicably agitated.

The tall proprietor—for I took him as such—nodded. "There are many tales, ship logs and diaries from his crew, and accounts passed down from the native Calusa people, describing certain details proving Ponce de León's discovery."

"St. Augustine," I said. "That's where the legends state the Fountain of Youth to be."

"Oh, please," the proprietor said, rolling his eyes. At last, he'd given an expression to his otherwise waxen face, although the act made me only want to slug him. "As Barnum said, 'There's a sucker born every minute.'"

"So, the sucker is he who believes the fountain is in St. Augustine," Roy asked, "but *not* the person who claims the fountain is real, but existing elsewhere?"

"It's real, all right, and it's out there. Whoever locates it will become rich beyond their wildest dreams!" The proprietor's eyebrows rose, waggling in a manner that reminded me of a dying Groucho Marx. "Ponce de León points the way."

Roy rubbed at the stubble on his narrow jaw, ran one finger across the thin mustache he kept groomed like an Errol Flynn movie extra. He looked almost to laugh. "I've seen about a thousand of these statues in your town, and they all point different directions."

The proprietor shrugged. "You won't have to worry about finding it. Tradition says that if you're chosen, the fountain will find you."

Now Roy's laugh did come out. "Well, that's helpful."

I gazed again into the carved figure's eyes and felt the unnerving sense of it gazing back.

"You look like serious collectors," the man said, relaxing. "Tell you what I know, the fountain is said to be northwest of here, in the swamps, as indicated by the original statue. I'd say around Deep Creek, off the St. Johns River."

"The original?" I asked. "Where's that?"

"You're looking at it. This original statue was carved out of a boat's mast taken from Ponce de León's fleet. Happens to be on sale, too. Half price, great bargain."

At that, I quietly joined in with Roy's laugh. We declined the offer and left *San Giblets*, the first store all day we'd exited empty-handed.

"Creepy," Roy said, and I agreed.

Dusk settled in around us, the Florida sky reflecting the great Atlantic overhead, but reversed in hue and design, slow-moving waves of irradiant pink and molten bronze and the shadows of lavenders that portend night's dreams to take rise. It was beautiful and opulent, and I felt that moment itself to be the realization of the Fountain of Youth, for time seemed to stop and magically infuse our being with the splendor of our ever-present universe.

Yet like life, the moment passed. We decided to get a motel for the night, one of those cheap motor courts that barely survived the decommissioning and now molder languidly under growing threats of mold, dust, rodents, and debt. I still didn't know what town we were in. There was no phone book in the room, just a pad of stationary from the State Tourism Department and a Gideon's Bible in which someone had crossed out the first page and scrawled, *Satan slept here* and below that, *Winky too*.

"This motel," I said, "Odd, it's at the end of the road we drove in on."

"I noticed that," Roy said. "What kind of town only has one way in?"

I took a bite from my take-out sandwich. "That shortcut was supposed to cross straight through to St. Augustine, right?"

"Sure."

"Wherever we are, this place isn't shown on the map."

Roy shrugged. "Eh, we'll ask in the morning."

IN sleep, I had a nightmare of Ponce de León pointing at me, his consumptive face waning to something skeletal. Laughter sounded, but it seemed not to come from him, instead surrounding me as an enveloping fog. Though not seen, I imagined it as coming from the tall proprietor we'd spoken with earlier. Ponce de León's arm lengthened, his pointing hand drawing nearer, nearer to me, and I, unable to move, watching his gloved finger grow larger by perspective, as if soon to impale me like a lance.

He turned, and one half of his face was of flesh, the other half skull, wet and glistening with vines and gray moss. The eyes were wooden, those of the statue. His other hand released the sword at his hip, and lifted a goblet, beautifully jeweled by smoky pearls, rubies shaped like falling tears, and cut diamonds as blue as the ocean becalmed.

The liquid inside the goblet began to overflow, as if a valve turned from within, and it became a great pool of crystalline water surrounded by a perfect circle of ancient stones and toadstools that were as immortal as the legends.

Ponce de León spoke, and his voice was my own. "Drink, forever."

IN the morning, we breakfasted and checked out.

"What's the way to St. Augustine?" I asked the motel clerk, an elderly woman with long gray hair and a quiet, dreary sort of countenance.

"*Weeell,*" she said, apparently thinking vigorously on the matter. "Y'all oughta take the 95, head down south and that'll get you near enough."

"We *were* on the 95. Map showed a shortcut coming through here."

She sniffled. "Nope."

"No shortcut?"

"Like I said."

"So, we need to backtrack to the 95?"

"That'll do you."

"Huh." I watched a horsefly the size of my hand buzz languidly around the counter. "Weird, the map doesn't show you listed, no markings of any town out here."

The woman swatted at the horsefly with a half-hearted disinterest. "Map's outdated, I'd say."

"Sure," I politely agreed. "By the way, what's the name of this lovely burg?"

She just chuckled. "Now you're gettin' uppity."

With that, I took my cue, and Roy and I left the strange little town, our purchased treasures packed down tight in the back of the rental.

Roy returned the map to its berth, unfolded across the dashboard. "Back the way we came."

"Easy enough," I replied.

It wasn't.

Imagine the tributaries of a watershed feeding into a larger river, or the shape of a chevron pattern with mirrored forty-five-degree angles abutting a central line. Following configurations such as this going one way, against the angles, is a perfectly obvious route; each junction seems to flow into the road behind you, all apparently leading toward the same location. However, changing direction and travelling the opposite way leads one to see every crossroad as a choice to be made, the branching of a letter Y, requiring the traveler to veer left or to veer right.

At first, we deduced to follow the asphalt, which at times turned one way before swerving to turn the other, but always seemed the obvious choice to alternative roads that were not much more than muddy trails. However, as I'd remembered from driving in the day prior, the asphalt soon petered out into a single dirt path, so now at each crossroad one direction looked as equally uninviting as the other. From a bird's eye view, the choice may have appeared obvious, but from our perspective the passage evolved into a labyrinth of wild hedgerows.

The ground grew rougher, rockier, while wetter, so we bumped over large stones one instant and splashed through puddles the next. Trees grew in closer together, and lack of sunlight caused them to appear wan, as if wasting from some disease. My watch showed an hour had passed although it'd felt to be three.

"We're lost."

Roy was beside himself. "There's not a single sign anywhere! What kind of a podunk corner of Hell is this?"

For the hundredth time, he balled the map up, then smoothed it back out onto the dashboard. "The road," he said. "It shows only two intersections along here. We've passed at least three dozen."

A movement outside the window caught my notice, and I thought I glimpsed a figure through the trees pointing away, but then dismissed it for shadows as Roy admitted, "We need to go back to town."

As I reluctantly agreed, Roy grabbed my shoulder and shook. "Jim, the gas. Look at the gauge, it's on empty!"

I don't know why, but my only reaction was to laugh. "Lewis and Clark, we are not."

It was at this point, the sickening comprehension of a terrible predicament began, for even after fifteen minutes or getting the giant station wagon turned around on that narrow path, and descending back the way we'd just come, we realized this particular road had also a vast number of crossroads branching off, identical thin trails snaking through dense undergrowth as if we'd become firmly entangled in the center of a mesh web of gossamer, where sticky lines seemed to radiate in all directions.

"This is bad," Roy whispered.

I stopped, and we got out to gaze at our verdant prison. The ground was soft, viscous, every tree wrapped in fat, ropy vines. Looking up, the forest canopy reminded me of the steep angles within a vaulted ceiling, while thin patches of daylight filtered down through their dark branches to reflect luminescent orange and white fungi spreading from beneath rotting bark.

"Our tire tracks," Roy said. "Look."

I didn't understand until he explained, "The ground is muddy, it keeps our prints. See the tracks behind us, driving this way? There are no other tracks in front of us, which means we didn't come this direction. We took a wrong turn in circling back."

"Ponce de León will be forgotten," I laughed with relief, "in the stead of discoverer Roy Prince's navigational brilliance!"

We got back in, and I turned the ignition, but the car would not start.

"That's it," Roy announced, unnecessarily.

Dark clouds rolled in, and it began to rain. We cursed and tried to get the car started, but to no avail.

"Should we wait out the rain?" I asked. "Follow the sun?"

He didn't answer, and we stared out the windows, glumly.

"I think we're going to have to hoof it out, Roy. No one's going to come looking for us out here."

He agreed, even as the rain worsened. We'd be able to walk back to town if we could find the paved road, which we should be able to locate by following the tire tracks. So we layered our clothes, brought out jackets; took off our shoes and rolled up pants to walk through the wet, and we left the station wagon. We followed Roy's idea, reversing direction along the dirt road, my feet recoiling at every step through the gelid, clingy mud. We went on like this for about two hundred feet, the rain plodding off our backs, the insects around us chirping and crikking and screaming in some orchestra of delirium, until I found where we'd missed a turn that had previously been made in the car. A shout of triumph went up that we'd ultimately escape this mess with little worse than loss of a few hours' time and the addition of blisters and some new gray hairs to our coiffures.

"Just keep following our tracks, and soon we'll be back to the asphalt," Roy said.

And that's what we did, successfully for about twenty more minutes. At that point, as we came through a clearing, we found the road in front of us—split by yet another crossing—to be flooding with rainwater, erasing the tire tracks.

"Damn this place, this entire state . . . " Roy groaned.

Suddenly I felt as if someone was watching us, some *thing*, and the cacophony of insects quieted. We decided the asphalt couldn't possibly be much farther ahead, so we chose the direction seeming most reasonable and tramped through the deepening mud, desperately hoping the paved road would return to sight at any moment . . . and then the path ended. We realized we were well and truly adrift in the swamps of eastern Florida with no sense of where to go. Visions of stalking pythons and monstrous alligators took hold and, as the daylight faded, I found my earlier fortitude to be a sham. I looked to Roy, and he was in equal spirits. We rushed back to find safety in the car.

Only the car could not be found. There were more crossings, smaller trails leading off from larger ones to turn small again, paths that could not be seen one way, but revealed themselves from the other direction, seeming to promise only immediate escape, but leading instead to darker dead ends.

Soon night fell, and the rain continued.

It was the longest night of my life, and I dreamt terribly again of Ponce de León. By morning the rain had not slacked, and our surrounds were seriously flooding, water having risen already above our ankles at every step. We spent another day and night, then day again, wandering the swamp, drenched and shivering, frightened of every sound, cursing every insect bite . . . and suspecting some presence to be watching us, following us, something made of gauntlets and arm guards, gorgets and doublets.

We quite reasonably began to speak of impending death. I'd known of men who could survive worse environments for longer periods of time, but neither of us were of that ilk. Every step was agony, the onset of a coronary. We were slowly freezing, yet still perspiring, starving, gasping, crying, and bereft of hope. I tripped over the root of a mangrove and injured my leg.

"Jim," Roy panted, "Jim, what is that?"

I shook my head without looking, examining my leg to ensure nothing was fractured. Roy walked away.

"Jim," he repeated, "I see something ahead. Light . . . "

Now I glanced up and saw a glow through the trees, a splendor faintly pulsing. Roy trudged toward it, then I got up to follow, limping behind. The glow became brighter, the air warmer.

"It's help," Roy said. "Someone's there."

An ethereal light shone from the distant vision, a light that seemed to have no source, for storm clouds above blotted out all else. A waver shaped the air, as if a ripple across reality, and I caught glimpse of a beautiful pool of crystalline water as pale blue as Mayan opals. The pool was surrounded by lush glades bordered by a perfect circle of ancient stones, ringed throughout by toadstools glowing fluorescent orange, pink, lavender.

"My God," I heard Roy shout, his voice moving farther away, "the fountain . . . it must be . . . it is the Fountain of Youth!"

I only stared as Roy broke out in a run, splashing through the swamp, shouting, "We'll be rich!"

I called to him by impulse, "Wait, it's a mirage, a rainbow after a storm—"

The rain hardened, another ripple seemed to radiate outward from the pool, and Roy was momentarily obscured. I wiped the water from my eyes, blinked, pushed onward and saw him nearing the strange sight.

"Roy!"

I saw then also the nightmare that will haunt the rest of my days, for in the center of that pool, standing on its surface, as if Jesus Christ walking on water, was Ponce de León in all his glorious conquistador regalia.

By what trick of perspective I know not, he seemed as near to me as to touch at arm's length, which caused me to shrink back. Beneath his feathered morion helmet showed a face no older than my own. He appeared healthy, vital, filled with prowess, yet it was the eyes that betrayed him; they stared out as fixed and unblinking as the statue we'd observed in the antique store. Ponce de León gazed upon Roy and pointed with a gloved hand, beckoning him forward.

How could de León still be here, looking the same as he did five hundred years ago? The riddle came to me all at once: *How does a person stop aging?*

And I knew there was only one certain answer... "Roy, come back!"

He was too far gone by then, either by distance so as not to hear my warning or by mania, caught in a dream of riches and immortality. He crossed the ring and stepped into the glimmering water where he would age no more.

I saw then there were others, hundreds more, also in that pool, flashing in and out of view: conquistadors, Native Americans, pirates, trappers, fishermen, tourists, all the seekers of agelessness, all the discoverers of death. The sparkles, the glimmer of the light around them were beings too, flying creatures like fairies, made of teeth and delicate wings and glowing fungi, the same bioluminescent attraction of lanternfish swimming forever in deep water brine.

Ponce de León's phantom wrapped around Roy like ropy, strangling vines and sank into the Fountain of Youth, pulling my friend down with him. "Drink," de León said, "forever."

Roy struggled and cried out for release, but he was gone in a flash.

I watched all this in horror, in the span of mere seconds, frozen by shock, by numbing disbelief.

By the time Roy was gone, Ponce de León's wooden gaze shifted to me. He pointed, gesturing me closer... all the hundreds of other ghosts in that pool pointed, gesturing me closer . . . Roy Prince rose back up, fixed in age for the rest of eternity, and pointed, gesturing me closer.

I turned and ran.

I wandered in the swamp for days more, fighting hypothermia, starvation, illness. I followed roads and paths that led nowhere, that led everywhere. At every juncture I saw the fountain, its distant pool of lights, watching me, following me, rippling nearer and nearer, if ever I stopped in one spot for too long.

By the most serendipitous of luck, a hunter and his dog were out tracking wild hogs and found me stumbling past. I told him what all had occurred, and he nearly laughed.

"You use drugs out here, some hippie commune?" he asked.

"Please," I cried, "help me, we must get away!"

"Sure, but you say your friend is out here too, drowned?"

"de León . . . the fountain . . . "

"Fountain of Youth," he muttered. "If I had a nickel, every treasure hunter—"

"No," I interrupted, "the fountain, it's found us. There!" I pointed toward a pool of ethereal light, appearing from behind a stand of nearby cypress trees.

The hunter looked, let out a little gasp, grabbed me by my arm, turned us to run . . .

But the path he'd come up now appeared split into fourteen different directions, each obscured by rising mud.

He gaped. "What the shit—?"

We were trapped together, as I'd been trapped already. The bell jar of such horrors and strain of the past several days finally crushed me under its vacuous pressure; I surrendered, crying, willing existence to simply end quickly so I'd suffer no more.

The hunter's grip tightened on my arm, and he yelled at me to get up, while I mumbled there could be no escape.

He whistled to his dog, some type of hound with small bloodshot eyes and a fat, lolling tongue. "Pointer, home!"

The dog sniffed around, then by scent moved to a path veering toward the right, and the hunter followed, dragging me along. Soon the mirage of the woods dissipated, and we were upon a main road running along the St. Johns River.

THE police never found Roy's body. They never found the station wagon either, nor the town we'd visited, although I've come to learn there are numerous small hamlets existing in isolation up and down the Florida byways, and it could have been at any of them we'd stumbled across that "wish to retain their own way of living."

Now, decades later, I still don't know what to make of all that transpired, but I think often of my friend Roy Prince, his ghost having found its own grim timelessness in never aging again . . .

He still looks as he did the day he died, for every so often I catch glimpse of him reflecting back to me in lone pools of water, his pointing finger turned beckoning, inviting me in for a drink.

RITUAL SACRIFICE TO THE GREAT GOD OF SKATES

Prologue

IT'S hot, sticky, ugly outside. Distant haze shrouds the valley, if one can see that far, past the festering shopping malls, teeming with languid, plotting patrons. They come, they go, belching exhaust-pipe fumes from their Pintos and Plymouth Champs at every turn. Imagine them there, sweating, broiling. Clambering in and out of stores like the morbid funereal procession of some sun-sickened cult. 90°, 100°, 110°—the temperature doesn't matter when Sears or J.C. Penney has a five percent discount off yesteryear's jeans. The streets are always packed there, crawling with cheap-suited workers, and insurance clerks, and bored housewives in their curlers and shapeless gowns. They step in unison, clumping and pacing, and mindless and dull. Screaming kids, befuddled elderly, dentists and actuaries and other broken-hearted, mobs of the clinging, clawing bourgeois, all circling each other like minor sharks turned toothless and terrified, watching, just watching for what will happen next. Such is the view in this downtown suburbia.

Rita San Glory knows this. It's why she drives the other way. Out on Route 63, where a few ancient trees still remind mankind of their place in this strange world. Past that to Cherry Blossom Trail, where an antique barn guards the crossroads like a timbered paladin. Past there and down the old fire road to a remote lot that's resplendent. Here, the air isn't brown with smog, but gold with dreams.

She parks and gets out, pulls from her backseat a velvet-lined box and carries it to the only building around, a single-story structure like a warehouse, long and deep, and maybe you can't see one end to the other, no matter how hard you try.

So just imagine it there where it doesn't belong, like the mirage in the middle of the desert, the rainbow sheen of an oil slick that if you touch sends ripples into radiance . . .

But the building, it *is* there, for real, for her, and four giant letters cascade down its front wall: RINK.

Behind her, in the parking lot, other cars snake in. Those who wish to skate, too, the initiates.

Rita enters, and they follow.

Rita San Glory in Her Element

SHE sits on one of those long wooden benches that's wrapped in carpet, mauve and maroon from another age. It's threadbare, to be sure, and that's from love. She sits there, and she takes off her flat pumps. She opens the box she'd carried in from her car, the one that's velvet-lined, and she lifts out a pair of roller skates that shares her name, and the others watch, those who have come before, and those who have yet to arrive.

When Rita San Glory puts on those skates, she feels her feet fitting into them—not the other way around. Not the oiled leather, dyed cross-stitched red and white, wrapping each foot to squeeze tight as she runs those double-knit laces up over her ankles helix-style, but rather her feet seem to shift inside the skates like something pliable, potter's clay molding between the hard shelled toe stop, flattening out over the steel plate, and then rising up in the boot, filling perfectly every indentation and slope.

Rita's used to it. It makes her fast, lets her *saiiil.* She stands, feeling the lift of those half-foot wheels, and it's on.

She rolls down a thirty-foot hall, past the endcap of lockers, past a video arcade, past a snack bar that sells a little more than what's shown on the menu. There's a gate up ahead, the kind where bulls might chute through before charging out into a rodeo field. She takes hold of the metal frame—it's cold, but warming up. She rolls her shoulders back, does a calf raise, cracks her knuckles and pulls a squat. Then she signals to the DJ; it's only a look, and that's all he needs.

The rink lights drop for one second, just enough overture for her to frame that gate, gold bangled arms held high for the explosion of light—it flashes three times, laser swaths of red, of blue, of green, and her face is a phoenix rising from the gloom. She hits the concrete track among the cheers, and all around it's flipped-up feathers, ducktails, locks, and now she's another bird blazin' past in blue spandex and a rainbow tee sportin' "Bounce Rock."

Charge and go, racin' in the front, racin' down the track, cross those wheels, kickin' from the back—

"Rita! Rita! Rita!" she hears the crowds cheer, all the prismatic eyeballs of the whacked-out world.

The lights, they're bright, and the sounds sizzle, but the smells are here too; yeah, the scents, they're effluvious. Bearing grease, slick lube, sweat, the sweet kind, perfumed from secreted dreams, and hair spray, 'cause those locks won't stay in place on their own. Snack bar smells, popcorn and pie; Coca Cola with fizz like fireworks; body lotion, cologne, and lipstick—cherry flavored, of course.

Rita swivels and swirls, double arm swings; she does "The Bus Stop," she does "The Get Down," "The Latin Hustle," "The Back Catch." She taps and drags her left foot, turns to the right, closes her feet together for a four-count, poses with her elbows pointed down, and shakes her goddamn beautiful ass.

Then she charges, races, speeds, and if her skates had throttles, they'd be opened wide, raising sparks on those inside turns, around a track with no end, looping and looping, and the faster the better, hurtling down the straightaways, cutting through the leads, leaning in, leaping out, for a back-spin and a flamingo, double-clutching those curves with a smile for a mile.

This is Lucky's 24-Hour Roller Daze, and in here it's strobe lights flashing, neon bright, 30,000-watt system speakers pounding out ABBA so loud you'll dream of that concussion in your sleep, but you won't be sleepin' for a long time, cause this club won't allow it.

So just groove on, baby, groove on, 'cause Rita sure will . . .

Craig Glibbsen in His Element

EASTLAND Shopping Mall. Clothing-Mart. Craig Glibbsen skims through pullovers. Twenty or thirty of them. Hung on racks, folded on shelves. Worn on life-sized busts of ivory-skinned mannequins. There's crew neck and fisherman's. Cashmere, merino. Ecru, Khaki, Desert Puce. Cardigans, button or no. Dusters, the cardigan's longer cousin. Buy one, get half off the other. Emboldened stickers inform that tweed has a traditional honeycomb Aran cable stitch. He sniffles, moves on. Once he was a size medium, but now he's a large, and that has to do with his gut, the softness, the flab that has somehow spread with insidious, yet inexorable, lethargy. His arms are too skinny, too runty for the larger size pullover, which just accentuates such unflattering proportion, but he must make do, since the medium would give him a look like he's gestating a spare tire. It's not fair. More pullovers. Here are alpaca fibers, natural fleece, unless synthesized. Basket-stitch or cable-pattern. Both beige as dust motes, and just as common. He nods appreciatively. Did you know sweaters originate from the fifteenth century, knitted by fishermen's wives to keep their beloved warm in those frigid realms off the Atlantic's Channel Isles? Craig didn't. Now such clothing is sold by design, by texture, by name. Talvikki or Neige, assembly-line precision from the child-labor of fashion supply camps. Craig thumbs through more. Polyamide, acrylic, elastin. There's a nice raglan. Saddle shoulders with a proper arc. Muzak hums from distant ports, "The Great Pretender" done on a xylophone. He sniffles again, gazes abstractedly at a Bouclé Knit sweater: Is yarn actually a better heat insulator than cotton? It's inelegant, what with the loopy patterns, but it's definitely a cozy touch.

MaryAnne touches his back, and Craig startles. "Anything?" she asks.

"No." Craig looks to his wristwatch.

They say no more, but in unison turn, and exit Clothing-Mart, into the walkway levels of other stores. Wall to wall, the stores connect, doors spaced twenty feet apart—optimal space for crowd control, for meandering before display windows, yet without impeding enthralled foot traffic. Here's Hallmark greeting cards and holiday ornaments. Here's Payless ShoeSource, the cheapest footwear in the hometown capital. Hickory Farms, food gifts of processed meat and saran-wrapped gouda cheese. Kay Bee Toys, VideoConcepts, and Zales Jewelry. A thousand more.

MaryAnne carries three bags. Craig stuffs his hands into trouser pockets. Her pullover is tight, fitting a nice form. It's admirable. A sniffle comes. He stopped wearing pullovers two years ago, opting now for flannel button-downs. He can't remember how she and him met.

It's crowded here, in Eastland Mall. Escalators hum. Children shout. Registers ring, clang, clatter. A girl in a paper hat and carnival-striped apron offers them corn dog samples.

"Yum," MaryAnne and Craig both say.

Wherein a pair of strollers bump together, and two mothers realize they haven't seen each other in a month. An old man heroically chooses to walk the stairs. A fly has somehow gotten inside the mall, buzzing and whirling, searching for food slop in which to lay its eggs.

"Wilson Leather is moving. Did you know that?" MaryAnne asks.

"No." Craig scratches at his ear.

A girl is handing out flyers. MaryAnne and Craig each take one. They're advertisements for Lucky's 24-Hour Roller Daze. *Come Visit! Fun for all ages!*

Craig sniffles. Sees MaryAnne give a quick wink to the girl.

He folds the flyer in half, then again. When they're out of earshot from the girl, he asks, "What was that?"

"What?"

"That wink."

"Just that."

He makes a face. "You wink at strangers?"

"I've seen her around."

"Where?"

"Lucky's."

"This place?" He holds up the folded flyer.

She shrugs. "It's fun."

"Never heard of it before."

"Of course you haven't."

"What does that mean?"

"Because I told you it's *fun*." MaryAnne gives a playful nudge into Craig's ribs. He pouts.

"Isn't skating for little kids?"

"Like the flyer says, Craig. It's 'fun for all ages.'"

They walk on, past a Harrison Draperies and a Foot Locker sports attire. Employees in mock black-and-white ref shirts motion for them to come inside. *Big sales! Big deals!*

"I didn't know you went there."

"It's not really your thing, Craig."

"I can skate."

She shrugs, lifting up her shopping bags in a sort of placation. "You have a pair?"

"Of skates? No. . ."

MaryAnne gives it a moment. Her voice is a singsong when she says, "They rent."

"Hm."

"If you want," she says very indifferently.

He glances back. The girl with the flyers has gone. He says, "Yeah. Sure, I mean, take me with you next time. I'll see what it's about."

MaryAnne conceals her smile.

A Moment of Vast Consequence

CRAIG pulls into the remote lot, off an old fire road, from Cherry Blossom Trail and Route 63. He parks the Datsun. Gazes there at a long building that seems like a horizon, way it stretches back and back until growing smaller and vanishing. Or maybe that's just the sinking sun, turning into dusk with a certain refraction through trees that surround it all like a great leafy palisade.

He rubs his eyes. "Never knew this place was out here."

MaryAnne nods. "Sometimes your surrounds can surprise you."

They exit the car, walk to the endless building. When Craig passes under the letters that spell RINK, he feels a quiet unease. An unsettledness he hasn't felt since childhood, lost and alone at night. There's a jolt like a small electric shock, and then it's done. They go inside. She already has the tickets, some sort of pre-sale, maybe. The place seems copacetic.

Until they reach the window for rentals and the unease hits again. MaryAnne walks off. He's taken aback. These skates, the ones to choose from, they're not . . . not *normal*. At least the way he remembers roller skates from his youth, teetering down the cracked sidewalk in front of his family home.

He leans in to look closer until a woman cuts in front, the woman who runs the rental counter. This woman, she dazzles. Snakeskin sheen on a rouge face, lips like a lush heart, beating with each breath. She's slender with muscles lithe as a wildcat. Eyes green as emeralds. Contacts? A trick of light? Those eyes, whatever they are, they search Craig, and they read *deeeep*.

"Here," she says. "Size nine. Wide."

She gives him a pair of roller skates that shares his name.

He stares at them. "How—"

MaryAnne returns, she's already on wheels, brought her own maybe. "Need help lacing up?"

"No," Craig whispers. The moment passes, he can't think of anything else to say. When he puts the skates on, there's a pressure that builds around each foot, not unpleasant, but unusual. It's warm, almost throbbing. *Wanting*.

"Ready?" MaryAnne takes his hand, pulls him down the hall, and then he's at the track.

He's never seen anything like it—swaths of light like shooting stars rocket down the lanes, flash-pops of brilliance pass and bend in waves that snap back behind. MaryAnne nudges him nearer.

He stutters, "Are those actual . . . *flames* inside the track?"

"Yes, Craig. Yes, they are."

And she shoves him forward.

Intermission

THERE are new gods as there are old, gods that are born, that are designed, gods that reincarnate or appear through collective vicissitude. Major, minor, providence or numen, the deities who are us, of our image yet magnified to titanic size and consequence. Is existence quantifiable? Or is it senseless as the filament of cosmic hair that retches out time and space? *There*, behold Ninazu, Mesopotamian god of serpents. From Enegi to Eshnunna, He doth go, as warrior and infinite son. *There*, witness Scáthach, Celtic goddess of combat. Temptress, trickster, heroine, She yet keeps the Fortress of Shadows in thrall. *There*, consider Xipe Totec, Aztec god of metallurgy. He cloaks himself in flayed human skin to depict the act of germination and of His nature in the sunken valles of Puebla, Mexico.

Here, regard Rink, Flemmish god of roller skating. See Him, if yon worth prevails. He proffers great bliss, both transcendent and of mortal felicity. At a cost. At a measure of worth. There are times—moments of astronomical significance—when Rink makes Himself known, when followers come to worship, times when distant moons and worlds align like the four spinning wheels of a boss-sprung ride.

It's said by theologians that worshippers love their gods for either external riches or internal consolation. Yet Rink towers above them all, undefinable. Venerable though haughty, volatile and so badass. Mosaic tiles depict him, skin of neon red, head thrown back with just enough smile to see fangs. There's a head of hair like a Texas tornado—bouffant up and duck tail in back. Lithe arms outstretch, one waving a goedendag sword, and the other holding a human soul like an hourglass; is it compassion he holds up this soul? Or perdition? The debate is as enduring as its legacy . . . and now look again at that skin, red as it is . . . You tell me: Is it blood? Flames? Cherry lipstick smears from Rita San Glory?

Maybe never mind that, but catch a long glimpse of those legs, all six of them, fifty feet high, and each colossal cloven foot sheathed in the bombest slick rigs you'd ever dream: golden skates jeweled with skulls, set on lifters and drag packs, with astronomical ratios that spring each bearing to the tightest of powerband.

Rink roars, he skates through the cosmos, cutting swathes through lesser gods with a pivot and a swirl, a split-squat-and-go. And sometimes he makes his way to Earth, where a coven of one hundred initiates emulate his ways and, once a year, grant onto him yearly sacrifice.

A Singular Moment of Realization

CRAIG'S been pushed from the skating rink gate by MaryAnne, and he lurches onto the concrete track. It's smooth here, glassy as ice, and promptly the wheels roll out from under one foot. He clumsily falls to a knee, says "Ow," is about to turn and yell at her for having pushed him—*I mean, why would she do that?*

Then the gate closes and it latches, and the moment strikes him as he rises, as he tries to steady himself: there's a vibration coming through here, like placing your ear on the steel rail of an oncoming train, thundering, pulsing, growing nearer. And this vibration isn't just from the track, but in the air too, a carnivorous beast breathing, and Craig has to turn, even with growing recognizance, MaryAnne all-but-forgot, looking *there!* where concentric blossoms of smoke whirl across the outside lanes . . .

A figure appears from the gloom, insubstantial as a wraith, until backlight catches the sparkling turn, and then it's sequins and spangles, blue spandex and iridescent sheen. The figure slides in like a rocket queen, coming upon him all at once in a blur, seizes his hand perfectly into her own, and yanks him along to skate at her majestic side.

A Singular Moment of Realization From a Different Perspective

RITA San Glory skates here whenever she feels the need. Whenever age has caught up, threatens to overwhelm. Whenever the world is slowing, and she needs to speed up. Whenever the sun reshapes seasons, when the calling is great, when the one hundred initiates gather.

Every year, one among them provides offering, sacrifice from the flock of the mundane—a mortal, assessed and found lacking, found inconsequential and unsaved.

And so here it is, the truth of the matter: Fuck confessional. You come here, you skate away your sins. You dance and you glide, and this is the purest vision of Xanadu you'll ever know on this side of existence.

Rita sees the sacrifice fall onto the track. He's unsure, dazed. Lost. Pale and pouting in his rumpled button-down flannel. He looks around, looks back. His fingers are limp, his posture strained. Those eyes blink like a sad toad's.

Rita leads the pack, the eternal hunt, and swoops upon him. "Baby," she says, her voice husky, smoky as the gloom. "You're about to lose your mind."

A Journey of Transcendent Flight

THE woman takes him and, at touch, he knows her name. The union is immediate, euphoric, entwining. They change lanes, and they fly, and the one hundred initiates follow, jostling at their heels.

And Craig can't help but scream, though he's not in pain. It's shock, facing the unfamiliar, which to this woman, this Rita San Glory, must *be* the familiar; fear, confusion, disbelief, it is the same for all whom she takes hold.

When he finds his voice, it's: "Wh—what's happening?"

She laughs. To ask Rita San Glory, High Priestess of the Sacred Circle of Rink, what is happening is to ask the stalking lion why it is hungry, or the ocean why it should storm.

And at which point Craig Glibbsen is transported. Another time, another place, another him. He looks upon himself, skating ten billion miles an hour. Ten trillion. More. There are no shapes around any longer, at least nothing discernible, but that existence has become a running blur, colors mashed and whirled together like passing through a great blender. He feels his particles trying to pull apart and understands that what's keeping him together, keeping him going, is the woman who holds his hand, and if she should let go now, he will be lost in the cosmic spiral of annihilation.

Craig Glibbsen was once a child, and before him lay the interminable entanglement of choices. Choices to turn right or to turn left, to speak a kind word or one cruel. Choices of books, of flavors, of friends; to act honestly or to lie, to walk or run or dance, to pet a dog, to watch a cloud, to kiss, to kill, to ignore. To choose the duster, the cardigan, the Bouclé Knit sweater. And with each choice made, how so does the future change, does it evolve or reset, or does it shrink by one, the decision made, the alternative foregone, and onto the next choice, and the shrinkage by one yet again, and the next and the next and the next, until the end of existence is but one final choice away . . .

And Craig sees the choices then, he lives them as he circles round and round in the lemniscate-loop of infinity. The adrenaline, the twists, turns, sparks showering all around, fireworks of celerity, and Rita San Glory who shifts and shows with spandex-clad limbs that grow and multiply and face him with the eyes of star-spangled vastitude.

Craig is an ant, infinitesimal, insignificant. Craig is a mote, a whit of dung from the bowel of a moon-slug. Craig is a fireman, a father, a hero. Craig is a primate on an island riven by catastrophe. Craig is a mayor, a mother, a lover. He is a spore. He is a wraith. He is a leaf of lettuce in the salad of a troll.

And so are his travels toward Rink, the learning, the yearning, each choice made, each choice *not* made, flying, flying through the laser swaths and fog screens, flying through the DJ pulse, the scree of wheels, the gold dust sparkle where he lives all the choices of that interminable entanglement of existence.

And he knows he's dead. He's been dead, hasn't he, just living in the purgatory of Eastland Shopping Mall, for years and years and years, all his venial sins collected and gauged, and charged back in due to a longing and deprivation from which there is no awareness, a yearning for more, of *something* indefinable, *something* out of grasp, a torment of banality and discount days in the dishware department.

But for MaryAnne, he's been saved, pulled forth from the distraught. MaryAnne, one of those hundred initiates, tasked and trusted to deliver him, to sacrifice him, to save him, and that he is free, he is flying in this moment, and he has learned the absolute singular perfect path of choices for his own existence, and thus is he spent, and Rita San Glory delivers him to Rink . . .

And why else would you skate but to live another life, of freedom, of exuberance?

Then the lights dim.

THE MOON OVER ANDERSONVILLE

Sep. 12th, 1864

FOG this morning, but the rain has finally slackened. The weather's inclemency brings more terrible disease with it and, I fear, worsens my dysentery. Mush for breakfast. The eating is poorer each day, and there is no salt left in camp. More Union prisoners arrive by train than can be handled. The new prisoners refer to the stockade as Andersonville, but I know it still as Georgia's Camp Sumter. I have been here one year today and have survived but by the Lord's preference.

Rebecca, I miss you so.

Sep. 16th, 1864

JACKSON died last night of diarrhea and scurvy. It was agony to watch, but I held his hand until death's merciful release. The moon was full like a porcelain plate, and we prayed under its radiant light. There is an open space in our tent and someone new may fill it. Wilson and I call it our tent, but it's no more than a ratty wool blanket stretched across wood stakes. Still, I am grateful I'm not lying under the sky with only my shirt for shelter, as so many others must pass their days. Smith stole a bottle of whiskey today and shared it around. The rebel guards searched, but we hid it well. Had a pleasant chat with a sergeant from the Iowa 5th Division.

Sep. 18th, 1864

THE weather holds at warm and rainy. We have a new man in our tent, a young private by the name of John Murray. I think he is Irish, but he will not admit to it. He was of the Pennsylvania 16th Cavalry. He appears healthy except for a large infected wound upon his arm. He relates he was bitten by a giant wolf two nights prior. The rebs found him sleeping naked in the forest. I think he must have got drunk, but he will not admit to that either. I consoled Murray to the horrors of life here, and he was scarce to believe it. Smith is very weak and coughing blood freely now. We both know he will not survive much longer. He wishes only that he may pass with dignity.

Rebecca, I still dream of you each night. I love you and think upon our fleeting time together.

Sep. 25th, 1864

TODAY, supper was peas and rice past their age, seething with bugs. A man went crazy and tried climbing over the camp fence. The reb guards shot him immediately. Perhaps he was not so crazy after all . . .

Sep. 29th, 1864

DEAR Rebecca, I have grown fond of John Murray. You would like him, for he is quite amiable. He owns a farm out in Columbia County with wife and two small children of whom he speaks about at every opportunity. His infected arm grows worse though, and I think it a very bad omen for him.

A crop of sweet potatoes arrived, and we each received a half of one as ration. It was a blessing.

Oct. 2nd, 1864

SMITH has died of dysentery, that dread affliction which will surely kill me if I do not escape this vile prison. Wilson and Murray volunteered for the burial detail. Wilson took Smith's clothes for himself, and he changed into them before me. His drawers were as black as the ace of spades from soil and grime, and under that he was one great sore crawling with maggots. I am told over one hundred and fifty men die here each day, but I would reckon to double that number. There is upward of thirty thousand starving prisoners of war now locked in Camp Sumter, and we are drowning in the rot.

Oct. 6th, 1864

THE weather is agreeable today. Mush again for breakfast. Wilson left this morning to draw rations for us but never returned. Marauders are rampant, and they prey on the feeble. Murray and I met a surgeon's assistant from the Minnesota 2nd Artillery. He was missing one eye and suffered from dropsy. We discussed the ghastly diseases that flourish in this camp. He related to us that infectious germs are transmitted through bodily secretions, such as waste and blood, even saliva, and through the air we breathe. Murray and I took to keeping rags over our faces that very hour, so as not to incur any further rotten illness.

I grow frail, Rebecca. My thoughts of you are all that keeps me alive.

Oct. 10th, 1864

MURRAY is wild with grief to return home to his family. He has terrible dreams of the moon, and I have watched a dark shadow of change come over him. The infection in his arm has spread rapidly through him, and his teeth have grown long at the root. I can only suppose that to mean his gums are receding, perhaps due to scurvy (I could discern no other reason why). He shivers and requires hospital care, as do I. However, I've known men who occasionally return from the so-called 'hospital'. Their testimony relates that even if a man is severely sick, he'd do better never to go there. My fluency of the English language cannot convey the horrors that building holds.

The sun was scorching hot today. I begged a man for a drink of water. He looked at me and declined. His fear of the contagious spread of dysentery was so great he refused to share his only cup. His is a sentiment shared by most of the stockade.

Oct. 15th, 1864

TWO spaces remain open under our blanket shelter although no man would wish to bed near us. Murray and I both lay on our sides coughing sickness. Murray has contracted the bloody diarrhea and can no longer make it to the trenches to relieve himself. He defecates all day outside the entrance to our tent. The stench of it would make me ill, were I not so ailing already. An old friend brought me two forkfuls of pork and molasses. I know not where he acquired it, but I cried tears of gratitude.

Rebecca, I love you so. I fear I did not tell you enough when we were together, which is my greatest regret. I fear I will never see you again to speak to your sweet face.

<u>Oct. 16th, 1864</u>

O! THE horrors, yet wonders! An event has occurred that one could never imagine. The moon turned full last night, and Murray became a giant wolf-man before my very eyes. He first screamed in agony, and I thought he was in the clutches of death, killed by his infection. But Murray grew and stood, fully twice in size. His eyes shone yellow, and large fangs extended from his mouth. He howled and ran from the tent. I crawled outside and watched him flee. Great shrieks sounded from the camp. Any man that stood in the beast's way was dealt with viciously, be it prisoner or reb. He leapt clear over the fence, twenty feet in height. Reb guards gave chase, but I am told they were either killed or retreated in terror.

I would not believe it had I not seen it with my own eyes. How can such werewolves exist in our modern times? Murray claimed to have been bitten by a giant wolf before he arrived. The infection had been transmitted. Our germs are everywhere in this foulness. I feared before that our illnesses would contaminate each other, but now I wonder how else the infection may pass by choice . . .

Lord, I ask you to understand and to forgive me. I eat of Murray's bloody defecation by the entrance of our tent. Rebecca, I pray I can survive until the next full moon cycle. I will see you again before this mortal life ends.

A STROKE OF DEATH

ODILE Thibodeau had once shown in the finest galleries in Montmartre and beyond, throughout the fringes of grand Paris, immersed among the Post-Impressionists at the Galerie Durand-Ruel, or amid the *demi-monde* depictions in the Musée des Artistes Vivants, and even the erotic grotesqueries hid beautifully within those thin shadows latticing Goupil et Cie . . .

But no longer.

His art, his masterpieces, they now received little more than a glare of menacing acknowledgement from one exclusive patron, Monsieur Bourguignon—the *loathsome* Monsieur Bourguignon—who stood before him that very moment. The scrutiny of Monsieur Bourguignon was, as always, unnerving while he waited, twisting at the curled ends of a heavily oiled mustache inside the sooty, soiled second-floor loft Odile called both home and studio.

"It is time," Monsieur Bourguignon finally said. His eyes seemed lifeless, his nose sharp as a shark's fin. "To see."

Odile breathed deep for this moment, the grand reveal: he whipped the protective white sheet off his newest painting. The act itself was a remarkable display of showmanship—the sheet billowed out with a flourish! It emitted a satisfying *whoosh*! Lighting from the overhead gabled windows shone down at just the right angle to illuminate his newest work, a stunning composition flawlessly blending impressionist ideals with the resonance of melancholy pointillism, that had taken Odile a month with little sleep to complete.

Monsieur Bourguignon shrugged, then wiped at his sharp nose. "It is fine."

"But . . . only 'fine'? See how I darkened the hues, added depth! The texture—"

"Must we? Every time?" Monsieur Bourguignon's exhalation of disdain was like the sudden gust of foul wind that rose often along the Seine, where the factory bulwarks discharged their steaming offal. At exhalation's end, he tossed over his shoulder a black satin-lined cape.

It was true, Monsieur Bourguignon was a notorious criminal, head of a gang of dagger-wielding brutes. The bakeries, the cafés, the clubs along Boulevard de Clichy, many of them were in debt to, or otherwise dread of, the petite man. It was true, too, that Odile was counted among that maltreated number. He'd long since exhausted weeping over the matter, had tired even of muttering liberally imaginative slews of denunciations and maledictions. The mutters were whispers of course, nothing ever so audible that Monsieur Bourguignon might actually hear.

He'd sunk instead into a deepening stupor of acquiescence.

"For you." Monsieur Bourguignon handed him a small velvet bag, the gold coins within a seeming lifeforce of their own, heavy, jangling, imbibed with conspiratorial deceit. "With other men, I would toss payment at their feet, the likes of a street beggar. But consider it a token of my regard, I present to you as a confrere. Hold my gratitude tight, *mon petit artiste*."

Odile took the money, looking down to the bare wood floor in shame. A glance back then at his painting, showing a figure—vaguely that of a man—filling a cobblestone road while nighttime stars the size of francs shimmered overhead. The painting's perspective narrowed, twisted behind an alley, from which could be seen the remnants of a shadow, perhaps a speeding carriage having just passed by, perhaps something else. If one should look at the painting upside down, it might appear the man was being dragged upward, his arms extended into the night. Otherwise, the figure was a smear of brushstrokes, crimson over umber, highlights jaundiced orange while the contours became muted, pushed into the cracks separating each stone of the road. It was evocative to look at, a whirl of fleeting shapes, an impression of despair, a gilding of release. A hope, tugging, like fog dissipating to reveal a great truth.

Monsieur Bourguignon whipped his hand at it twice. Odile

thought a fly must have gotten into the studio, until Monsieur Bourguignon said the words Odile knew would come:

"Now destroy it."

ODILE'S mother had been a nun. Once. Before she died. Before she was excommunicated. His father had been a priest as well. Odile never knew his father, but that had been no one's fault but for the divine vagary of the god both his parents had given their lives to serve. Odile's father had died young, early, as punishment, some denounced. For what he'd done, the corruption, the seducement. As far as Odile knew, there had not been as such claimed, at least from the secular sense. His mother had not been raped, there had been no abuse of power, as was often said to occur in the sacristies of the church. His parents had simply fallen in love. As man and woman. As nature designed. They'd left the church surreptitiously, eloped down to the lake shores of Aix-les-Bains to wed, where his father promptly drowned in the icy clutches of Lac du Bourge, the night before they were to take their solemn vows, but not before a certain premarital coupling had already occurred, leaving Odile's mother alone, penniless, and swelling visibly from her weakness in sin. A bleak future had foretold the poorhouse for her, a brutish orphanage for infant Odile . . .

Yet instead, she'd bravely returned to Paris, no longer a sister of any Consecrated Order, but rather as Mademoiselle Cécile Thibodeau, reborn in certainty to persevere, to provide for her child. To leave her mark. In art, in work, in life, until *la vie* became *la fin*.

IN the morning, Odile went out for a café crème and buttered croissant. It was a beautiful day with warming skies and pigeons and martins snuggled along the shop eaves, cooing, warbling. He almost whistled in reply.

A boy in felt cap, with buck teeth much too large for his crooked mouth, paced on the street corner, calling out to passing shoppers, strollers: "*Nouvelles! Nouvelles!* News, read all about it!"

"Here," Odile said. He recognized the boy, one of several who circulated the boulevards twice a day with their newspaper-filled slings.

"Un franc," the boy said flatly.

"*Oui*, as always." Odile took the paper, unfolding it as he walked along the street. He enjoyed to walk and read in the same motion. He found he enjoyed things less and less these days, ever since meeting Monsieur Bourguignon. But this was nice, at least, to get outside, feel the sun after so much past rain. Perhaps it was a good omen.

He browsed the headlines, that the level of the Seine was rising, imminent flooding if spring rainfall should renew. The next page, announcing premier opening of the Vélodrome d'hiver cycling stadium. The page after that read *DES MORTS*, and showed a photograph, a slightly out-of-focus image in blobs of black and white.

Odile gasped, a horrible oily burn racing through his chest. He balanced himself against a streetlamp, staring, sweating suddenly. The event of this death was not unexpected, not by this point, but to see it in print, this—*this* was the horror: the photograph was a copy, perhaps not exact, but rather a "reimagining" of his painting, if not more concise, more realistic, grainier. The actualization of a dream. The cobblestoned road twisting away, narrowing in perspective, crossed by an alley. A body, crushed most obviously, lay in its center. The only difference in newspaper print was a policeman's cloak draped over the carnage, leaving in wonder at only how those lumps underneath could be so misshapen, so . . . distanced apart.

"Gods," he cried out. "Gods."

The death was of Aloysius Jeanneret-Gris. A banker, age 46. Run over by a speeding carriage, weighed down by produce. The driver had not seen Aloysius in the dark hours of night, when Aloysius had apparently emerged from a reputed den of vice. An accident, all agreed, a dreadful accident.

But Odile knew better. For this was his great secret, his blame: Odile Thibodeau painted deaths before they occurred. He *created* the deaths.

At first, he'd believed he only foresaw them . . . the images simply seemed to come to him, coalescing as he wandered the streets of Montmartre from Rue Championnet to Rue de Châteaudun: performers bright with rouge, shopkeepers, smiling, calling out their wares, children in short pants, rolling hoops along the streets. Inspiration was rich, then, tendrils clutching for his senses, heady with tangs of perfume and fresh baguettes, vigorous in sound, clanking gears and whinnying steeds. The sights, the feelings, *c'est la bonne vie!*

And so he painted them, macabre portrayals of men electrocuted, women decapitated, children froze in icicle shrouds. It was avant-garde, shocking. Brutally honest in depictions of peoples' frail mortality. And from his artwork, he prospered. Received stipends, adoration. And his conscience was clear all the while, for everyone died. What did it matter if the spirit of premonition should make itself known through his art, the prophecy of strangers' deaths that he simply put to the brush . . .

But all that changed. Such "la bonne vie" darkened to the grave, when he learned he was, instead, the actual agent of such fatalities.

His instructor of this knowledge was none other than Monsieur Bourguignon—the *loathsome* Monsieur Bourguignon. If only Odile had deciphered the horror on his own merit beforehand, it would have brought immediate abstinence. He would have fled for the coast and hurled his paints and bristles into the icy depths of the English Channel! Instead, it was arrogance that had proved his undoing, the conceit that foreshadowed its own sort of demise, the annihilation of all that was good in his life. Too much vin, perhaps, had blinded him. The absinthe, cold as sleet on his feverish brain. The accolades, the money. The charm of his favor; who could see past such things, who would think to *search* past them while in the throes of joy, scrutinizing for some invisible disease festering underneath it all?

And the grand revelation by Monsieur Bourguignon . . . beyond all else, who could have surmised such a criminal overlord should have a love of art, a refinement toward the radical painters displaying, late at night, works of progressive thought, of response and reform through abstraction? And that Odile's work had caught his eye . . .

THE night after Aloysius Jeanneret-Gris's grisly death, Monsieur Bourguignon returned to Odile's loft-studio. "*Bon travail,*" he applauded Odile. "Well done, well done."

The rainfall the newspaper feared had returned. Lightning split the sky outside the gabled windows while tempestuous wind buffeted the building.

Odile never knew how to reply to Monsieur Bourguignon's praise. To say nothing was discourteous at the least . . . but to acknowledge the act repudiated any hope Odile had of convincing himself it had all been hapless coincidence. Tonight, Monsieur Bourguignon was not alone, so Odile finally settled on a whispered, "Merci."

The other two men who had come inside the studio with Monsieur Bourguignon said nothing but stared at Odile intently.

Mon dieu, do they never blink? Odile thought of them in alarm. He nervously stepped backward, turned away, glanced at the plaster wall upon which their shadows loomed twice larger than their physical bodies. Odile knew them both: Cearbhall, whose closed fists were the size of anvils and as powerful as such. Anatomic impossibility be damned, Cearbhall had once pulled a rival's spine out through the man's jaw. The second of Monsieur Bourguignon's henchmen was even worse: Vlak' Mikel, towering though stoop-shouldered, immaculately dressed in a suit of pin-striped periwinkle and white, a gay violet kerchief around his neck. Upon his head was a straw boater's hat, pulled low, crowning the black hood that covered all his face but for those staring eyes. It was said Vlak' Mikel had no tongue, although Odile could not attest one way or the other—he'd never heard either man speak, even when Vlak' Mikel had once sliced off the top of Odile's ear with a knife.

"People will liken you to Van Gogh!" Monsieur Bourguignon had merrily said then, over a year ago. What he said now to Odile was even worse. "A new commission is arranged."

Monsieur Bourguignon then lifted his hands, palms upward, a small reckoning of regret as he continued. "For the problems this man has caused cannot be undone."

"Please, no more," Odile begged. Cearbhall and Vlak' Mikel made no movement, yet the vigor of their stares was a physical force of its own, a fiery optical backhand striking him along the cheek. Odile tried again: "I mean, just . . . not so soon. I beg, I must rest."

"I am not asking some favor of charity to remove this man," Monsieur Bourguignon said, twisting at the ends of his curled mustache. He spoke gently, reasonably. "This is a duty, and I pay you for it. Considerably. My job is to make sure our business runs without interruption. This man I give you is an interruption. Like him, if you become an interruption, you will be removed—"

Odile knew what would come next.

"—as will others."

Cearbhall then held out a photograph, and Odile took it, a sepia-toned *carte de visite* mounted on cardboard, showing an elderly man in a waistcoat standing in front of a luxurious chaise lounge. The man in the photo was smiling, a sweet, genuine bearing. He could have been anyone's handsome grandfather.

"One month to complete?" Monsieur Bourguignon asked.

"*Oui.*"

The three visitors turned all at once and exited to the outside stairwell, opening frilly parasols to shelter from the stinging rain.

Odile stared at the photograph for hours, as the candles waned under shallowing wax, the storm outside swelled, as memories surged, and hopes mourned, and failed wishes taunted him from the edges of despair, over a gift only gods should possess. He stared at the photograph until weariness took him to slumber, and even then he kept the photograph with him, staring until his eyes collapsed, and the photograph stared back in dreams.

MADEMOISELLE Cécile Thibodeau had raised Odile in the artist clubs where she herself found work and developed a remarkable talent for expressionist visions of the Holy Hereafter. She promoted in employ from venue to venue, first a type of slop-and-scullery maid, then a waitress of hors d'oeuvres, and then bottle service, then assistant to the flesh-baring girls of burlesque, and onto hostess of the house, and then, finally, a contract in entertainment, as set designer for the bawdiest of nightclubs, and then muralist for the snootier ilk, until finally—*truly finally*—gaining grant as artist-in-residence at Montmartre's celebrated *Cabaret du Ciel.*

Should one's life be summed up by a single occupation, such would be this culmination of profession for nun-turned-artist Mademoiselle Thibodeau (as well as being the initial and strongest impression upon young Odile, at his first visit, which set him on an immutable course of art, death, and the inscrutable, celestial hand that issues judgment upon us all). For the Cabaret of Heaven was this: Garish bells chiming, robed men thundering, cherub-actors flinging toy arrows about the room. Cracked plywood clouds, lacquered shining white, hung above dining tables. Globed lights mimicked stars. Harps and organs abounded, as did revealing women pirouetting throughout the club; gold slips curtained off their hips, and cascades of bright and fragrant flowers fell from their hair. Gothic façades tapered to points at every corner, and a pulpit stood on one side, adorned with a great sacrificed pig; blood and sliced apples hung off its chin. And the crosses! The crosses were everywhere, on every surface, on every chair. Gold, silver, great, small. The bar was engraved with them, where patrons would spill cognac and le Soixante-Quinze onto the Holy marks. And never was *Cabaret du Ciel* empty! People clanking glasses, confessing sins, dancing, eating, shrieking with bellows of laughter.

All glory and false fronts and fresh beef à la roti.

Never had Mademoiselle Thibodeau imagined she would end up in such circumstance; but she did it all—sacrificed modesty and divine enlightenment—for her son. For both their sakes, she did not try to shield him from the nightclub's depravities, but explained them for his own prudence.

"Expressions," she said. Her voice was soft, always so placid, like wind upon a dreaming sea. "We express ourselves in what we believe. God and good. Or lust. Envy. Pleasures. Of the mind, the body, the spirit. We express through deed, through song, through art, to share visions and ideas. I paint to give meaning. To this and *us.*" She embraced Odile then. Her warmth, her scent of parfum and safflower oil, filled him. "Art transforms us, both the creator and the audience. Our inner state, existence, and the hint of beyond."

Her subjects for painting were of Christ, crucified, eternally-suffering eyes cast Heavenward. And spirits ascending, angels bringing forth the revenant of man. Christians tormented for their beliefs, tortured, fed to lions, speared, beheaded. Their souls glorified. Martyred.

Always the sacrifice first, then always the rebirth.

She taught Odile to paint in such ways. She sang hymns, and quoted psalms, while they painted. Spoke of the resurrection of man, of forgiveness, of all God giveth and what He taketh away.

Mademoiselle Thibodeau and Odile lived in the rooms behind *Cabaret du Ciel*, and even when she was not working, and young Odile scampering underfoot, he would still sneak into the club, to mimic his mother's art there. He copied her styles, her beliefs, and his subjects were of the afterlife, or on the throes of reaching such. He painted their portraits while scripture filled his head, and angels on guy lines swung overhead, playing lutes in the high, arched theatre ceilings and smoking cigarettes there too when on break. Ash dropped on him, and girls with no shirts, less even brassieres, blew him kisses from gold-gilt cages. Always the life, the love, the essence! Expressions, indeed, he practiced on all he saw.

He watched a man die, a heart attack from gluttony. He watched a performer fall from a balcony and break her neck. He watched revelers turn to violence, and knives flashed, a pistol. Two more dead. Then a waiter, murdered in a lover's feud. Then a diner, choking on chicken bones. And more; he painted them all.

By age twenty, Odile called himself—without any uncertainty—an "artiste," and his mother approved. By twenty-one, he showed in exhibits, and she turned ill. By twenty-two, galleries made bids for him, and she went to a private hospital. Odile paid for her room. By twenty-three and twenty-four and twenty-five, his fortunes improved, while hers declined. And then she died. Her face, at the last, had shown acceptance, grace, and something else . . . ascent. Fate—he saw her die in his mind, saw her death, and others, so many more, as he held her hand, and watched into her eyes as the event came to pass. His paintings, they became more macabre, grim. And the deaths came to him then, like a divining rod of doom. And his patrons loved them, they cried, "*Et plus!*" Skulls, gore, morbid aberrancies, Odile painted them without pause. Drownings, burnings, disease; swordplay, strangling, suicide—Odile was exhilarated by almighty annihilation.

And all the while thinking they were but shadows of foresight . . . until Monsieur Bourguignon appeared.

OVER the next month that current Spring, Odile painted the death of the handsome grandfatherly man that Monsieur Bourguignon had ordered.

Odile had thrown himself into his work, for he had little else; his self-care was faltering, though by painting he clung to some vestiges of normalcy. He no longer scraped the residue of pigment from beneath his nails, but he bathed. Sometimes. He did not bother to launder or even straighten his clothes. When he shaved, his reflection showed eyes seeming incurably red-rimmed and sunken. But painting! At least engaging in his craft was escapism from this dreadful plight—by art, he managed to rediscover some withered pride in improving technique, in expressing vision.

When the latest painting was complete—the exquisiteness in the gradation of value, the transcendental gaze of the subject being impaled on an iron lattice after slipping off an icy step—Monsieur Bourguignon visited, inspected the work, and paid Odile his wage in gold coins before directing he "now destroy it." Destroying the artwork was not necessary to the process, but Monsieur Bourguignon wanted no evidence to remain, took no chance that a rival loathsome criminal overlord with an eye to the arts might happen upon his prized painter.

"Of course," Odile allowed. It was another dagger thrust into his soul, but he dared not disobey. The painting went into a small furnace and burned.

The following morning, Odile crossed the street to the newsboy and read about the death in the paper. Denis Gaston LaFromboise. A judicial clerk in the Council of Ministers, age 63, instrumental in the fight against organized crime in Paris. Husband, father, grandfather. An accident, his falling off the slippery steps, a dreadful accident.

And that night Monsieur Bourguignon reappeared at Odile's loft, new photograph in hand. "Another commission for you, *mon petit artiste . . . mon petit assassin . . .* "

And so, the cycle went.

Odile painted a police sergeant exploding into a hundred chunks by an errant stick of dynamite. He painted a rouge-cheeked strumpet with her stockings tied off around her neck. He painted a vexing witness to robbery choking on his own written testimony. He painted a card-shark being eaten by actual sharks while bathing at home. An accident, such terrible, terrible accidents, all! Monsieur Bourguignon had the news publishers in his pocket.

And with each painting, the gold coins flowed in. Monsieur Bourguignon paid well and promptly—for that he was irreproachable. But the more riches Odile obtained, the less he felt any care for them; the guilt, the damned crushing self-condemnation allowed no pleasures but to drink himself into a stupor at home each night, enslaved there as a captive, as a murderer . . .

How could he escape such a fate? The answer was obvious, that if Odile could paint people into death, he should take up the next canvas and depict Monsieur Bourguignon suffering the most horrific, agonizing annihilation imaginable: pierced through in the Iron Maiden, or quartered over The Wheel, or sat upon the slowly impaling Judas Cradle . . .

But, *non*. That answer, unfortunately, was *too* obvious, at least to one who had risen to such heights in the criminal underworld. It was the first precaution Monsieur Bourguignon had taken: If he should die, whether by accident, tragedy, his own hand, then Odile would be next, as would others. Such was the problem of many-headed monsters; once one falls, another takes its place. Someone would accede into Monsieur Bourguignon's role and reap revenge . . . and if that someone should fall, someone else would move into position. The world was filled with Cearbhalls and Vlak' Mikels and their lot. Odile could paint them all into fiery death, but he had to *see* them first; he'd be helpless against unknown assailants.

And in any case, it was becoming harder and harder to wish to see *anyone* at all. He began to shield his view from faces, he kept himself locked within his loft as much as possible, going out only to procure food, drink, and paints. Until even that became too much to bear... for the weight of malaise, after all, is a crushing load. Odile soon found himself stricken with immobility by the mere task of trying to take the knob of his door to exit. How his heart would race! How sweat would bead upon his brow... outside, he would see faces, imagine horrible disasters! His hands trembled at the thought of death-visions shrouding every visage he chanced upon.

While, all the time, his back room filled with those little black bags of gold. He thought often of his mother, her words, her own rebirth to art from the Church. Sacrifice and judgement. And forgiveness... ? *Bah,* he spat at himself for even imagining such a thought.

Finally he went to his window and saw the newsboy passing below. "Boy!" he cried out. "Garçon! Come here, please!"

The boy came up the iron steps, and Odile left the door wide open before retreating into the farthest corner, eyes cast away.

"*Oui*?" the boy asked hesitantly.

"What is your name?"

"Louis."

"Louis... " Odile repeated it, letting the sound of the name hang between them. "I wish to hire you."

"A job?"

"Yes. I am much too busy to leave this studio, for my work is found necessary. You must shop for me, groceries, supplies. I will give you a list each week."

"Perhaps."

"I will pay well. Anything you need."

The boy's eyes grew wide at this. Odile waved into the back room, where through the doorway could be seen Monsieur Bourguignon's payments of gold. Odile thought so little, he'd thrown them to the floor, having no place, need, nor care to hide any of it. The gold helped not with his sleep, his conscience. Many of the coins had even fallen free, lying there like glistening, molten puddles.

"I would be very happy to help you," the boy announced with an immense smile of those buck teeth.

With that stroke of accordance, Odile no longer had to step outside. He slept fitfully, drank more. His face grew pale, haggard. But he painted.

WHEN Monsieur Bourguignon had first approached him a year-and-a-half before, Odile was in the center of a great and depraved gala of drunken ceremony and hysterical boasts. Odile's face was ruddy, flush with vigor, his speech slurred from champagne. He laughed with friends: " . . . and the fellow said, 'To be frank, I'd have to change my name!'"

Cackles burst throughout the hall.

Then Monsieur Bourguignon was there, introducing himself, neatly steering Odile away from the others. Odile thought the man effeminate, some sycophant fan looking to curry favor with a rising célébrité.

"That painting there," Monsieur Bourguignon had said, pointing to a framed work on the gallery wall; in it, a top-hatted man held his own severed legs, while a great sawblade sprayed blood upon onlookers. "When did you make it?"

Odile shrugged. "Two months ago, or so."

"And that one?" Monsieur Bourguignon asked, pointing to the next work; in it, a woman's pelvis split apart as a two-headed child emerged.

Odile was bored with the hanger-on. "I don't know, the month prior, I suppose."

Monsieur Bourguignon tilted back his head, stroked a clefted chin, calculating something with a twiddling of fingers. "Yes, yes, I thought as much." He smiled. The expression was ghastly. "I have a request, a custom portrait, done in such your style."

"No requests. I am too busy, monsieur."

"Please, it is for a friend. A prank on them. I always pay well, *very* handsomely."

Odile tried not to scoff, but his dainty lip curled up. "How so?"

"Gold."

Odile now was attentive. Monsieur Bourguignon handed him an image of a druggist in medical apron. "Do you think you could have it done in a month?"

"Hardly. Exhibit deadlines are barbarous."

"One month," Monsieur Bourguignon repeated. "And I will pay double."

"All for a prank? A caprice?"

"Quite. He is rather . . . important."

"*Très bien.*" That was the moment Odile sold his soul, and he never even knew. He painted the druggist, ensnared by a loose tether and dragged on his back by an elephant escaped from the zoo.

Two days later, Odile was visited at his loft by Monsieur Bourguignon and his two "associates"—how they'd found his address Odile never learned. The associates, of course, were terrifying: Cearbhall and Vlak' Mikel.

Monsieur Bourguignon explained that the druggist was recently found dead, killed exactly as Odile had painted it. Odile would have thrown out Monsieur Bourguignon for such a notion, but with the others there, his choice of response was much limited. He settled with, "Absurd!"

Monsieur Bourguignon shrugged. "Absurd, yes. Also true."

"A coincidence then. I had nothing to do with it."

"Not wittingly."

"What are you accusing me of, monsieur?"

"It was luck, serendipity I believe, that I discovered your work some time ago. I recognized a man you had painted, the circumstance in which he succumbed. I think, perhaps, you did not know. He was a schoolmaster, you painted him stuck in a chimney as flames licked at his feet."

"*Non . . .*"

"I too thought it a coincidence, surely. But since then, I have watched you presage accidents. And now this," Monsieur Bourguignon held up the photo of the druggist. "Whatever power you have been gifted can be controlled. *Directed.*"

Odile denied, he repudiated, he waved it all aside. Monsieur Bourguignon then informed him of the unsavory business he was in, his iniquitous dealings. Odile's scoffs faltered. Monsieur Bourguignon next informed him that effective immediately, Odile would be in his employ.

"An exclusive arrangement, I'm afraid. No more galleries, exhibits, shows. Just *moi*. But I pay well."

The first time Odile rejected the offer, Monsieur Bourguignon simply repeated it. The second time Odile rejected it, Vlak' Mikel sliced off the top of Odile's ear. Such act brought about a sort of immediate and implicit agreement. Details were worked out, rules. Promises. Threats. Besides Odile's own life at stake, there were others. A cousin in Montreuil. An old friend in Sarcelles. A lover in Créteil . . . they could all be made to suffer at Monsieur Bourguignon's whim.

NOW, Odile kept painting. Insipidly, self-abhorrently, drunkenly, perhaps. But he painted.

He painted a deceitful jeweler disemboweled while riding a horse.

He painted a baker, starved to death while surrounded by mountains of bread.

He painted men of a rival gang engulfed by a volcano inexplicably erupting from the Louvre Museum.

Each an accident! the newspapers declared. *Such terrible, terrible accidents, all!*

Scene after scene of mortal carnage issued from Odile's hand, while depression left him bare and stripped of any cares. Even his lingering fastidiousness toward the perfection of craft, of expression as an outlet for his stupor, fell to the flames of ennui. Somewhere between painting a laundress drowned in a vat of bubbling toxin, and a sailor succumbing to skull-faced sirens, Odile found his brush strokes becoming no more than drags of the wrist. Once-exquisite faces turned now to infantile blobs punctuated by dots for eyes, a wavering line for a smile—or frown—as was usually most fitting the circumstances of their composition.

By the time he painted a man cometing from the sky to crash into the Sahara Desert, he did not even mix colors any longer, but slopped on a layer of umber one direction for the sand, then a layer of blue going the other way for the sky.

Monsieur Bourguignon arrived for inspection. Odile opened the door then flung himself back into the farthest corner of the room with as much haste as his lethargy allowed. Cearbhall and Vlak' Mikel followed behind, breathing hard. They carried a steel safe, a 500-pound deadweight they'd had to lug up the flight of stairs that ran from outside the building.

"A gift," Monsieur Bourguignon told him. "Your gold, it is everywhere, a mess. They say this term in America for a slob, he is called a 'soup sandwich.' That is you, *mon petit artiste . . . mon petit mess . . .* It would not do for the wrong person to get whiff of your prosperity, your well-deserved revenue being so exposed. The wrong dagger in the back is, after all, our business, not our wish."

"Very well."

The two brutes set the safe into the back room, gathered up Odile's gold, and began to neatly stack it within, tallying numbers into a ledger.

"And now the latest work?" said Monsieur Bourguignon. "Dazzle me with your brilliance."

"I . . . I've not been so inspired of late," Odile admitted. He dragged away the protective white sheet off his newest painting. The canvas was warped, saturated with linseed oil on one side, dry and parched on the other. Black swaths ran across it haphazardly, with generous speckling of spilled rum. Purple curves in the sky may have meant birds in flight . . . a stick figure lay on some sort of overlapping scribble, impaled with a spear through his neck. Each eye was a simple X.

Monsieur Bourguignon squinted, pointing to a series of blobs. "What are those?"

Odile coughed. "Flowers. See how they beautify the hillside?"

"And the line, here. A river, then?"

"A long snake."

"And this, the red . . . heart?"

"A devil. *Le diable.* Watching."

"I see." Monsieur Bourguignon twisted at his mustache. "And how long did you spend on this masterstroke?"

Odile's mouth began to feel parched, the certain dryness that only a fine Chartreuse or Armagnac can slate. "Twenty minutes. At least."

"Your effort of late, it seems . . . lacking."

"Since when do you care for refinement, or for method, for *éclat*?" Odile snapped. His retort visibly stunned them both, though each for different reasons.

Monsieur Bourguignon's lifeless eyes had even flared, but he nodded his acquiescence. "You are right. The technique matters not, as long as the vision is *effective*. And it still is, may I presume? Even in such an . . . uneven state?"

"Yes. *Oui,* I feel it now. And faster too. The death, I can tell, it has already occurred. The more I make, the faster they respond."

Monsieur Bourguignon's smile could not have been more elated. "I see."

Odile realized his mistake, but he had collapsed already back into detached lassitude. Nothing could be done. Cearbhall and Vlak' Mikel joined them in the main room where their glance lingered with surprise on Odile's painting before moving to Monsieur Bourguignon for instruction.

"Your next commission," Monsieur Bourguignon told Odile. "A bit delicate perhaps, but nothing you cannot manage. Business as always, I say. Another interruption that must be removed."

Odile nodded once.

Cearbhall held out a cardboard photograph, and Odile took it. For a second, the subject did not make sense. It was too small, out of scale. Then the crash of realization struck, and his listlessness turned to frenzy.

The picture was of Louis the newsboy.

"N-no . . . but why?" Odile cried. "He is only a child!"

"A nosy one, yes."

"Surely there must be someone else, a policeman or politician. What could the boy have done to deserve murder?"

Monsieur Bourguignon took a step nearer, and Odile fell back. "We see the boy watching us, talking. Coming here."

"He is a paperboy! He must do all those things. He brings my groceries, so I may paint uninterrupted."

"Yes, the steadfastness needed for your *pieces de resistance.*"

Odile began to reply, but Monsieur Bourguignon cut him off. "And has the boy seen you paint?"

Odile sucked in a breath. Perhaps not the act, but surely his works had been on display on their easels when the boy made deliveries.

Monsieur Bourguignon nodded. "And by the state of this space, I assume he knows you are burdened with so much wealth you cannot store it properly and must resort to leaving it strewn for the cockroaches to make their home?"

Odile sucked in another breath. He couldn't form words to speak.

"And do you think," Monsieur Bourguignon continued, "the boy from his street corner, aware of your eccentricities, particularly now notes the individuals who come here to visit? Myself for example? Cearbhall, Vlak' Mikel? Do you wish to endanger Vlak' Mikel?"

Odile could not face that black-hooded monster. He only shook his head.

"We will now bring your supplies, your foods," Monsieur Bourguignon said. "For your protection. Your service."

"*Oui.*"

"The boy, he is a danger. You may, at the least, make his death gentle."

"*Oui.*"

"One month?" Monsieur Bourguignon asked.

"*Oui.*"

Monsieur Bourguignon tilted back his head, stroked a clefted chin. "*Non*, that is too long. Considering your condition, the waning of quality . . . all that is needed now is one day."

Odile sobbed.

"One day to complete," Monsieur Bourguignon repeated, and he and his thugs departed.

THAT night, Odile could not sleep. He drank. He prayed. Begged for divine intervention, for answers. Drank more. Hurled a bottle of Chateau Latour to explode against the wall. The horrors he had induced, but never to someone he'd known, and never would he to this child! In deepening stupor of vin, and the dolors of desperation, he found the Bible his mother had given him when a boy at *Cabaret du Ciel*. Opening to random passages, he read verses, exaltations of God's glory, His will, His retribution. Acts 24:15, ... *there shall be a resurrection of the dead.* Isaiah 26:19, ... *dead shall live.* 1 Corinthians 15:52, ... *the dead will be raised imperishable.*

If only it was that easy.

If only his mother was still here. Her love to strengthen him, her wisdom to guide him. He poured another bottle, mixed brandy and bénédictine. Thought then, too, of what rebirth might mean. And of God and such mysterious ways: He giveth and He taketh away ...

If Odile had been granted the power to paint death, what *else* could he do, had he not thought to try ... ? His mother's sacrifices, and God's, that He had given his only begotten Son.

Odile polished off one drink, then another, and then he painted as he had never painted before.

THE following night, Monsieur Bourguignon arrived at Odile's loft. He found the door locked. Two hard, pounding knocks later, and the door was still locked.

"Odile, *c'est moi*. Open!"

No change.

Cearbhall put his weight against it, shook his head. They stood on the outside stairwell, and from there pushed together, but the door held fast. Something blocked it from the other side.

"The fool," Monsieur Bourguignon hissed. "He has thought to barricade himself within."

Behind them, Vlak' Mikel cracked his knuckles.

"I know you are within, *mon petit artiste*," Monsieur Bourguignon called out. "You never leave."

No response.

"Cearbhall, the narrow ledge here," Monsieur Bourguignon pointed to an eight-inch-wide brick extrusion. "It runs around the building. On the other side is a great window. Can you break through, come let us in?"

Cearbhall nodded. He placed one foot onto the brick ledge, testing its weight. On his toes and gripping the rain gutter, he eased along the wall until turning out of sight around the corner.

Monsieur Bourguignon twisted at his mustache, sharp teeth showing under a ghastly smile. He said to Vlak' Mikel, "I only wish I were inside to see the look upon that fool's face when Cearbhall smashes in."

A distant creak sounded and a shattering of glass. Monsieur Bourguignon's smile turned greater. Ghastlier. "Quick, let us in!"

They heard next from inside the loft a thud, and something toppling over. Then footsteps—too many. Another thud, louder, and then a scream—shrill and shocked and horrible, the prying of rusty nails from a wood crate after rain has set in.

"Cearbhall, what is it?! What is going on? Let us in!" Monsieur Bourguignon pounded on the door, and Vlak' Mikel kicked it until the frame shuddered. "Cearbhall!"

They were met with silence. *Dead silence*, as Monsieur Bourguignon's father used to tell him. His senses sharpened: this was wrong, a trap; Odile Thibodeau was causing problems, that rat-heart-drunk-sniveling-painter... but he was inside; this, Monsieur Bourguignon was certain. Hiding, disobeying... *painting*. That was the fear, was it not? No matter the threats made, the intimidation shown, the soothing over with gold, this, *this* was the danger of trying to subjugate such a power, a gift of the gods to a dolt, this *sac à merde*.

He could not wait to let Odile finish whatever he was doing within.

"Stay here," Monsieur Bourguignon told Vlak' Mikel. "I will be back."

And he was.

Twenty minutes later, Monsieur Bourguignon returned with eight more of his men, all lumbering, hard-hitting, scarred brutes of his gang: Boneyard Billie. François Guignol. Matheu the Mad. And the others. They brought with them a battering ram.

Four of them took up the ram and smashed through the door in seconds. Display hutches and shelves had been stacked there, but the battering ram went through them all. One of Monsieur Bourguignon's men laughed. Another cheered. They poured into the filthy, shadowed loft.

Then Monsieur Bourguignon froze. His emotions shook, erupted in a wild tempest of inner conflict, each vying for dominance as what to feel most: horror, shock, fear, revulsion, bewilderment, for there was too much to see all at once . . .

Closest was Cearbhall lying on the floor, surrounded by the glass he had broken through. He was motionless and smoking. No blood was visible, no fire, only smoke rising from his skin. *Smitten*, Monsieur Bourguignon thought wildly. Cearbhall had been smitten . . .

Behind him, the corpse of Odile the painter was stood up and splayed backward over a large wood easel, crucified. His hands were outstretched, his feet crossed at the ankles. Each was impaled by the handles of paintbrushes. The painter's eyes had turned upcast, perhaps a final sight of the crown of gold coins he'd sewn upon his scalp. Blood dripped from his mouth, his wounds, to mix with the paints splattered over the floor. It would have been impossible for Odile to have done that to himself, and yet . . . yet . . .

Odile was also across the room, watching them.

A wood stool had been painted gold, and covered in crosses in some homage—or mockery—of a throne, which Odile sat upon. Silently. Fingers splayed beneath his chin, as if in contemplative judgement of those he faced.

One of Monsieur Bourguignon's men cried out. Another gasped. Boneyard Billie whispered, "*Zut alors*!"

Smells came to him then, not just of Cearbhall's smoking body, and of painter's oils, but something strange, something that did not fit: heavenly fragrance, lilies and lavender. And even then, as he took in those scents, and the men around him shuffled and muttered, he realized movement forming; besides dead Cearbhall, and dead Odile, and—seemingly alive—Odile, were a group of people, vaguely "normal" people, though expressionless, streaming in from the back room to stand alongside Odile on his gold throne. At glance and quick estimate, there were perhaps thirty men and women, of all ages, all clothing styles, all familiar . . .

A druggist in medical apron. A police sergeant. A rouge-cheeked strumpet. The handsome, grandfatherly judicial clerk. All the dead Odile had killed . . . resurrected. Reborn. A golden glow issued from their eyes.

"What have you done, *artiste* . . . what have you done? The dead . . . the dead!" Monsieur Bourguignon roared. His hands flicked up and out, a dagger suddenly in each. "No matter, we will kill them again!"

His men, they withdrew knives, brass knuckles, revolvers, pipes.

Those aside Odile lifted their arms in supplication, and great feathered wings unfurled from behind their backs.

IT ended in no time, and the final sound was of Monsieur Bourguignon shrieking, "Seraphim!" before demise.

The paintings, if he'd had time to see them, surrounded him and his smoking men, his *smitten* men.

For there was every death Odile had painted, undone. Every murdered soul, reborn on canvas. Risen from the malfeasance that had cut short their mortal existence. The Lord giveth and the Lord taketh away, and so too did Odile find he could return life just as he had ended it.

By his own sacrifice, he'd painted himself, crucified, in which all the human pain he had caused came back, marked as his stigmata. He'd painted all the others, quick sketches of lives spliced back together, martyred, saintly and angelic. Halos and harps, and wicked retribution, his host of seraphim angels.

Odile now took a brush and dipped it into a jar of ebony black and carefully painted onto a new canvas a thin, separating line. He must take care for his craft again, he knew, return to the mastery he'd so assiduously once held himself, the ideals of composition, the focus and tapestry of beauty comprised by hue and depth and value.

With the next stroke he released his host of reborn into the streets of Paris, his eyes—the seraphim—decreed to avenge all wrongs, to seek out all evil, and to smite it.

And he hoped—as he began to compose the first face he'd ever known, the face of his own divine mother—that there would still be persons left remaining to enjoy all of how he would repaint this grand city.

THE SHIMMER OF TREES

THERE'S something to be said about immersing yourself into deep wilderness, to allow your soul to transcend its mortal confines and meld with ancient surrounds, to commune with the shadowed pockets of our nativity. There's a relationship between spirituality and human health, an instinctive process that runs through nature, through the lichen and sequoias, the luminous violet, the tranquil toad, the soil, the stone, the seed.

It's what I believed. What I still do, I suppose, though now tempered with fear, with despair, for there are *things* out there that cannot be explained. I say this not to frighten you (as I know I won't be believed), but as fair warning. Confession, as well, why my Columbia gear has long gone to Goodwill, and my trusted alpine boots to the dump. Why I kick my feet up now in flip-flops or slippers in the central midst of choked suburban sprawl, far, far away from that wilderness I long ago considered bliss.

Looking at me now, it's hard to imagine I was once hale and adventuresome, but so too does time twist us all to unrecognizable shapes. In my youth I was an Eagle Scout, later a Ranger in the army. When I was twenty-eight, I set out to hike Pacific Crest Trail alone one summer, a 2,600 mile route tracing some of the highest crests of the Sierra Nevada mountain ranges, stretching all the way from the American border at Mexico northward to Canada's brim.

I didn't make it. I was lucky, in fact, to make it home at all. Two months into it, I was somewhere between Nebelhorn and Echo Lake. At 7,600 feet elevation, California's granite ridgelines are spectacular, blanketed in lavish folds of Douglas fir and black oak, groves so old, they're said to be prehistoric. I'd just forded a craggy gulch, surrounded by the music of blackbirds in aspen. Suddenly, ahead, a red fox raced past, a curious phenomenon since the animals are nocturnal, and it was nearing noon. Next came sounds of crashing through underbrush as mule deer chased after it, then a wolverine, chipmunks, snakes, all escaping something off to my right.

I froze. Stared hard into the dark thickets of unmoving trees that had caused those animals to flee, trying to see: What was in there? Something incredible? Something dangerous? The blackbirds went silent. A tension filled the air, as if a current of galvanized wind plumed its breath upon the slope. The moment passed, yet still I stared . . . there was something, I knew, *something* had happened, had appeared or changed around me . . . I felt such depth suddenly, unnaturally, and a substance . . .

And it may be in the mind, you'll say, staring at any pattern long enough will cause the eyes to think it moves. There's science behind that, especially for striped patterns; and what other pattern can the branches and trunks of so many trees form, but of stripes? It's called "gamma oscillations"—a word I've heard a hundred times since—the repetition of intensely-striped shapes that triggers distortions in the brain. For I was staring into those trees, through them, searching for the source of such disruption that would panic wildlife, and I stared so long that those trees began to move.

In the blink of God's eye, I saw them waver, saw them reform, overlapping each other in vision, like looking through shifting waves. They *shimmered.*

I was startled, but not terribly so, thinking it a mirage, like heat cascading off desert sands, or the glare from frozen snowbanks. The shimmers grew brighter, the trees around me coming into focus, then fading away, so that trees behind them became the focus, before the process reversed itself to bring back into clarity the nearest ones.

I slowly extended my arm to touch one—what hideous disaster would have befallen me, I dare not consider—but thankfully, I stopped short. The shimmer was spreading, encroaching nearer, flanking me at the sides, and then, only then, I saw in that blinking sheen, there were small creatures, no larger than beetles, but humanoid, tiny, scurrying about in incredibly fast motion up and down the trees, *building them.*

I cried out, "Hell!" and had the strangest impression that was exactly what I was witnessing . . . I leapt back, trying to understand. The new trees were materializing, gaps of space filled in with some oozy, tar-like residue the creatures vomited out, that replicated physical properties, while the real trees that had stood in their stead were dismantled, *vanished*, as if consumed by hideous appetite. The creatures, they were building a mirrored reflection of what I observed.

And, as with any mirror, the observer looks upon themselves.

Those creatures, tiny blurs of pale turquoise, molded a tar-like statue that became me, that turned its head to face me, that opened eyes that were mine. Meanwhile the shimmer flowed, reaching for me, and I knew, doubtless, that should it touch me, I would be dismantled like the trees, and the duplicate take my place.

I bolted, but the trail was blocked! New trees had spread across the way, the shimmer of their inception already fading. I turned and sprinted away, into the forest opposite, bounding deep through thickets and sedge. At the last, I'd caught view of my replica reaching for me, opening its mouth to mimic my shrieks, while pushing, pushing to get through the shimmer.

I tripped over the tangled roots of manzanita, sprawled, leapt up, dashed again, downslope, through the woods, and I ran and ran, and only then while running, wondering . . . how much had such a mirrored reality spread already? I could be rushing further into it, rather than away; and the animals I'd seen taking flight . . . were they of biological form fleeing disassembly, or were they already of the tar and spreading out into our world?

And even now, years after I escaped that horror of the wilds, I ponder such things, of the dreams and riddles of life, as to what is "natural," and what is not, and what has come before us, and what shall yet befall . . . and in the course of those years since, of time, to wonder if it is my imagination, or have the striped patterns of rising buildings, of modular furniture, of books, of roads, of clouds—or that reflection gazing carefully back from the mirror—ever begun to shimmer?

OMMETAPHOBIA

DARKNESS, darkness, darkness, and then light.

The terror, the euphoria, the shock of that morning: as chaotic as it had been when Dean discovered he could suddenly and inexplicably see, after being blind from birth, amounted to mere shrugs of indifference when faced with the growing awareness that everything—*even inanimate things*—possessed eyes.

And even *then*, as unimaginable as that recognition had become, was *still* not the most worrisome consequence of his most sudden and miraculous vision . . . No, the greatest distinction of his trauma, that which suffocated what should otherwise have been cause of life-affirming euphoria, was the ominous wonderment of why such eyes stared only and entirely upon him.

FOR half a year Dean watched the eyes while they, in turn, watched him. They watched each other, though he knew not why. Eyes of every size, of every shape, blinking through every color surrounded him; they emerged menacing from walls and from tiny cracks and from all the places in between, and only Dean could see them.

The eyes were a lunacy by which all the rest of life was now measured, and the longer he examined them, the greater in number they seemed to appear. He was terrified of what he saw, but the terror, at least, had dulled to a distant sensation, detached, like knowing a large frothing dog rages on the other side of a leaning, rickety fence; as long as the fence holds, you're safe, but Dean wondered what would happen when the fence holding back those eyes might finally give way.

So he contemplated, lying in bed, looking up. A vast aqua-colored iris returned his contemplation from the ceiling. The eye was uneven, as if bags of ethereal skin puffed around its edges, flaring out into heavy lids that receded within the plaster ceiling. Its gaze was solemn, like the stern glare of a disappointed elder, and Dean wondered again as to its meaning.

"Why?" he whispered out loud.

The great aqua-eye blinked and, in unison, did the eyes on the wall blink, the eyes on the lamp, the eyes on his blanket, the eyes on the Braille book he held tightly, *Encyclopedia of Vision*. The eyes he laid upon blinked as well. He felt their movement as the lids crinkled close and reopened beneath his back. His own eyes blinked, too.

"What do you want?" he asked.

Again the eyes blinked. Dean wondered for the millionth time if this would be the moment they might finally communicate with him, whisper some great and terrible secret.

"Do you understand me?"

The eyes did not blink. He had asked the question before and never received a response. Sometimes the eyes blinked when he spoke to them, and sometimes they did not. Perhaps it was only a random action, the reflex blinking of an eye to keep from drying out. He found no reason in their action or even in their existence.

Dean thought back to when he saw the first eye . . .

He was born blind and knew nothing but darkness. Six months ago, a morning, he moved through his apartment by rote memory and opened the bathroom door. A dim light struck him like a knife, searing his brain, and he beheld what other people had tried in vain to describe: a mirror reflection of himself, hanging above the sink. At first, he cried out in fear, not comprehending what he saw. Then he screamed in joy. He stepped closer to the mirror and waved his hand in front of the reflection, watching in awe as it waved back. His sight was shrouded, as if seen through the mist of a dream, and he continued using his hands to explore and understand by touch, as he had done all his life.

The mirror overlaid the medicine cabinet's door. He opened it and looked upon things for the first time that he used every day: a toothbrush, a bottle of vitamins, deodorant. He closed the cabinet and looked again at himself in the mirror.

Something like a small, dark eye protruded from a corner of the glass surface. He wondered at that.

Then his vision became clearer, and a second eye erupted from the towel rack hanging next to the cabinet. It swelled from the metal bar the way he'd been told a rubber balloon might expand.

A loud pounding sounded at his front door, and a muffled voice called in. "Dean, are you all right?"

He crossed the apartment and opened the door. His neighbor, Diane, stood before him. She looked nothing as he'd imagined.

"I thought I heard you scream," she said. "Just wanted to make sure you were okay."

He leaned close and stared into her eyes—they matched the color of the sky above. "I can see."

He watched the movement of her face, the way her lips opened wide and her nose flared. He always loved the sound of her voice and found it surprising now that sight of her was not appealing. He used to imagine her as a radiant thing—so far as he understood what radiance meant—the diametric opposite of the darkness he lived in.

"You can see?" she repeated, her lined mouth falling open.

Diane took his arms in her own, and the collar of her blouse opened so that Dean glimpsed another eye at the base of her neck. It turned up to watch him. He pointed to it, asking, "What is that?"

"This? She pointed to herself and smiled. "This is my neck. Oh, you poor dear, you don't know what anything is."

"I know what a neck is," he replied, feeling suddenly embarrassed. He looked down, aware of her examination. His vision continued to grow brighter, more concise. She wore tall dark boots, and a rolling eye popped from each instep, like a buckle, winking in unison. "Diane, how many eyes do you have?"

"Two, of course," she said. She took his hand and led him to her car. "I think I should take you to the hospital."

An hour later, Dean sat on a silver table in a white room, colors that were stoically identified to him. He smelled chemicals and felt uncomfortable in the antiseptic enclosure with strange eyes staring at him from the light overhead and from the drawers filled with instruments, from the door, the walls, even from framed artwork. He did not understand the sensation, yet the world seemed to watch him.

Doctor Jansen shook his head. "It's a miracle. I really can't explain it any other way. We'll run more tests, but for you to suddenly have vision is simply an act of God."

"I realize it'll take me a long time to figure out what I see, to correspond sights with the sounds and smells I've lived by," Dean said while looking around the room. "But why do the eyes stare only at me, and not at you?"

Jansen followed Dean's gaze. "What do you mean?"

"That's an eye, right?" He pointed to the sink where a cyclopean orb bulged from its faucet.

"It's called a spigot."

Dean paused, then pointed to the ground. "And that is the floor . . . but I've never been told that we walk upon eyes."

Several more eyes dotted the rubber floor mats like coins tossed into a fountain. There was no order he could discern; they protruded in different dimensions and hues at irregular intervals.

"There are no eyes on the floor," Jansen said.

"And the counter?"

"No."

"And your clothes? You're wearing eyes, covered in them."

"There is nothing like that on my clothing," Jansen replied. He scrunched his face, clicking his tongue. "Hmm, it's no stranger than what has already occurred . . . but, with your circumstances, it may be some rare effect."

"Of what?"

"Ommetaphobia."

Hours later Dean sat alone, returned to his apartment, thinking of what Doctor Jansen had told him.

Ommetaphobia: The fear of eyes.

Dean was diagnosed with a condition that did not make sense. How could he explain something he saw that nobody else could, when he had never seen *anything* before? How could he understand—much less describe—this, when he did not know what should appear *normal.* Even Diane had made an unnerving face when he asked her about the eyes that watched him from the dashboard of her car.

He should be elated having vision. It was true what the doctor said: it *was* a miracle. But a miracle with a price . . . the sensation he was being watched, *judged*, grew increasingly frightening. More eyes appeared, and they scrutinized him. He shouted at the eyes like a madman, cursed them, threatened them. The food he ate caused him to gag: apples or buttered toast looked pleadingly at him before he lifted them to his mouth. The eyes were incessant.

The only relief Dean found was when he closed his own eyes, and the world returned to darkness. He then felt normal, and life resumed as how he once knew.

When a child, Dean became aware he lacked a sense most others possessed. It didn't bother him. Doctors told him he would never see, that his eyes were deformed and useless, like loose ball bearings rattling in sockets. But Dean was not affected by his condition, and he knew of no life different than that as he had been born. He grew and went to school, laughed and cried and loved as all sighted people do. His parents passed away when he was twenty-three, and he struck out on his own, determined to live like everyone else. The term "handicapped" was attributed to men or women who could not walk, or who suffered mental illness, never to himself.

Had God really granted a miracle, or was this a curse, or a test? Dean opened his eyes knowing there should not—there *would* not—be any eyes watching him.

But they were there.

They blinked, and he shouted, "Leave me alone!"

They blinked again.

Now, after six months of light—of sight—of *things* surrounding him, Dean felt his sanity fray like the loose thread at a cloth's hem. Slowly, he was unraveling and knew not how the threads could be sewed back where they belonged. The eyes *were* real, but he questioned why he alone perceived them. After several more visits, he broke contact with Dr. Jansen; Dean refused to accept the eyes were merely some phobic manifestation of his sight. No, something else was happening, something greater.

The eyes waited for him, they *wanted* him. Their appearance was foreboding, and he expected a terrible revelation would soon occur. Still, they spread more, erupting like blisters across burned skin . . .

They crowded to him, seeming even to climb over themselves as they multiplied. The eyes bulged from every dimension, as if a force pushed from behind each retina. Many eyes shone bright in luminescence, twinkling as faraway stars, though there were many, too, that appeared blood-shot, dull, or colorless. There were large eyes, such as the one above his bed, and there were many-eyed clusters like masses of tiny bugs. Dean recognized eyes in every color, irises gleaming chestnut or emerald or haunting black as the void. In some, the colors reversed, so the iris was white, while the surrounding sclera was blue or gray or purple. Some eyes appeared humanoid. Many did not.

The thread of his sanity unwound further, loosening, then dropping, it seemed, into the empty eternity of moonstruck chasms.

Dean cried out for the return of darkness. "No more, no more!"

The eyes bulged and blinked and multiplied more.

He broke for the kitchen and flung open a drawer of utensils. The things inside were living, seething with flickering eyes.

He took a fork, and its beady pupils glared at him, wavering on thin, silvery stalks like the tendrils of a snail. They seemed to perceive his purpose, and they were enraged.

Dean wanted to return to his world of darkness, the comfort he had lived in since birth. He knew, if it was not too late, he must restore himself, before his mind became nothing but a single, disconnected string floating in madness.

"I won't see you anymore!" he shrieked to the room.

He stabbed the fork deep into his left eye and pulled it out. Seething pain overwhelmed him, and he screamed until his throat seemed it would rip apart. Nausea and unconsciousness surged like sharp pulls of a riptide, and he felt himself falling away into its depths. He thrust the fork into his other eye and pulled it out too before he passed away into darkness.

When he woke, it were as if a dream. The world seemed bleary and his head throbbed. A hot wetness ran down his cheeks. Dean did not understand the things that flickered and moved around as he blinked over and over.

He tried to stand but a sense of vertigo sent him crashing back to the ground. He looked at the brown carpet that he laid upon, but the sight was not like it had been over the past six months. He lifted his face from the floor, and he saw the carpet as if from a distance. He realized, then, he saw *himself* lying face down on the carpet. The vertigo twisted his perception as the sight doubled over, looking at himself lying there, but from a different perspective, as if from a parallel plane. Dean moaned and then also observed himself from below, looking up, watching as his mouth opened and shut with each sound. He saw himself from the floor, and from the ceiling, and from the walls, and from the fork he still held in his hand. He saw himself in a dozen different ways and watched from afar as he rolled over and rose to his knees.

Dean saw his own eyes were gone, just bloody black holes where the organs should have been. He tried to close his eyes, but there was nothing to close. The flaps of the lids fell down and rose as they should, but they did not block the sight of himself as he frantically turned in all directions.

He found himself, again, looking at eyes as the eyes looked back at him. They were everywhere and they were *him*. The eyes—his eyes—looked at himself as he buried his head between his arms. The great elder eye in the ceiling blinked. Dean waved his arms frantically in front of his face, terrified that he could not see them from his perspective, but only from the perspective of the multitude all around.

His vision spread outside, radiating like strands from a spider web, spreading and multiplying in sticky lines from its hub. Dean saw the apartment he lived in laid out like a hundred dots, with each dot sharing new details: the cracks at the bottom of the wood door, a line of ants trailing along the cement sidewalk, blades of grass growing in the courtyard. He regarded the street beyond, then the supermarket a block away, and then the airport twenty miles past. He saw the details in all, and he saw, too, their distance and relationship to each other. Dean observed the people moving outside, driving in cars, sleeping in beds, arguing, reading, making love.

The eyes that were Dean's eyes opened everywhere, and he felt himself going mad. He discerned a power—an endowment—grow and spread across his consciousness, the way his vision spread across the world.

Omniscience.

It was the power of a God and through it he saw all: the beauty and the light flung against the hideous and the dark. He observed not just things he knew, but undiscovered animals, unexplored depths and, on a smaller scale, microscopic insects, grains of sand, the molecules that make up life. He beheld Earth in its place in the galaxy and then all the other planets and galaxies spread across celestial skies.

He saw everything and he saw himself, a man lying on the floor in a pool of blood with his eyes impaled on a fork.

It was too much, and madness pressed further into his mind... Dean tried to close the eyes of the cosmos, but they remained open, and he wished desperately only for the darkness.

Though blind, he stood, and watched himself rise. He lifted the fork and plunged it into an eye on the floor. He felt the white-hot pain return and screamed and screamed. But that eye blinked out, and more blood fell from his sockets. He crawled to the couch and stabbed out its eye. He shrieked again, and stabbed out the eye on a wall, on the lamp, on the radio. His vision went black from each point of view as it extinguished. But there were many, many more eyes that remained.

A knocking sounded at the door, and Dean saw Diane's eyes peering on the other side.

He raised the fork and understood: he would stab them all and return his world to darkness...

THE ASCENDING LIGHTS OF YU LAN

CULLEN'S Pub stank of old brine and whale oil and hard ale, cheap chowder and rotting fish, sordid sweat and cigarettes and dog shit, and there on the filthy, thick air was the worst of it, that dark-earth whiff of colcannon like his mum used to cook.

The sailor Johne Fieldworth closed his eyes, bit the side of his mouth, grimaced. He hated that smell, the stinking bitter scent of quartered potatoes, softened by goat's milk and a head of boiled cabbage—he could never get far enough away from its trace, even here on the other side of the world . . . It was the memories of home the smell brought, his home from so long ago.

He cursed the damned eatery next door, downed his mug, and a lightness took hold, his brain dulled in relief until, too soon, the gloom of it all flooded back. He'd need more than a few bottles tonight to hide from the nightmares, though at least, unusually, he had the fare for it, nearly eight dollars won in a round of Dead Man's Hand. He let his hand slip into the pocket of his trousers, caressing the wad of bills for reassurance. For this night, he was good as rich.

The crowd—the men, his *lads*—roared as they crushed against each other in the pub, lurching, swaying, bickering, dancing. Some twat sang a verse to Saint Bernward, whoever the blazes that was. Someone too near blared a mouth harp like a siren that's been bludgeoned a few times with a flue iron—just dented and out-of-tune and somehow made the louder for it. Deckhands from every nation belched and cursed and bet and chanted, the sound of it all like twin barrages of fusillade; he'd not been in naval battle before, but Fieldworth could well imagine it were the sound of this night, in this hall, of his mates blustering before they all shoved off in the morn to a thousand different ports.

From the bar, he swept his eyes around the room. *His mates . . .* bloody hell, not a one of them gave a rosy fart about his arse. A doxie whore who hadn't bathed the last week would be better company for his time and cares . . . though he didn't much care for that option either. All he really wanted was to get blotto, find a room or privy to pass out in till the sun came up and he shipped out.

Fieldworth sucked in a sharp breath and turned abruptly back, his hand clenching the heavy glass mug until the veins in his wrist stood out. He lifted the mug in an overhand arc and slammed it onto the bartop, bellowing, "Where the gob-fuck is that barkeep?"

As bellows go, it was not impressive, but it managed to convey the sort of insolence that Fieldworth enjoyed imparting on the local serving men; for even if no one cared, he at least liked to make himself known.

The problem forthwith, though which took Fieldworth a full moment to realize in some sort of slow dawning cognizance, was that he'd somehow leaned away at the last, and bellowed his question straight into another fellow's face, a longshoreman who was bloody big as a bugbear.

A spray of foam and droplets had splattered on the other man's features, though to be fair it was mostly just Fieldworth's spittle, a bit of backwash perhaps, but not a drop of ale had spilled from the slamming mug (which should have counted for something).

The sodden longshoreman rose over Fieldworth, somehow growing even bigger, while wiping a runny line of saliva from his scarred brow; his was surely a better bellow of note, when he retorted, "You goddammned lack-about!"

The fist that came crashing between Fieldworth's eyes was somewhere near the size of a masthead, somehow *weighed* like a dropped Union Anchor . . .

Fieldworth did not gain consciousness for quite a time.

WHEN he did, it was early night, just past dusk, and the full moon already beginning its rise. He lay in the drain of the street, a trickle of brackish gray sludge soaking through his pea coat to his back; someone had pissed on his trousers, and his head felt to have doubled in size. The Pub was across the way, all jolly lights and laughter and warmth, a reminder of what he lacked.

San Francisco . . . the fucken' pisspot of the Western world as far as he was concerned, but where else could he go? Never far enough . . . although perhaps tomorrow's ship would sail beyond that horizon of despair to find some mystical port of absolution, of oblivion.

His mum's voice came to him then, of course, unwanted, ghostly, near-forgot but for this anniversary: *Don't go out on nights of August's full moon, Johne. Nothing good ever comes from being out of doors on the Grain Moon . . .*

His mum, his sisters, reading fortunes in sheets and flames, what did they know? Turned out, it was the peril of him staying *indoors* that night long ago.

Soft footfalls came from behind. "Mister, mister, you need move, or you get run over."

Fieldworth spat. Cursed. Rolled over. A Chinaman looked down on him. The man was dressed real nice, better than he should've in this part. Effeminate too, like a broad, but with a nose flat as a pancake.

"Beat it."

The Chinaman took a step nearer. Offered a hand. The other hand held a small box wrapped in tissue paper. "You need help?"

"You a moron, or just off the boat? I said scram." Fieldworth's throat was dry, he ached all over.

The Chinaman shrugged and turned, walked away down cobblestoned Market Street without looking back. He had a limp.

Fieldworth rose on grating joints, glaring at the Pub from where he'd been tossed, till a couple mariners came out the huge wood door and sneered at him. "Ahoy, a drowned Mick!"

Fieldworth dropped his head and shuffled down the road the way the Chinaman had gone, the sound of laughter fading to ships' bells tolling all around. He saw rats' eyes glittering from the cracks of alleys, produce carts turned over, the moon rising higher, the sea mist drawing in.

He put on his wool mittens and watched the sparks shoot from the chimneys of crowded shops: cigar houses and gambling halls, lodges and taverns.

People milled about, going in and out of doors, glancing his way, if at all, only to scorn or scoff. It was 1917, what the papers called "Dilly Times" for all the high-nosed bastards, 'cept here, for those who had been sloughed off almost as much as himself, relegated to the slums of ports. There was much boasting that could be done, but Fieldworth didn't want any of it, the noise, the show, the fucken' slag-off city and its airs.

"A lad needs a drink," Fieldworth muttered, "to brace himself for this night." And he continued down Market Street that led away from the wharf, the sea, the carousers, and then he touched the eight-inch knife sheathed in his coat's pocket.

That big-knuckled bastard, he thought of the man from the bar. *Let's see him try something like that when I'm at attention . . . just caught me unawares is all . . .*

As such was the world, always trying to pull one over on him, the goddamned rest of the world with their sneaky ways, fleecing him, knocking him down when he wasn't ready . . . But he kept getting back up. *Oh yes, I'll keep gettin' up, till I get my own.*

He passed some tipsy bloke in dungarees, who held open a lodge door for others going in. When the bloke turned, Fieldworth lifted a billfold from the man's pocket. Around the next corner he unfastened it. Inside was nothing but a love letter to a Chicago dame and a photograph of a child.

A bust, that was. Still, he remembered his eight-dollar-winnings from Dead Man's Hand to blow through, so no better nor worse was he yet.

He felt a sudden presence and stiffened, thinking the bloke had fingered him after all. When he looked over, it was the Chinaman from earlier.

"You should not do things like that. No good." The Chinaman shook his head. "No good."

"You wantin' trouble, following me?"

"I thought you follow me. You come from behind."

"You're loony. This street's just the fastest way outta the wharf."

"I know. It's why I go this way."

Fieldworth rolled his eyes. Flung the billfold to the road. "There. He'll probably find it. So no harm."

The Chinaman shrugged, a curious movement that made his bare, thread-like eyebrows wobble up and down. His head was shaved high on the sides until giving way to heavy locks of oiled hair styled up over the top and crown. His suit looked crisp, his shoes clean. He wore round spectacles. He said, "Why you not with others, make jollity?"

"Jollity? What the fuck is that?"

"People like yourself, back on the wharf, with friends. Merrymake all night."

"They ain't no friends of mine. I hate it here."

The Chinaman nodded, but Fieldworth didn't know if it was from agreement or commiseration. He still held the small box. The tissue paper wrapping it was plain, unadorned, but for a line of twine circling into a bow. He said in an offhanded way, "People do funny things here."

Fieldworth's temper spiked like his headache. "What's funny about it?"

"Your people, your history, you ignore what is around you. Like tonight, you out here, you do not honor ghosts. You do not remember them."

"Ghosts?" Fieldworth ran his hand under his chin, scrunched up his eyes until the Chinaman was just a blob of pale skin, trying to figure if he were real or a figment of ale-sodden dreams left to haunt him. "Why in blazes would anyone wanna honor a damned haint?"

"Family. Ghosts of loved ones."

"Crackpot," Fieldworth said and turned to go. "That's what you are, a fuckin' crackpot."

"It's why no one happy here. The ghosts, the living, no harmony. No balance. Just a line with a wall in the middle."

Fieldworth felt the urge suddenly to flee, as if he'd be held responsible by hearing whatever was said next.

"This night is special. Ghosts come back," the Chinaman went on. "They are happy should you give them respect, *feed* them with love, with honor. Without that, ghosts turn very bad. Hateful. Their necks grow long and thin from starving."

Fieldworth had enough. Couples or other lone men bashed on mash wandered by. He reminded himself where he was, who he was talking to. Something else was on his tongue, but instead, before he walked away, he just admitted with some strange fit of grace, "Your English, it's pretty good."

The Chinaman shrugged. "It's where I live now."

"Yeah. Well. S'long," and he went past the Chinaman, giving him a wide berth. For a while Fieldworth heard the soft footsteps behind, and knew the Chinaman was still going the same way as himself. It was getting to be outright irksome.

A drink, a bar, shelter for this night, but where? The longer he was out, the worse it'd be, the memories, the dread. There was The Cracked Lintel, only he'd been thrown out last week, a scuffle over some disparaging words. The Railroader's Tavern, only he'd run up a bill that he wasn't quite ready yet to settle . . . The Creek and Watershed, only that one was full of dandies and Italians . . .

Fieldworth moved deeper into the city, where the streets narrowed, grew darker, roaming past 1st and Fremont, the cold of the sea air beginning to nip at his face and neck, the night growing darker, the gloom settling in. Grocer stalls here were empty or chained shut, loose awnings clacking in the breeze, and he thought of ghosts like charred logs, his mum and his sisters, but with tall, wavering necks like serpents rising to strike. He drew up the collar of his coat, tightened his arms around himself, kept his head down, eyeing the doorways for the lonely, the disparate, like himself, or the vulnerable. A lone Packard puttered by, and the driver honked once, though if it were in greeting or in annoyance at him impeding the way as he staggered headlong through the street's center, Fieldworth could not say. He profaned and spat at the car nonetheless.

In doing so, he drew his eyes from the surrounds of the land to the sky.

There shone lights in the distance. Many of them.

The lights were faint, glowing orbs floating in the darkness, some moving upward, ascending like ships' lanterns vanishing in a fog, though others seemed tethered, just shimmering stars pulled to earth, near enough to touch.

He'd never seen anything like it.

He felt himself drawn to them, down, down the road, beckoned by their strange beauty, past the boxcar fronts of Bush Street and the raised wood sidewalks of Montgomery. He thought fleetingly of tales of leviathans in the deep, monstrous fish as large as trawlers that spent their entire lives in the darkest of depths where even fishing lines could not reach. In some way, those beasts grew bulbs of light from their heads like bargemen holding lanterns in a fog, luring lesser fish, susceptible fish, right into their great-toothed maws.

He touched again instinctively the knife in his pocket. *They'd not get me.*

The streets, now emptied of people, became just towering shells of buildings like monoliths to dilapidation: soundless, lightless, neglected. None but himself seemed to move toward the sky lights, none but himself seemed to care and, as he neared, the lights grew brighter, larger, more in number. Balloons is what they must be, some kind of balloons made of sheet or paper, and what they radiated to Fieldworth was not just soft light, but . . . peace, the sorta feeling he dreamed of one day encountering. It was a peculiar thought indeed, though something that if he tried to understand might prove the very undoing of the impression it created; it was a matter of acceptance, it just *was*.

He kept walking awhile, and suddenly Fieldworth found that without his knowing, his surrounds had become foreign, and not only in ways of unfamiliarity, but that the buildings were colorful, the windows festooned with ribbons and heads of gold dragons, the writing above shops nothing but squiggles and crossed lines. He'd not been payin' attention and had let himself cross into the quarter of Chinatown.

Even worse than where he'd come from, here was the greatest blight of the foul city . . . and yet, this, this was where the lights led, and the compulsion was strong as any drink to find their cause.

For now he saw there were thousands of the orbs. Bubbles of star shine floating up a pool of night to the pale high moon above. A splendor, and the things he tried to hide away began to float up in his mind, not just the nightmares, the fears, the anguish, but even worse, a touch of what he'd lost, what he'd done: his mum in the kitchen with her fire-red hair wrapped in scarves so deep it looked as if she'd lost her head in a cloud of plaid wool; he'd hated her, though she'd looked down upon him in love, once . . . before she'd turned to fire herself.

Here and there were people again, these with pale skin and black hair, narrow eyes and clean faces, smiling—Chinamen well-dressed in loose broadcloth suits and strange flat hats and tassels, the women in long flowered dresses and bonnets or kerchiefs of silk. They seemed themselves, no costumes, no airs.

And still, it came: *You're out on the Grain Moon, Johne . . .*

Flashes of his mum, cooking her colcannon, reading visions in the steam of boiled roots, and his two sisters, building a great fire in the cottage so to throw in chestnuts, to presage a life of marriage or of chastity. The ninnies! He'd scoffed at them all. Bother their folklore and superstitions, even as a boy he'd wanted out, to go runnin' the world . . . *But the Grain Moon, Johne. August's full moon: I've seen it end for you. Don't ever go out-of-doors that night . . .* and hadn't she whupped his arse that very day for sneakin' out to pilfer a bottle from Old Man Clemmens down the way? That was the end all right . . .

Yet there wasn't a sign of ill omen here, not even that goddamned bitter scent of colcannon, the milk-curdled potatoes, to remind him of the fire, of her. Why the fear, why the worry every year? It seemed here it could all just evanesce if only he'd let it.

A small boy moved from the shadows of a stairwell, saw him, and darted away. Fieldworth cried out "Hey!" for no reason other than nerves. He almost gave chase just to know why the boy had fled from him.

But he knew better, and suspicion rose . . . he wasn't familiar with this place, these peoples' ways. Sneaky foreigners that they were, anything could be a lure, take him down into some cellar, put a hinky jinx on him, or worse, press him into an Emperor's sloop as *their* slave, the way the English used to take lone Chinamen and Shanghai 'em, sellin' each to steamer sea captains for labor. Wages were paid by not getting flung overboard in the middle of the drink.

He looked back to the rising lights and felt calm. They shone orange and white, or yellow, red, all warm colors against the chill air.

He moved on farther and noticed some of the shops actually had names in English too, below the Chinese script, and he marveled that here was a reflection of the streets along the wharf from where he'd come, but reversed, the perspective in all things of a different people. They had their own taverns with such names as: Yuan's Corner; Jiǔguǎn and Eat; Long Bar on the Bend. There were many more.

Then he turned under the flood of a streetlamp, around an intersection, and came upon their crowd.

A thousand Chinese? Two thousand? More? People filled the streets, all calm, happy, standing in small groups. Some of them had fires lit in brass pots in the roadway centers, others seemed to pray in front of photographs and ornate altars. Plates of fruit and bread and drink lay on the street too, on little altars at the base of each pot or bonfire, and Fieldworth's stomach grumbled. He hadn't eaten all day, and here was food being left out for the flies.

He took a deep breath and headed closer, into their midst.

Incense smoke swirled upward as if the very force propelling the balloons to the sky. And the balloons were some type of lanterns, he saw now, made of rice paper with lights inside, strung along the eaves of tiled buildings and hung to the many wash lines crossing the street. The lanterns all had faint writing on them, but in that foreign script language he couldn't understand. His heart hurt all the same.

Soft footsteps, and a voice. "You change your mind?"

Fieldworth turned sharply, like he'd been caught in the act of doing something he shouldn't. "I, what . . . you again?"

"You decide come here to honor your ghosts?"

Fieldworth's voice came out funny, quiet when he replied. "I just . . . I was just walkin' by."

"You keep walking my way, we no longer strangers."

Fieldworth made a face at the Chinaman, conscious that he'd let himself be surrounded, although no one else seemed to pay him any heed, except for wondering glances of curiosity. As far as he could see, he was the only white man in sight.

"My name, it is Bai. I was born Sun Yat-sen Bai, after the rebel leader. But, you see, he was later disgraced, found a traitor by some. I do not use that name anymore. Just Bai."

"All right."

Bai waited for more, his thread-like eyebrows going up, prompting Fieldworth. Fieldworth didn't give in.

"You know what this is?" Bai finally asked, extending his arm around.

Fieldworth shook his head. Even that small of a movement brought the ache in his skull back.

"Tonight is Yu Lan," Bai said. "Feast for Hungry Ghosts."

Fieldworth felt a chill from within. "Why . . . I mean, tonight?"

"It is our lunar calendar, middle of Chinese seventh month. Full moon in your August."

A coincidence, Fieldworth thought. *This and the Grain Moon, a coincidence of nights is what it is.* All peoples had beliefs in the full moon, even if for different reasons. No need to get twisted up over it. He asked, "Why all the lights?"

"Spirits are released this night, and lanterns guide them to us from the afterworld for communion, then guide them back. Without the lanterns, without loved ones lighting the way, ghosts would get lost. Those lost ghosts are the *pretas*, the ghosts unloved, unmourned. Lost to existence, wandering forever in the dark."

Fieldworth grunted. "Sounds dreary."

"Very old custom, told in ancient scriptures."

"Never heard of it."

"It is like your Hallowe'en," Bai said, moving closer, "that ghosts are released for one night to find their way. But Americans, you stir the ghosts up, call them down and then hide in fear when they come. Our ancestors come this day when we call, and we will not leave them unwanted. We celebrate Yu Lan today with our ancestors, though we wish their spirits could be with us for every day."

Fieldworth unbuttoned his pea coat. It was warm here, in this place, among these people. "What about the food on the ground, the waste of it?"

"The ghosts, they are hungry. We make sacrifice, burn food and drink to them so they remember enjoying it. Burn possessions of value to them, to share. We burn money to them, to pay their expenses in the netherworld."

"Bloody shit! You burn money?"

Bai nodded, stepped away, walked a half dozen feet to an iron brazier. He held up the small wrapped box that he'd been carrying since the wharf and carefully undid the twine bow. Underneath was the box case, a fancy thing of red velvet and gold thread. He opened it, and it was filled with paper bills.

"You must love others to be loved yourself, to not become a *preta*," Bai said and dropped the first bill into the flame. It blazed for a moment before curling up in a wad of black ash that a gust of wind carried off to the sky.

The shock, the revulsion of this was almost more than Fieldworth could bear. Bai turned a smile to him as he burned his money, as if all his life were easy street, and he knew it, he flaunted it, even.

And Bai was not alone in this, for Fieldworth could see the others setting things to flame in their brass pots, and he knew now, horrified, it was actual currency.

What if . . . what if he could do it too, he thought. Make amends, just this once, sacrifice something to his ghosts, give honor, give remembrance . . . ask for forgiveness. For a moment he even fancied he could see them, ghostly figures in glimpses of his mother, his sisters, nearing, like trying to catch shapes out of mist.

Then Fieldworth chuckled, an ugly giddiness filling him. *Imagine! Setting scratch to burn* . . . No, he was done with this. The spectacle of the lights had worn off now he knew what they were and, as he'd thought, Bai had proven his people a nation of backward crackpots.

Fieldworth had almost lost sight of what was important this night, to obliterate his consciousness, forget all till morn, not invite the haints back into his head.

He'd have to walk back, let the smell of the sea guide him from this pissant place, for it'd be hell if he were caught in an Oriental joint. Find a new tavern where no one knew him, maybe up on Clay Street by the cigar factories.

Fieldworth let his hand slip into the pocket of his trousers, feeling for reassurance the wad of his money.

His fingers felt nothing.

A wall of despair fell upon him. He swore furiously and rechecked the pocket, then all the other pockets, then the ground upon which he stood. Tears blurred his vision, panic brought a moan. The eight dollars were gone.

His mind raced faster than it ever had, calculating, figuring, retracing his steps . . . he'd touched the money while in Cullen's Pub, and afterward thought about the money, but not actually checked again if it was still there. Something had happened . . . Realization filled him, and the sensation was like falling through a crust of ice into the cold black waters below: That big-knuckled bastard who'd knocked him out. Fieldworth knew then, not only had he been sucker-punched, he'd been mugged.

That money was all he'd had, and now there was nothing . . . nothing. The world again, kicking him when he was down!

And his mum's voice, mocking: *See there, the fortunes don't lie: Nothing good's to come from being out-of-doors on the Grain Moon . . .*

"Where the fuck else can I go?" he roared.

Bai looked up at Fieldworth in alarm, his hands frozen gripping bills above the flames, and by slow degrees the Chinaman's expression turned into something that could only be read as the broach between concern and spare pity.

Fieldworth turned away, arm raised to cover his eyes so Bai would not see him weep. He knew he'd not escape tonight through drink alone . . .

He'd been so angry that night his mum had kept him inside, in their little hovel on the hill, when she'd said the fates spoke of bad omens, that very night of the August full moon. Other kids were out in the fields, hunting under the lunar light, having fun. Instead, his mum and his sisters hung sheets in front of the fireplace, to read the shadows of flames. When they'd gone down to the cellar for their chestnuts and augur roots, he'd kicked the sheets into the fire, where, to his horror, they'd suddenly caught blaze and spread into the room, faster than he could decide what next to do.

His mum would've known it was an accident, although he'd fled. Of course he'd snatched her scant jewelry on the way out, but he'd fled nonetheless. In all eyes, he was guilty, even if no one knew truly what'd happened once their charcoal bodies had been found. Fieldworth didn't even know where they'd been buried.

Why couldn't *they* foresee *that? Rubbish, their presaging was all rubbish!*

He hadn't meant for things to go the way they had, but he hadn't felt much contrition either. But the goddamned date, this goddamned anniversary, their ghosts returning to remind him year after year of what he'd done!

Why couldn't they leave him, like Bai had said, go wander forgotten, lost to existence, *pretas*, he called it . . . Or, maybe, they *were*, and hateful for it, released this night with no one to guide them, no one to remember them . . . The impossibility of the thought somehow jumbled itself into making sense.

Fieldworth's breaths came heavy, panting, his chest hitched.

And now his lost money; every goddamned time he got ahead, he fell back again . . . and here's this fucken' Chinaman *burning* money to ash! And a spittin' smile on his face to boot!

Fieldworth clenched his hands to fists, gulped air, tasted the ash of money, and imagined that to be the taste of ghosts themselves: charcoal and soot and cinder, hot and dry and choking.

He cleared his throat, calmed himself, made schemes. "Say, Chinaman, where can a fellow get a drink around here, and I mean *real* drink. None of that noodle juice."

Bai just looked at him.

"Hard stuff, I'm sayin', not tea, or whatever it is you people drink."

"Inns, places to imbibe are all around," Bai answered. "Stay away from the laundries, they front for opium dens. You never come out."

"I mean, well, can you lead me to one? I don't exactly fit in, right? I don't wanna get lost." Fieldworth thought a moment as if considering the magnanimity of what he was about to offer. "I'll even buy you a round."

Bai pointed at his own eye. "You okay?"

Fieldworth forced a grin, forced himself not to bring more attention to the tears by drying them with his arm. His voice came out strained. "Yeah, sorry, old memories. I'm ready to just settle in now."

The Chinaman smiled, nodded. "We don't get many of your people here at night. Mostly the curious in daytime, or those wanting brothels. You want too?"

"Naw, no. Just a drink, take this night's edge off. You can tell me about these ghosts, this ritual, whatever else you want. It's real interesting."

"Well, yes. Okay. East Star Keep is good for you. Just next block over. I take you, but then I must come back."

"Oh, sure."

Bai put the money that he had not yet burned back into the little velvet box, put the box under the crook of his arm, and led Fieldworth away from the square, the crowd, back in the direction he'd entered.

"I'm a foreigner myself, y'know," Fieldworth admitted. "So I get it, the hardships of a new land. Come from a little town outside Galway. That's in Ireland, on the coast." He let a hint of lilt return to his voice. "Land of the Celts and leprechauns. Ain't seen it for twenty years."

"It's been twenty years since I too left my homeland. I come from the province of Shanxi along the Hutuo River. Each morning I go out to pray at the Wutai Mountain. Many temples there. What they call mountains here, we call raised paddocks. I miss it."

"Twenty years for each of us, huh?"

"If I had a drink, I would make toast!" Bai said.

Fieldworth laughed in spite of himself. He asked, "Earlier tonight, what were you doing at the wharf?"

"Seeing off my uncle and aunt. They sail back to home in China. I help watch their children. Families care for each other here to survive."

"Yeah, your kind seem real generous to each other."

Fieldworth watched the rising lanterns pull his and Bai's shadows along the street as a child might stretch apart circus taffy. Firecrackers blasted in the distance, and the jangling echo seized his nerve. He looked around. They were alone and passing an alley where the lantern light was blocked out by high false fronts of clapboard shops: a meat market, a peanut roaster, a dentist. Bags of refuse poked out from the alley entrance, trailing backward into the gloom within.

"Hold on," Fieldworth said. "Give a lad a moment. I got some business to attend."

Bai looked at him, perplexed. He opened his mouth to speak, but Fieldworth cut him off. "I gotta piss."

Fieldworth didn't look back, just walked straight into the alley, lost immediately to the shadows and the moist, moldering smell of rotting garbage. He noticed with some disquiet that walking into the darkness, with the festival's light blocked from behind, was like watching his own hands and feet, then arms and legs, vanish into nothingness.

He brushed the feeling away and made sure to kick things hard as he blindly walked by, making all the ruckus he could: bottles clanking, barrels overturning, rats scurrying away. He muttered for effect to his plan, then cried out. "Chinaman! A hand!"

"My pardon?" Bai's voice came confused.

"I tripped on somethin'," Fieldworth groaned. "I fell, it's my ankle. I think it's broke. Can you help me up, get me to a doctor?"

Bai didn't like it, Fieldworth knew, but the Chinaman came in anyway, haltingly, arms outstretched, the light at his back. From where Fieldworth turned and crouched, he could make out Bai just fine, a figure silhouetted against the lanterns' light from the mouth of the alley. Bai called out, "Where are you?"

The Chinaman almost tripped himself, and Fieldworth suppressed a mad urge to just let it all out, laugh and laugh for the rest of the night. Instead he answered, real pained, "Just a little farther."

"I can't see you," Bai said.

Fieldworth lunged out with the knife from his coat pocket and roared, "Then open those slant eyes!"

The blow sunk into Bai's chest, just below his ribs. The sound Bai made was a squeal, a heavy, unused door on rusting hinges being pushed open. Instead of falling back, Bai twisted, spinning, tripping over the mounds of garbage. Fieldworth lost his grip on the knife as the Chinaman collapsed, taking it with him impaled in his chest.

Fieldworth gave him a moment to thrash around, make a gurgling sound, before moving in to retrieve the blade and that box of money.

The Chinaman was just a dark shape on the ground, barely visible through the farthest reach of glimmering distant lamplight. He was trembling, bleeding out, his hands wrapped tight around the knife's deer hoof handle.

"Need some help?" Fieldworth asked, crouching down next to him.

He placed his hand over both of Bai's, yanking the knife out from his chest. Bai jerked, gasped something in his language. Fieldworth moved the knife slowly up, his hand controlling Bai's own over the handle, savoring the sound it made skimming along the Chinaman's fancy suit until coming up under Bai's throat. Bai's hands were weakening already, loosening their grip.

"Time to go see those ancestors."

Just as Fieldworth lifted the blade, something erupted around him. A sound like a shriek on the wind, heard over a great distance, but unmistakable for what it was: his mum and his two sisters flashed before him as a flicker of light, a mirage, but they were there, and they were hideous. There were no wounds on them from fire, but rather they appeared as if they'd starved to death, emaciated figures with stringy patchwork hair and sunken skeletal faces. *Pretas*, unmourned . . .

Their necks stretched up like twining vines that slowly strangle trees, each long and thin and terrible. His mum, she splayed her fingers at his heart, as if only to startle him, to rend that which she once loved. Then the ghosts winked out of existence.

It was just a moment, just that flicker, a finger snap really, but it was enough. Bai had some last adrenaline surge while Fieldworth was taken aback, and he turned the knife; it twisted and spun and went deep through Fieldworth's jaw and up into his brain.

Fieldworth almost screamed, *It wasn't fair!* The Chinaman had caught him unaware, the sneaky bastard, but instead his last thought was of his mum's warning, now her vindication: *I told you not to go out-of-doors on the Grain Moon . . .*

He crumpled over Bai's stilling body.

WHEN he woke, for the second time that night from unconsciousness, Fieldworth felt numb, his body heavy, sluggish. He looked up into a sky that seemed impossibly black, but for the sweep of those ascending lanterns like a swath of falling stars in reverse. The beauty of it made him turn away.

He saw another figure rise not far from where he lay and limp off in the direction of the lights, his back to Fieldworth . . . the Chinaman.

His first thought was that Bai was escaping to find help; city police would come for him. Fieldworth felt around for the knife to give chase but could not find it.

A dimness crept over the field of his vision, and when Fieldworth looked up again he saw the lights of Yu Lan begin to twinkle out, like candle flames being blown upon, one by one, to a sky empty even of the moon.

A dryness took hold in his mouth, a fear in his heart. He rose and followed Bai as darkness grew. "Chinaman, wait!"

Fieldworth stepped forward carefully, mindful not to trip over the bags of garbage and *really* break his ankle, until he realized there was nothing to impede his progress. His footfalls seemed even barely to touch the ground, and he wondered at the absurdity of someone cleaning the alley while he lay there . . . until he realized next he must have somehow left the alley already, as neither were there any enclosing walls, nor even any buildings. The land was empty, and the fear in Fieldworth's heart became a strangling fist. He moved faster then. "Chinaman!"

Bai outpaced him, impossibly somehow, advancing without running, even with his limp, as if propelled upon a wind. Bai pulled ahead effortlessly. He never slowed. He never floundered. He became just a glimmer of sight surrounded by those guiding lanterns, the ones nearest him, for the others had already flicked out.

Fieldworth ran for all he was worth. “Bai!”

But Bai did not turn back, showed, in fact, not the slightest sign he’d heard the call.

“Bai!” Fieldworth shouted again, louder. “It was a mistake!”

At that, the last of Bai’s lanterns grew fainter, or moved farther away, and Fieldworth halted to study, with all his singular effort, those final pinpricks, committing them to memory precisely, for he knew there’d be none lit ever for him.

Then he blinked, and the universe extinguished, and Fieldworth saw nor felt anything else thereon but for that unceasing black void of the lost and unloved.

TWO HEARTS MAKE A HALF; OR, GHOSTS OF A RODEO CLOWN

WHEN a Rodeo Clown dies, he creates not one but three ghosts, a division of the self he maintained while alive: one-part imprudent jester, one-part steadfast defender of the bull rider, and one-part testament to frailty of the human condition. Each of these three parts goes on to become its own entity-spirit within the transcendental realm of mankind, being specters illimitable and omnipresent, yet bound forever to the reaction of their one-in-three development, the essence of their once-mortal self: jester, defender, or testament. But when Teddy "Dove" McGuinn died, his division produced an exceptional anomaly, a development as astounding as it is ironic . . . his being—what he'd *been*—divided not three ways, but instead *quartered*, forging an additional fourth ghost. And that ghost was of the beast Dove McGuinn had equal-parts loved and tormented, for this fragment of his soul turned into the haunting creature known as . . .

The Were-Bull.

Listen close, and you may hear faraway echoes of its thundering hooves or the bellow of its indignant rage. Feel the whispered exhalation on your cheek of heated breath from its ringed nose. Look hard enough into the shimmering grass fields, when the sun hits dappled crests just so, and you may even see the ghostly glimmer of the were-bull, a foreleg lifting half-cocked as if to charge, reddened eyes glowing, watching, intent. Lost. Adrift. Alone.

Though surely majestic, the were-bull is a cursed creature, a shadow of its once functioning, vibrant human form. Is it punishment? Karmic justice? Such reflective comprehension is no longer capable for this one-quarter of Dove McGuinn-turned bull-ghost, so it must wander confused and abstract, like nuzzling mist on a cold, dim day.

Until transformation.

The fourth quarter of the lunar cycle (as akin to this fourth quarter of himself), sees the were-bull corporealize! Now you need not listen close, for the bellow of its indignant rage turns chillingly real, a noise equally resonant as it is terrifying, for transformation into any new form is a painful process for all were-creatures.

One week a month, the were-bull exists in living form, in all appearance a massive, prominent example of the *Bos taurus* species, swaths of rippling muscle, gleaming black hair, horns the length of sabers, and just as deadly. But imbued, still, with the human psyche—albeit a quarter—of the consciousness of he who used to mock the bull, chase the bull, ride the bull, provoke the bull. What Dove knows is only that he is broken now, confused, somehow cast adrift in cosmic anthropomorphism. He has tried to communicate before, has brayed sounds constructed to mean "Help me" and "Where am I?" but instead causes only fear or laughter from any human who hears them. In fury or disgust, he charges them. They flee in terror. A sense of gloating floats up into his consciousness, of pride. He may be a monster, but he, at the least, is formidable.

It is not long before he finds himself shunning mankind anyway, grazing deeper and deeper into rich, wild prairies, away from the commerce and troubles of mortals' living. Grazing and brooding, until the fourth lunar quarter waxes away, and he dissipates back into the spectral.

Such is the cycle that perpetuates. One week a month. Twelve times a year. 120 transformations a decade. Two decades elapse. More.

It is thereafter at one of these shapeshiftings, as the moon wanes gibbous, that Dove is seen metamorphosing in the meadowed vales of Pawnee National Grassland, a hundred miles northeast of Denver Coliseum, where he used to work the circuit of the National Western Stock Show. Finding his voice once again returned, the were-bull roars across the night, a cry of pain and wariness, a searching, repeated call for other splintered fragments of himself or others of his kind . . .

IT'S night. Dark but for the moon and the fireflies flitting across the plains. A dashboard clock reading midnight. The flickering smolder of a Marlboro Red dangling from the corner of Rod Reams's mouth as he sits in his 4x4 Silverado. Rod "The Bod" to the ladies of line dancing, the mini-dress-wearing, high boot-scootin' boogie aficionados of Denver's rodeo cow*men* (they ain't boys in Denver).

Rod's just staring out the windshield, not really looking at anything, but just thinking. Thinking and smoking. He's got a Sig Sauer P226 in his lap; the clip's two bullets light. The body of his whore girlfriend is outside on the cold ground, wrapped in a tarp. Coupla shovels are out there too, a pickaxe, a chainsaw. A 50-pound bag of quicklime. He's heard that's urban myth, that the quicklime won't dissolve a body in the earth, but hell, why not toss it in anyway? It's gotta help, and Rod's all about maximizing his odds. *Play the long game*, he thinks, as he smokes and stares out that windshield to the prairie, a wind-ruffled realm of shifting grass and shooting stars.

Suddenly a roar sounds, and Rod almost shits himself. The cigarette falls from his mouth to land and burn a smoldering hole in the leather upholstery. The sound is a fucking building collapsing. Or an Abrams tank fighting for traction on a gravel road. A grizzly with its nuts twisted off. The roar comes again—pained, angry, beseeching in its timbre. Rod knows he ain't in any position to ask for a benevolent favor right now, but goddamn!— he prays whatever that thing is goes far away.

A third roar sounds and (ain't karma the bitch she's always said to be) it's instead gotten closer. Or louder. Or both . . . Rod's nerves light up. He was already on edge, but this heightened sense is like the icy tingle of silence before the chute gates open up, before the shot and shout of the announcer over the P.A., the moment that somehow spans an eternity, when the bronc is already rising up, and he cinches tighter the flank strap circling the beast, all before they shoot out into the ring; that's the sense Rod is feeling, but a hundredfold, and if it wasn't for cheating-filthy-whore-Brenda outside, he'd drive off right now, but instead he's got a grave to dig, and upon further reflection, he's a *man*, and hell-no he ain't gonna be scared off by some animal.

He gets out of the truck, steps over the tarp, and walks toward the bellowing sound, a Maglite in one hand, the Sig Sauer in the other. He tops a knoll of wheatgrass, and as a frayed shroud of silvery cloud floats away, he sees—there under the moonlight—a giant creature emerging from the air. Rod flicks off the Maglite just in time, while sucking in a breath so sharp the back of his throat prickles. He's heard the legend—every kid growing up in Denver has—and even known some folks claiming sightings, though most of them, Rod wouldn't give a piss for their claims.

But it's here now, in his sight—bigger than he'd imagined, more hideous too, though unarguably imposing, majestic, in the way a hunter may espy a devil-fanged 20-point buck across the range.

The Were-Bull.

His gasp is some word-combination of "Shit," "Christ," and "Holy-fuck-me."

He takes two steps back, more a reflex than any reaction to get hidden, his mind reeling with a whole slideshow of outcomes based on what he should do next.

His first thought is to kill it and hang its head in his trophy room. But the Sig Sauer feels small suddenly . . . how many shots would it take to down that beast? A solemn certainty tells him way, way, more than he's got, if it's even possible to do at all.

But going beyond that—using that big brain of his—he thinks, shit, this, *this* is the were-bull . . . Rod's been breaking broncos since his teens, riding bulls before he could drive. Always someone else's stock though, and that dream of owning his own show, his own ranch, had day by day slipped through his fingers, like cupping your hands in feed, and watching each grain slip away over your palm. That image is the golden cascade of bad choices, missed opportunities . . . 'til now. He could catch the were-bull, showcase it, ride it in front of a hundred-thousand roaring, cheering fans.

The long game just got longer.

He fumbles out his cell phone, *prays* for reception here in the boonies. One service bar hovers, flickers. Rod dials his little brother. The call goes through. "Bobby," he says, panting and whispering at the same time, "get your ass out here."

"Where you at?"

"Pawnee. I'll text you my coordinates."

"At this hour? What'cha doin' there?"

Rod falters, stutters. "Alright, first, there was a problem, and I was going to take care of it myself, but you're gonna see something when you get here, so don't get mad or nothin', but that *thing* I said might happen someday with Brenda, well . . . "

"God, no," Bobby says, his voice so small.

"I warned her!"

"You was drunk, you said that!"

"I was drunk again, it happened."

"Rod, you—"

"Right now, that don't matter! Why I'm calling you is our lives just hit stratosphere-rich, if I can count on you. 'Cause I honest-to-God just found us *the were-bull!*"

Bobby's silent. Rod thinks the reception dropped, then a crackle sounds, and the remnants of a sputtered reply, "I can't believe—"

"Lord's truth," Rod interrupts. "It's real. Bring the tranq guns, rope, prods, everything you got. And the cattle hauler. You get down here, we're gettin' this sum-bitch."

"All right, I'm puttin' on my boots." The call drops. Rod texts his GPS location while watching the were-bull paw at the ground, swish its tail, rear back on hindlegs and arch a massive back.

Rod scrolls his phone to camera setting, takes a picture. That big brain of his must've forgot there'd be a photo flash like lightning. For a hair's-second, the world goes bright, but the were-bull is still black. Rod's heart drops about twenty feet. The were-bull's head snaps to him, there's a snuffling sound, a tensing of its enormous body.

Rod knows what that tensing means.

He turns and runs.

THE quarter left of "human" Dove McGuinn is torn further, weakened in the way that something already shattered will be additionally compromised: the after-effects leave compound fractures, rent edges, irrecoverable lack of emotional underpinning. The rodeo clown-part of him sees a man in fear, running for his life, and that part of Dove seeks to protect the man, to throw up a floppy hat and goofy grin, or find a steel barrel to roll around in, call off the bull with flashing lights and taunts . . . but such a flimsy revenant of thought, so weakened and confused already by vivisection of the soul, and in conflict with the mythical beast he's become, has little hope of allaying the monster bull's natural instincts.

It was the man's fault, his sudden motion, the flapping of his clothes and jerky movements—like any cat drawn to a fleeing mouse—is what induces the bull's impulse to charge, engorges the chemical syntax of the brain to hunt him down. Dove has chased other men before as the were-bull, enjoyed it even in a toying way, but this is different somehow; this fleeing man doesn't feel like a target of capering fun, but rather a mark—a *bull's eye*—for blind rage.

The were-bull gallops, gains on the man rapidly—in only moments he will strike, he will lower his head and slam the man head-on, with force not unlike an artillery cannon's discharge at point-blank range.

The man spins, there's terror in his wide eyes. Dove sees the man is holding a gun, recognizes what that means, and tries to stop the drive of the bull, tries to turn away, but the were-bull-part of him is determined, and continues on, and the man fires the gun, again and again.

Dove feels the bullets strike—every one a hit. Pain detonates across his breast, his shoulder, his dewlap. A shot furrows his nose and pierces his neck. A shot shatters a carpal joint. A shot drills through his skull. A bull is color blind; it's a misnomer they're drawn to the color red, but nonetheless, it is Dove's memory of pain that colors the world shrieking, explosive red. His legs teeter, collapse, he plows face-first into the ground, the acceleration of his charge propelling him several yards more, to end in a broken mass at the man's feet and the man's clicking, now-empty gun.

The were-bull's vision flickers in and out, matching the convulsing waves of agony.

The torn muscles, shattered bones, frayed nerves . . . as Dove lies there under a clouding black, he feels them begin to repair themselves.

"HOLY fucking shit," Rod gasps. "*Holy fucking shit!*" he repeats with emphasis.

He's still twenty yards away from his truck; there's no way he would have made it there in time. Even if he did, that creature would have demolished the vehicle. Rod's life most definitely had flashed before his eyes, and it was not a pleasant view.

Plan A, at the least: Rod can hang this bastard's head in his trophy room. And he was wrong, he supposed—the Sig Sauer *had* worked just fine. Never doubt the power of German arms manufacturing.

He takes another long searching look at the downed were-bull, then makes his way to the truck. To the chainsaw there. That's what he's going to use next.

On *two* corpses, now.

Moonlight plays funny tricks on a landscape at night, especially with a wind; it moves shadows around, distorts objects, causes things to appear and disappear. Rod knows this, *thinks* this, when he sees the tarp that was covering Brenda is gone, blown away or vanished—that part doesn't matter so much. What's of more concern is that Brenda's gone, too.

"No," Rod whispers. "Shit no, no, no." This night is getting well and truly screwed, and visions of his long game are shortening drastically.

He left the Maglite behind in his mad flight, dropped his cell phone too, he realizes. He just cannot believe it . . . Thank God, he'd at least called his little brother. Bobby can help him find these things, clear away any other evidence, but first, of most pressing importance, where the hell did Brenda go? The bitch whore was dead . . . he'd shot her twice. He's never killed anyone before though, didn't even think to check for a pulse, just assumed she was gone. *I'm a fuckin' mess*, he realizes. And the Sig Sauer—what the fuck? Who survives two headshots from that?

Then Rod hears a moaning, a shuffling. A scrabbling in the dirt. A sob, a whisper, some plea.

Oh, she's right over there, doing a sort-of worm crawl through the prairie grass, pulling herself along on torn elbows, dragging unmoving legs. All is not lost.

He'd loved Brenda once. Thought she was "the one." She'd been smart, sassy—but not too much. She gave what he asked for, anything. But then she'd two-timed him. All that fire and love he'd shared, that part of himself he'd given her, fervor and devotion, and secrets and dreams he'd never told anyone else. But it wasn't good enough for her, he—Rod Reams—wasn't good enough for the whore. He'd thought before she was seeing someone else, but she'd been sneaky, he could never prove it, 'til tonight, he'd come home early from the bars, and seen someone leaving, someone getting their ass out fast through the bedroom window . . . but not Brenda, no, she'd had nowhere else to go . . .

"You got nowhere else to go," Rod tells her as he hefts up one of the shovels and brings it down clanging on the back of her neck. Her worm-crawl stops. Rod hits her again and again, just to be sure. And then he hits her a few more times.

DOVE wakes. The were-bull wakes. He is whole again, in physical terms, regrown, repaired in body. The bullets pushed out by healed flesh have plunked into the soft dirt he lays upon.

When he opens his eyes, the first thing he sees is murder.

The man he'd chased, who'd shot him, brings a shovel down onto a prone young woman. Her neck snaps at a horrifying angle. Her head splits apart with a sickening crunch. The rage the were-bull had earlier felt seeps entirely into Dove.

He begins to rise, then stops, frozen by sight of something incomprehensible . . . something he himself experienced but never witnessed.

The woman's soul.

It rises up, visible to Dove, but not to the man who is still slamming down the shovel on her flesh, screaming obscenities, shrieking with rage and regret and fear.

The woman's soul, it begins as an ethereal thing, an unwinding exhalation growing in the night, something so insubstantial, yet a vast vale of shining eternity that glows and spreads, expanding, evolving, *dividing.*

Dove understands so much now, memories locked away find escape to uplift him. The woman's soul is a cloud, morphing by divergent pressures, billowing upward, and outward, and within itself, a thousand faces, a million faces, every face of every moment of her life, in love, in dread, in wonder, in lament. The face of a child looking into dewdrops at the curve of a rainbow beyond. The face of a woman staring into the eyes of another, seeing the refection of herself, dimmed, distorted, honest . . . faces yet to come. Faces never to be.

It is too much. Nothing as such can be contained in only one afterlife. The spreading realm of her existence begins to divide, first into two great clouds, then into three. Dove knows nothing of her life, who she'd been, what she'd done, only that she is ascending onto three separate paths, to three separate planes.

Dove had become the separate selves of jester, defender, and testament. And then the were-bull. What she might become would be yet another inexorable mystery of the universe to him.

But there, there, even as Dove watches, as the madman continues beating her mangled corpse, there, feeling unable to behold more, the woman, her soul, spirit, the dividing cloud, it does not stop at three parts . . .

A fourth tears away, like parting veils of mist. A quartered part of her sinks back down to the ground, mere feet from her killer.

The cloud begins to form, to solidify into a shape, large, risen on four legs. Skeletal bones appear of their own accord, encasing organs, supporting muscles. There is a bovine head, a swishing tail . . .

The man has stopped with the beating; he's standing there, frozen in some terror, some recognition . . .

The forming creature lets out an anguished *mooo*, something of pain and confusion, that Dove understands well, that Dove has been searching for, pleading for all of his abhorrent existence.

The man raises his shovel once again, and advances on the were-cow. He does not realize the were-bull has revived . . . until the were-bull charges with a shriek that is as human as it is beastly.

HEADLIGHTS stab through the darkness.

Bobby Reams drives his Ram Diesel Laramie, 370 HP, and a tow package that could pull half of Colorado; the trailer he's hauling is a 53-foot steel box, reinforced with iron girders at every seam. He's gonna need it, if what his brother said was true.

Bobby's got a .450 Marlin hunting rifle, and a .458 Lott, manufactured for the sole purpose of bringing down the largest game ever known on the face of the planet. The bore cartridge of each could punch a fist-sized hole through a hemi engine at a quarter-mile away. Hell, he even brought his FN M4A1 automatic machine gun, and 2,000 rounds of ammunition. Can't be too careful these days.

What Bobby's thinking though, what he's really wondering about, is who's he going to use it on? The were-bull, if his brother isn't full of shit, and this isn't a set-up, and if tranq guns and traps don't work, is the obvious choice.

Or is he gonna use them on his brother? His miserable, shithead brother, who was never good enough to lick the mud off Brenda Turner's boots?

Rod never treated her right, never deserved someone like her . . . and *how* had Brenda fallen for him in the first place? Rod was handsome, she'd said, and charming. Rod could be funny, vibrant in a stuffy room, and he was confident; loud and brash to a fault, but *compelling* . . . that was all true about his brother, but still . . . after a couple months, she'd seen the real side of Rod, the pettiness, the ugly, condescending speeches. The drinking, the explosive outbursts; the controlling demands, the insults. He'd never harmed her before though, and Brenda kept believing he'd turn it around, act better to her. He didn't.

Bobby knew too, this was his own fault. No one should mess around with a brother's girlfriend, but it had just happened, one night, him and her ran into each other, and Brenda with that smile, like an ode to moonlight, melancholy and sublime. The upturn of her eyes when she laughed so easily, so honestly. Her fingertips, just a brush was all it took—softly across the back of his hand. The smooth, sun-touched skin . . . and then the touches intensified . . .

And Bobby wasn't any great catch either—he'd be the first to admit it. Brenda didn't need either of the Reams brothers, rodeo men-hustlers that they were. She'd been raised on a farm among cows, and had built a greater career from it, a name in the cattle industry, devoted to livestock breeding programs at the university, even quoted in magazines for her dairy work, her involvement and passion for domestic ungulates.

Bobby's headlights pick out Rod's truck and the tire tracks of crushed grass leading from it. Then he sees the blood. Everywhere. Literally. Blood on the truck's fender, blood on the wheel wells, blood splattered and soaking over a shovel and across the ground, where he sees some misshapen lumps; one of them looks like an upturned hand, broken fingers splayed toward the sky, and the other lump, imagination be damned if that's not a head. A man's crushed head.

Bobby drives in a little closer and sees there's two bodies. One he recognizes by the floral dress she'd been wearing . . . the other body, there ain't much left—and what remains is scattered over a couple dozen feet—but he knows it's his brother out there, mutilated and ravaged. Bobby feels sick, fearful too, wondering what could have done that. He turns the steering wheel a bit, flicks the beams from low to high, and sees . . . *it* . . . *them* . . .

Massive and monstrous. Nightmarish, the were-bull most certainly. But there, too, is a second creature, and just as large, but without the horns. A cow. The two beasts are staring into each other's eyes, muzzles nuzzling in communion, something more than harmony passing between them. The two creatures, they look up, slowly, straight into the beams of Bobby's truck. Maybe it's a trick of the light, or a wistful fancy, but for a moment he swears that cow has a smile like moonlight.

The were-bull, it exhales a breath of steam, paws at the ground in challenge to the newcomer.

But maybe it's not Bobby he's pawing at, since Bobby glances movement at the edge of the beams, a third creature that's materialized, something also monstrous and deformed, writhing on the cold, dry ground. Something with eyes on wavering tentacle stalks, and a skirt of slimy fringe; something culled straight from his vegetable garden, but the size of a log; something that strikes him with impossible familial association, and maybe Bobby can still smell a hint of Marlboro coming off it . . . He has no other name but to call that other thing out there a *were-slug*.

Bobby Reams doesn't know what went down here, but he no longer wants anything to do with it. He silently wishes Brenda all the happiness she deserved in life, and he speeds away as fast as he can.

PERCHANCE TO DREAM IN VOICES OF A FIEND: A FANCIFUL EPILOGUE TO FRANKENSTEIN

To Mrs. Saville, England.

September 15th, 1799.

MY dear Sister,

Scarcely two days have passed since all occurred that I'd written you of regarding those fantastic meetings with, and chronicles of, my ill-fated and admirable friend Victor Frankenstein and the unnatural creation he brought to life.

And yet, though surely I thought that chapter of fate to have met certain completion, as the ice loosened, portending my return voyage home to England and to your cherished sight, but most unexpectedly should I meet with the very same dæmon once again!

September 11th the passage towards the south became perfectly free, and by the next day we endeavoured to sail such way, but after only a meager distance, a new and terrible cold spell blew suddenly down within the night, and once again the ice seized around us, so that we were stuck as before, as if underneath an endless glacier pushing down from the north. The only respite was the moonlit glimpse of open waters some miles farther away so that I thought with hope our situation to be mere temporary.

It was as I strolled the deck, investigating the ship's condition, that a commotion caught my attention. One of the watchmen espied a figure, motionless on a flat and frozen berg off stern. Under glow of the man's lamp, I saw thus a dark figure of gigantic stature below and immediately knew who—or *what*—he was. I called out to him, but there came no response. I feared he already had met that great and final doom he spoke so eloquently of heretofore. I gathered six of my most trusted hands, and they caught him underneath the arms with rope and hauled him aboard.

Even amidst the noise and clamor of the action, the strangest sensation came over me, that it seemed I could hear a whispering, a muttering coming as if from a dozen voices within the creature, though his mouth did not move. But in a moment the impression was gone, and I found myself needing to attend more urgent matters.

For at sight of the creature, the sailors grew afraid. I told them however he was but surely a man as themselves, giant as he may be, but one afflicted with scurvy no doubt, pointing to the castaway's bloody gums and discolored flesh and blackened lips—known symptoms of the disease—and the other men found truth in my falsehood.

I ordered the creature to be removed to my cabin for further study, and swore the sailors to secrecy, as I began to fear their superstitions could grow bold.

Once I was alone with him, and my cabin's doors barred, I began to examine the dæmon up close, as I had been only at some distance on our prior meeting. I brushed aside the long locks of his ragged hair and beheld a grave wound upon the side of his loathsome face. Just as I determined surely no creature could survive such a mortal infliction, his eyelids fluttered apart and he gazed at me with such mixed feelings as one can imagine from his experiences: fear, enmity, wonder, and the gravest of pain.

O! Margaret, what can I express to you, but to hear a man surely thought dead, who should never have been alive to begin with, look upon you suddenly and speak your name!

"Captain," he said. "I thought my eyes never to behold man again."

"Do not flee," I said. "I wish you no harm, but only for you to recuperate."

"For my heart, there is no recuperation."

"But that you have experienced the worst of man, know you yet still may realize the best. You spoke before of cheering the warmth of summer and hearing the warbling of birds, and I say those are but triflings to the beauty this world has still to offer. You, here, have been given a second chance—do not think immediately of past torment, for every day is a new beginning."

Where such words flowed from, for hope of the creature, I do not know, but at that moment, I felt the magnanimity of charity, to see but a smile on the wretch, to see for him yet a chance for redemption. He hesitated, and it were as of our ship mired in ice, caught in a moment of indecision.

"To that, I will speak," he began in a voice as faint as ever I'd heard. "For but yesterday, I sought my own demise while the ice floes began to break apart. I climbed to the highest precipice there abounded, contemplating how best to ensure my demise, when suddenly a ledge gave out from beneath my heel. I lost grip and tumbled to the frozen sea far below. Thence, it were only but darkness, until I opened my eyes to thine, yet while in that darkness I found myself within myself... And should I have been accursed before, my miseries have thus manifested by the hundredfold."

The creature must surely have seen the perplexity upon my countenance, for his scarred brow crinkled and he sighed so terribly, the sound were as if that very ice around us did moan. "Who was I? What was I? Whence did I come?" he cried. "For that, I found cruel answer, knocked loose by some mysterious force of the beyond, that in the death I searched, instead I met the lives of whom I have been formed! It is my own body, and I discover that I cannot die, but have awoken instead this host of many . . . "

I found myself unsure how to respond, for surely my wits were not as quick as those of Victor Frankenstein's. The fiend sighed again, and he whispered, "The voices, the voices, they are in me."

And before I could react, he reached out and kissed me full on the lips, and this is what I heard all at once on the breath of his mouth.

(1) From the Hands of Sebald the Mason

I was a craftsman, a mason of stone.
By my hands did I strive to bring beauty to this world, sculptures of opulence and grace.
It is my hands that carved the figures of Atlas and Caryatids atop the garden front of the Sanssouci Palace. It is my hands that fashioned the exalted guardhouses flanking the Doric columns of Brandenburg Gate.
And so do I recall that to caress the lineaments of polished tourmaline is bliss. To touch the smooth spire of jade is sublime.
'Til a loose ceiling tile from an unsteady apprentice fell upon my head while repairing the Church Maria de Victoria in Ingolstadt.
My last touch was of its baroque manoualia.
Or so I thought.
I find myself still alive in my hands, and what are they now, these gentle means that once wrought only grandeur?
What are they now but the murderous cudgels of a fiend?

Margaret, I tell you I tried pulling back so suddenly from the dæmon, I near knocked over my reliquary of sextants. But the creature's hands held me fast, his lips held me still, and a second voice immediately flowed thence upon the first.

(2) From the Legs of Johan Adam Riepe

As a boy, I could outrun any other in all of Ingolstadt.
As a young man I could leap and dance the Zwiefacher or the Schuhplattler across the waning of the moon.
And as a soldier in the army of the Electorate, my legs carried me,

marching or climbing or kicking or vaulting o'er the peaks of Wasserkuppe and Fichtelgebirge, fighting the Habsburg Monarchy who attempted overthrow of Karl Theodor.
Then I learned of science, and the era of enlightenment called forth, and I sought to scale the greatest heights of the Fatherland, in pelt-lined boots and a coat of heavy fulled woolens, and on these legs that never knew fatigue.
It was my hands that slipped. It was my neck that broke. It was my mind that cried out, But too soon!
My body was returned to Ingolstadt, to the cold and still of the tomb.
And yet now I awake in my legs to the chance
To Run again! To Leap again! To Climb again!
O! Blessed fiend, carry us to the lofts!

Besides the horror, the revulsion of having my lips endeared by the flesh of the dead, I found myself imploring to the fiend to make those aberrant voices stop! He did not, or *could* not hear me, perhaps, while our mouths were enjoined. And so did the voices continue in a tumultuous roar within my own mind.

(3) From the Backside of Peter Gottfried Autermann

In life, I did not sin.
I did not carry on unbecoming of my kin.
I lived simply, ate simply, attended service at Liebfrauenmünster, and fell before my savior on pleading hands for mercy, for absolution, when called upon for such . . .
And even if I did not believe entirely in His almighty creed, I thought surely there must be more.
For the stars do gaze back upon each swelling night tide,
And the splendor of a petal ever conquers the pall,
And perhaps we may drift forever in the cosmos o'er the moon,

Or perhaps we may find ageless rest in the shade of Elysium.
But never would I have thought, a fate such as cruel:
For I to come back as the posterior of a wretch!

(4) From the Eyes of Jobst the Chandler

What is light but to make clear
the filth of life for all to behold?
The dung of the ass splattered across this wheat used for bread.
The running sores of orphaned children sickened in bed.
The foul muck of existence we cry to adore, until lost in those
shadows where no glow can take hold.
And I, who toiled as chandler, forming candles from myrtle wax . . .
Daily dipping wicks to molten tallow,
earning welts and boils, blisters and burns, but to see things best left for the murk.
Yet I dipped for my duty and watched this horrid world turn,
watched the filth spread, like fungus at edges of an odious moor.
And in the warmth and the light of those candles, I loathed it all,
until that great shade Oblivion came, and I was finally made glad!
. . . Thence my eyes opened anew, to loathe this world all again.

I could not scream, I could not cry, but that my lips continued to be encased by the fiend's own. I could not understand, could not fathom what was occurring, nor where would this lead? Was he filling me with demon possession? With sickness, with madness? Was this whole night madness, this entire expedition, and I lie instead in a fever-dream within a hospital in London?

I could satisfy no other explanation, and even while I thought this so, the voices continued upon me . . .

(5) From the Arms of Melchior Kühn

For love is what's found, beyond our life lived,
a new breath, when the last is come at hand.
What hast gathered from a smile, from a star,
Or yon halo of dawning light,
piercing the chill of perdurable gloom.
The empress of this undeserving heart,
by my arms that held your cheek, I knew thee.
By my arms, I embraced the sea
of felicity,
And by my arms, now, I live on!
As if, by your sweet touch, I have found eternity!
Thus know, somehow, this dæmon, this brute, is one of destiny,
For I am here, and you are near, yet if only I could hold you once again,
as I did that night of moon and mist,
When our tears froze together in rapturous demise . . .
O Lyse Maria van Brandt! Paradise is my stay, with you alongside,
together in this carcass of a fiend!

(6) From the Brain of Lyse Maria van Brandt

What horror must I endure, what trial,
and for why?
I who laundered the linens of those better than me,
to afford food for siblings and orphans Poppa took in.
I who had little, and wanted little else.
I nursed the boy giant, Melchior Kühn, whose rib was broke as his heart,
and I gave him a smile of cheer.
And he took that and warped it, and tried to force more, through

mucus and horrid tears and threats of obdurate love.
He warned his seed brooked no rebuff,
and wakened me each night, whispering maudlin verse from outside my sill.
'Til finally he stole me and plunged a knife through both our breasts,
and called my tears tragic joy . . .
Thence do I wake, hearing the verse still of that murderous boy
whispering up through his arms . . . !
Mark these words, O Fate, O Fiend, O Creature Foul,
Some day, whilst though are unprepared, whilst thoughts are of drink or of pleasantries, or of the banalities of friendlessness,
Some day, whilst you think not of me, I will take your arms against the other, and rend them from the sutures of ligament and bone, from muscle and flesh, and hurl them to the depths of the abyss, whence they will rot unclaimed, and never again be of burden to my mind, to vex the peace expected, upon my life that was despoiled!

When finally the creature released me, I fell to the floor of my cabin, gasping. It took some moments to compose myself to speak, and though at first my tongue prepared itself to berate him with the roughest of curses, naming him truly for the vile beast that he was, I was instead immediately overwhelmed by some sympathy that, by his act, he had opened himself to me, allowing me a glimpse into his tortured soul. By his own way, it was his cry for help, for compassion.

I wiped at the sweat on my brow and said honestly, "I do not understand . . . Those voices, they were in my head, they were of others, men, even a maiden!"

"And of those, Captain, who should I listen to, who should I please?" the fiend asked in fright. "That voice which loathes me, or that which loves me? That which calls me a wonder, or that which names me their nightmare?"

His own voice rose to a wailing, a shouting, a pleading, all wound within itself. "Tell me, dear Captain, what manner of *life* now to expect, and I will bade you my retort! For there are more, ever so many more, I'd never have thought . . . every piece of me has a voice, and their volume seems overrun, parts unused, parts spliced where they should not have been—And now, they clamor so!"

The creature's torment was so grave, I dared not look into those pitiful watery eyes, as he continued his laments. "My chest, my head, my heart, even my stomach and toes do speak, they sob, they plead, there is no respite! Do I charge left, or veer right, do I taunt or cry or kill?"

An idea then took suddenly hold, and I girded my fortitude, and stiffened my knees so as not to give way as I rose, and met directly the creature's gaze. For if I could not find glory in my great Arctic expedition, perhaps glory could be found here at least in exorcising this creature's affliction.

"I understand now," I said. "I understand in your story the reason for your tumultuous emotions, your conflicts of peace and rage, murder and tenderness, want and grace, confusion, self-deplorability. It is true, you were brought into this world a wretch, and I can wish no man, even yourself, such further torment as I detect corrupting what humanity you have remaining. I foresee only greater calamity, should I not offer what I can to assist, so in that, I will offer everything at my disposal.

"Firstly, no longer are you a fiend, but a person, a *life* as am I, one who is tempered by all means of emotion, yet more turbulent than any should bear. Sir—*friend*—as you henceforth shall be named, I give you this: For when your lips took mine, and I inhaled your breath, know that my breath too exhaled into you. Thus of you, I am forthwith part from such exchange, and I have given you voice of my own.

"Take these words and make them yours:

From the Breath of Captain Robert Walton

Though your burden is great, I allot you with more:
A calming voice, which I hope
lends use to navigate these gale-driven seas of your psyche.

For you must take what you are, a marvel, a wonder, a being of
reckon,
And make better in this world of science, of faith, of hurt and wanted
salve.
I ask thee: Aren't we all composed of a sum,
of different parts from our forebears, our dreams, our
experiences, our plans?
Don't we all hold pity and passion, anger and love, corruptibility,
hope, pain, lenity?
Just as your creator sought to push through realms of mortality,
and have I striven to bypass these frozen Arctic realms,
so too must you circumvent your unwanted agencies, and take
hold;
Seize control for rapture comes only from within—
I say, Age si quid agis*!**

Margaret, perhaps I spoke too hastily of my self-perceived flaws, for as I heard my own voice thence, I thought my wits surely at that moment to be as equal to those of Victor Frankenstein's.

The creature—no, *being*—looked at me most ardently, and I felt from him a relief within like a frost thawed beneath the sun.

Yet by the very next instant, the melancholy returned as heavily as before.

"How can I be part of mankind, when I look as such?" he asked, wiping one hulking hand across his misshapen face. "How can I function, under these legion cries?" He then placed both hands on the sides of his head, as if trying to wring the ghosts from his senses. "It is my creator they call for, they wish to question or berate, and surely were he here, he could control them through his wiles . . . and to think, it was Victor who wished to discover those secrets to overcome death, yet it is he who slumbers in oblivion, while I, who wish to die, must live on."

"Truly, friend, do you consider such things so?" I asked quietly.

"Yes, though for me I know not how to be relieved."

I thought on the matter for some moments, and then I asked him to wait for my return.

I called for the ship's surgeon, a burly man with whiskers as wild as a thorned bramble, and a constitution of equal note. We quarreled sometime over my proposition, but as he was one who could be plied malleably through the generosity of spirits, and further had some unsettled debts I offered to satisfy, we came to an arrangement.

I brought the surgeon into my cabin and introduced the *being* as son of Victor.

The surgeon was named Merton. The two did not shake hands but nodded at each other warily. I saw misgiving in each other's eyes.

"Your father," I said to the being, "is dead, yet his body remains here on ship for autopsy and burial. His body is still . . . *fresh*. Supple."

The being's expression was unreadable, so did his features freeze. It was shock, no doubt, perhaps considering what I was next to suggest.

I continued. "From Victor's own account, related days ago**, he said that you discovered his journals, minutely detailing the progress of work that led to your creation, the descriptions and details, the *means*. Do you recall what was written there?"

"It was the account of my birth. How can I ever forget, no matter how accursed the memory?"

"Then herein lies your chance," I said. "For you to gain what is necessary. To find balance and some certain satisfaction for all."

The surgeon lifted his scalpel.

"Victor's body is in the next room over," I said. "For I believe you, I believe *all* of you, that the greater good can be satiated. Victor owes you that much, and I believe, too, it's what he ultimately desires—a new chance to extend his own journey, a destination as such to make amends, which is not closure in itself, but offers an approach to closure."

The being nodded. Then he began to relate precise instructions to Merton in a voice without emotion, and we three moved to the next room over . . .

And when the being woke, I looked upon that face of a once-dead friend, now of a *new* friend. I bent to his new lips, and this is what I heard:

From the Face of Victor Frankenstein

I yearned to learn the secrets of immortality,
And now it is so.
I live on, in that which I've wrought,
As from the start, we were twined too inexorably together
to ever be apart.
Thus know then, in what you do,
Is what you become, though a champion or a fiend,
or both, most like, as such mortals we remain,
Though time anon will determine which, and only when looking
back.
So now I thence guide
by caution through this tale of woe:
Be mindful! Be gallant! Yet above all else, shun pride,
and seek not me further, though know I live on,
for truly I see, the Fiend is me!

And so I conclude this letter, dear Margaret, as the hour doth grow late.

For since last, we have buried the creator Victor Frankenstein at sea in a shroud, so as not to reveal the profane vivisection of his features. Of his most strange and wondrous creation, I sense he will be maltreated little further—Victor was quite handsome, as you recall in my writing before, and the surgery highly successful. And, as his creation believed, Victor's added presence has been enough to mollify the conflagration of those voices, to temper their stings through redress, explanation, understanding, and rallies of virtue and blessing.

At the last, the being cried out, "This horror, it is me, though will be set forthwith to apt use!"

And he sprang from the cabin-window as he shouted this, and

thence was seen no more by sight, but for my prediction, should live on by all else.

Your affectionate brother,
Robert Walton

(* *Do well, in whatever you do)*
(**from: *Frankenstein; or, The Modern Prometheus*)

INCIDENT AT THE RED HAWK ROAD STOP

DEAD-CENTER on that stretch of Route 66 that slips through New Mexico barely seen, in the barren scrubs and ghosts of grizzlies and snakes and widow spiders, the indignant cacti, the livid cliffs, the ragged and rough loam that hardens every scorched-sand day and hoarfrost night, sits a trading post named Red Hawk that most drive by with great speed, unless desperation or a need to get fleeced lures them into its loose gravel lot.

Or maybe they're part of a sideshow caravan traveling from Lubbock to Flagstaff, separated from the rest of the trucks and jalopies, lost and running low on gas.

That's how Madame Karla ends up here, as a quickening dusk folds over the land.

She turns the wheel of her midnight-black Chevy pickup, and it and a nine-foot mini trailer steer into the parking lot, churning through pools of grit and dust and the occasional slab of pot-holed asphalt. Both sides of the truck and trailer are painted with the bright pin-striped logo and name she works for: *Sweeney Circus Sideshow and Marvels.*

The jumble of small buildings and shacks ahead with one single dim light is fronted by a giant windswept sign, that only by squinting and twisting up her face, can she read its faded letters.

Red Hawk Road Stop—Rock Shop and Indian Trading Post and Visitor Center. A secondary sign exclaims: *Gas! Ice!*

A third: *Dinosaur Fossils for Kids!*

Her sigh is mixed resignation and aversion. It's by her own ways that she recognizes the trademark signage of a huckster. So by the sort of prescience she's known for, as well as a damn good eye for reading people, Madame Karla envisions it:

Red Hawk is the sort of place tourists slobber over to tell they've visited, to snap off an entire roll of Kodak film showing candids of their children centered below a rusted Coca-Cola sign, flanked on one side by a stuffed buffalo and the other by a hard-nosed wooden Indian Chief with a quiver full of carved cigars. There's a photo-op for the wife, alabaster arms and florid face, a great billowing gown of polka-dots and whimsy, leaning on a brick teepee that houses the largest collection of rocks and minerals this side of the Bandelier National Monument. There's a photo-op for the husband, wearing that oversized cowpoke hat (price tag still fluttering by a line of dull twine) and fending off the broken glass sculpture of a rearing scorpion with agate eyes. *Click-whir*, goes a picture: a line of kachina dolls with raised spears. *Click-whir*, goes a picture: notched frontier logs punctured in shoot-out by the genuine bullet of Kit Carson. *Click-whir*, goes a picture: the jovial, fat proprietor with a bulbous, ruptured nose from binge drinking, big fake smile and a redneck twinge in his voice; shit-kicker snakeskin boots and a bola tie with turquoise pendant.

And here comes that very same fat proprietor now, exactly as she imagined, walking through the gloom of falling dark, to the front of the nearest building—the Trading Post, she guesses—the one with a single gas pump and a sign reading TEXACO. He's putting up a new sign on the door, one that says: CLOSED, COME BACK AGAIN.

Damn.

This is the sort of place she despises, the lowest rung on the carnie ladder—the cautionary tale even—where showmen with the flair of a dung beetle and even less prospects for gainful employment finish out their years. It gives her the willies.

But, so too, is she almost out of gas.

She spits out the cigarette butt that's been smoldering between clenched lips, turns on her biggest rube grin, and drives across the lot, careful not to jostle her cargo, until pulling alongside that single gas pump. Pokes her head out the window, and a gust of wind pulls at the kerchief tied over her hair. The wind out here is beastly.

"Howdy-hi!" she calls out, chipper, with just a lil' twang of carefully placed vulnerability.

The proprietor looks at her, does a big show of scratching his whiskers and inspecting the CLOSED sign still in hand, just so she knows he ain't fallin' for it.

Double-damn. The bright-eyed damsel card's not going to cut it with this chum. *But that's okay, she's got a full deck to pull from.*

A gust of wind rocks the truck. She changes tact. "Mister, I need gas, and I've got cash. Wanna do business?"

He whistles two notes. "Well, ain't you the prettiest thing in a circus car I've seen all day."

She cocks a penciled eyebrow. "You seen more of us, or you bein' smart?"

"No need to get feisty. Group of you drove by couple hours ago. Some sight."

Not so lost after all, Karla thinks.

He goes on. "Running a little behind, ain't ya?"

"Blew a tire on the stretch out of Santa Rosa."

"Someone else ridin' with you?"

She opens the carnie truck door and it squeals loud, and she steps out and smooths down the pleated rose skirt she's been wearing two days straight. "I can change a tire myself."

"Dressed like that, say you can."

She shrugs, and the gold hoops in her ears tinkle. "So, you open for gas or not?"

His lips purse and he takes in a great, long breath, leaning back on boot heels in the deepest of contemplation. He glances at her, then past, his eyes darting back-and-forth, searching. "No need to stand out in the wind, I guess," he finally says. "Come on inside while I turn the pump back on."

He doesn't look back as he saunters inside the building.

She hesitates. There's something about this man, something she doesn't like, even more than his crude yokel manner, something… *dark*, something she can't quite yet read, but it's unsettling to her instincts, her *prescience* …

It's a talent she has, some spiritual or mystical awareness, letting her see things occasionally about other people. A faculty her grandmother's grandmother passed down all the way back from the ancient pagan tribes of whatever old land they hailed from. These visions aren't altogether absorbing, aren't profound nor consistent—and she knows this—but it's enough to get by, enough to bring in the price of admission.

She'd rather stay outside, with her truck and the circus trailer and its cargo, rather than follow the fat proprietor into his lair, but, so too, is she hungry. Tired. She hasn't showered or changed clothes since they packed up in Texas. It'd taken the strongman's best efforts to close the trailer door, it was crammed so tight, and of course all of her own things and the cages are wedged far inside and unreachable until she arrives at Flagstaff to unpack. No time for sleep either, so bagged food and a cup of coffee—if the yokel's got some inside—could do miracles to help her drive on, catch up to the others. The rest of the troupe will be setting up soon on a new parade ground, and she has all the circus flags and sideshow banners stuffed in her trailer, things they'll need to start off. She has everything, of course, *except* any money . . . Really not a penny to her possession. It'd been a rushed packing, and not much for planning, but there'd been that inconvenience of an irate crowd of locals beginning to organize, all in a huff over some communal sense of having been bilked and beguiled. Shotguns and baseball bats were indeed the modern-day tar and feathers.

So Madame Karla follows the fat proprietor inside, though all her senses scream not to; for reassurance, she runs a finger along the edge of the razor knife hidden up the sleeve of her dress.

The man goes rustling underneath a counter. Its top overflows with highway maps, cactus spine magnets (*I'm stuck on you!*), Route 66 matchbooks, hard peppermint candies, sundry other junk her eyes skim quickly over and register.

When he speaks, the counter muffles his voice. "What d'ya do in this circus?"

"Read fortunes mostly, some other acts."

"Don't say?" He reappears, standing tall in front of her, his turquoise bola tie at level with her eyes. "Like a Gypsy, then?"

"More a psychic."

He grunts. Reaches for one of the peppermint candies and knocks over a stack of unshelved postcards; there's a flash of: *Red Hawk Road Stop—Best Piñon Nuts in the State.* He mutters and bends down again behind the counter to pick them up.

She says with a no-nonsense assurance, "Really appreciate this, mister, uh . . . "

"Name's on the sign."

"Hawk? Mr. Hawk?"

He scowls as he comes back up. "Ain't you a psychic? It's Red. Name's Jimmy Red."

"As they say in the biz, 'It only works when it works.'"

He looks at her strange. His eyes are murky, hard to read, and she guesses him now for a poker player. *That's good, he likes to gamble.* She holds out a hand to shake and is pleased to see his eyes dart to her fingers.

When he takes hold of her hand, he doesn't let go, but lifts it up for a closer view, scrutinizing. Each of her fingers is ornamented in garishly bright jewelry. The ornamental rings are carved gold, inlaid with rubies, opals, diamonds. To the trained eye they're well-crafted shams, but to John and Jane Public, she wears a sublime exhibit of precious, glittering gems—a good impression while her hands are reading someone's future.

"Quite the frill you're modeling," he admits.

"Thank you. I tell people's futures, and they pay me well."

He grunts, but it's a dead giveaway he's interested when he turns her hand over.

She plays the line. "I appreciate exquisite jewelry." She now becomes the gracious socialite, the purveyor of taste and culture, and only by happenstance to be involved with a carnie sideshow. "Being a travelling entertainer, I carry all my wealth with me. Better to keep it in sight, rather than hidden away in some shoebox, wouldn't you say?"

He nods, seeming impressed. "Well, pump's on. How much you want?"

"I'll take twenty's worth."

"All right."

He bangs open the cash register, stares at her expectantly. "Twenty's worth costs twenty, lady."

Problem being for Madame Karla, is that lack of funds.

She opens her mouth to reply, ready to purr out an unfeasibly magnanimous opportunity of selling Jimmy the Yokel one of her rings for the gas and maybe fifty bucks small cash from the register, but he cuts her off.

"You ain't gonna try jawjackin' me again like you did on those phony rings?"

Her breath catches, her skin prickles. She screams at herself, *Goddamn it, misread him again!*

She's overly aware of the buzzing from the fluorescent lights overhead, the cold draft sneaking in through unsealed windows, the smell of *him*, whiskey, oil, a cloying sense of musk and mothballs.

She fumbles for words, and finds they pour out easy only by reflex. "I'm real sorry, Mr. Red—Jimmy, can I call you Jimmy?"

He snorts, curls a lip.

"I didn't mean to try hustling you but, fact is, I'm caught short. I lost my purse while we were packing, and you're right, I wouldn't be senseless enough to walk around with a 'Mug Me' sign on each hand. I mean, I *have* riches—" She thinks to everything she's hauling, desperate to keep him interested: "My real treasures are locked in the trailer, just none of it's regular currency, you understand."

He flicks a tongue over his lips; *now* she's got his interest, and she won't be wrong again. From here on out is just a matter of patter . . .

"I *need* gas, so how about this?" she says. "You fill up my tank, throw in a handful of these candies, couple soda pops, and I'll tell something about your future and your past."

"I prefer currency."

"Miss out on knowing what awaits you by Divine Fate?"

"Miss out on you fillin' my head with a load of malarkey," he replies, real flat. "Say you're gonna tell my future, when you can't even predict your own, like thinking to bring an extra can of gas on your travels?"

"It's the wit of soothsaying: A medium cannot read her own future."

Jimmy laughs, a short and hard sound. "Well, you telling me something I don't know is gonna happen until it does or doesn't, don't sound like much value to me." He flicks a tongue over his lips again, giving her the eyeball. "Seems you're at a disadvantage, lady, stuck here, needing somethin' from *me* . . . "

"All right, I'll level the field, give you a chance, so to speak," she says. "Twenty bucks bet at straight odds: Write down a number between one and ten, and I'll guess that number."

Jimmy scowls, considers, calculation in his eyes. "You're just indebtin' yourself to me even more."

He takes the stub of a chewed pencil, hides one hand behind the other, and writes on the back of a receipt. She doesn't need to see his hand; no one thinks how the elbow moves also, betrays penmanship: a tiny jerking motion means a seven, a slight bounce is a three, a swivel is a two, and so on. The unimaginative always pick the number seven or three anyway; she's been playing this a long time. His elbow gives the tiny jerk.

"Seven," she declares, very cool.

Jimmy curses. "How'd you know—"

"Because I am Madame Karla, it's what I do. Now that's twenty *you* owe *me*, though I'll give you a chance to get it back, double or nothing."

And she could keep this up all night . . .

"Fine," he concedes, frowning. "I'll take that bet, double or nothing, against my future, but how can you prove it—"

"By your past. I'll also tell something that's already occurred, which will *cause* the named future event."

Jimmy's frown deepens. He crosses his arms. Something crashes outside. The wind picks up, loud and shrill.

She shows him her bejeweled hands—even with phony rings, they're distracting, mesmerizing. He blinks, and a crystal ball appears, held in her palm.

All sleight-of-hand from under her sleeve, and her hands are quick.

"How'd you do that?" he asks, taking a step back.

Now she's on familiar ground. Now she's the one with sway, assertion over this sad, wondering, fat bumpkin, and she's going to milk it—*enjoying the bettering of this bastard who tried to get the better of me*—"Because Jimmy Red of Red Hawk Road Stop, I'm a magician."

"You said you're a psychic . . . "

"I'm that as well. I keep three vocations, such is the case of a true showman."

She rolls the crystal ball slowly around the palm of her hand, *sensually.*

Jimmy gulps. He's bewildered. "Is it . . . real? It's so small."

"Crystal balls in movies overcompensate, doll," she tells him, enjoying the flash of crimson at his neck. "You don't need a large surface to prognosticate."

And Madame Karla feels a certain prescience coming on then, a warm, lethargy in her brain that spreads, like a dream, as visions cross over. The foresight comes and goes, and half the time she can't figure what any of it means, but Jimmy Red doesn't have to know that.

She's going to toy with him, use the whole reason she was slow behind the rest of the circus caravan, and not just because of the crummy packing in Lubbock, the flat tire after Santa Rosa, but that she has delicate cargo, a *side*-sideshow attraction, and she must drive cautiously.

Madame Karla looks deep into the crystal ball, makes her eyes widen, roll up, then down, crazily.

"Your future, it is not long," she says. "I see death. *Yours* . . . I see splendid wings . . . you will die . . . by a butterfly."

"Die, what? A *butterfly*?" he sputters. "What the hell does that mean?"

"I'm sorry, I don't know more, but I have foreseen it. It will occur." Inwardly she laughs. Next, she needs to reveal something of his past that will cause the future-named event, something she may have figured already, or . . .

And it happens at once: Her brain is ravaged, ripped open in a sudden, immense prescient-wonder, a rapid-fire series of images shuttering forth—*It only works when it works*—and Karla draws back, gasping. Jimmy's past has shown itself to her:

Wayward, lone travelers stopping here who never leave . . .

She drops the crystal ball, her quick hands flicking out that razor knife from under the sleeve of her dress—

Jimmy Red yanks a snub-nosed pistol from beneath his coat and shoots her through the forehead.

HE hadn't meant to kill her. At least, not yet.

Hell, getting to know someone before you pulled the trigger was half the fun. But the broad had pulled out one damned mean-lookin' blade, and she looked ready and quick enough to use it.

Though not quick enough . . . Jimmy laughed.

He often thought a woman wielding a knife to be twice the danger of a similarly-armed man. A dame got heated, let her emotions take over without giving much warning, while a man liked to boast about what he was gonna do, gave you time to prepare, time to act first. Over the years he'd put the brakes on steely Huns with barraging rifles, hatchet men with Tommy guns, and private dicks who should've known better, but he feared most of all a fired-up woman with a skewer.

Some psychic Madame Karla turned out to be anyway, Jimmy thought, and his laugh turned to a giggle. He was giddy with adrenaline. *Couldn't even read her own future.*

And some mess she'd left behind, too. Before reopening in the morning, he'd have to wipe down the spatters of blood and dusky hair she'd sprayed over the rubber tomahawks for kids and best piñon nuts in the state, sold by the pound.

Such is business.

He left her there, bleeding out on the checkered linoleum floor, and went to the front door, peered through its window to the darkening sky and distant stars and a sliver of moon rising behind puce-spired mountains, while storm clouds and long shadows grew obscure, melding to the night, and a distant coyote's howl meant everything was all right.

And there, forty feet away, just at the edge of light spilling from the store's window and sitting plum in the middle of his otherwise-empty lot, was Madame Karla's truck and cargo.

My real treasures are locked in the trailer, she'd said, and that made him smile anew.

It wasn't the first time he'd killed a late-night traveler, all alone and lost, and he supposed it wouldn't be the last. This country had too many rich tourists to miss a few now and again . . . *and what was that crazy talk about dying by a butterfly?*

Jimmy pushed open the front door and walked out to the bleak, dark desert. The wind kicked up, blowing a spray of dust, a patter of gravel. It clinked like loose coins. He flexed his gun hand.

A ghostly sigh came down the mountain pass, and even from faraway it prickled goosebumps on his tensing arms. He rubbed his eyes; through the deepening gloom, Madame Karla's slat-side truck was long and blockish in shape, but the connected trailer was turned at an angle, and from his perspective the two vehicles appeared as one, curled inward and facing him, almost alive like some giant creeping slug, or . . . caterpillar.

You will die by a butterfly. The thought came sudden.

The moon winked out behind leaden clouds. He rubbed his eyes again in the darkness. Another gust of wind, stronger, tried shoving him aside; the night was cold and smelled of creosote, and it was noisy in the ways of deserts with crickets and creaks and billows. Arid wind brought odd sounds: one moment a whoosh like shaking out an old blanket, the next like a great intake of breath. Worse, it distorted things so you couldn't hear a crash two feet behind you while listening to the groaning of a settling crag half a mile away.

Wait, no need to go stumbling around out here blind. Jimmy turned and went back inside the trading post for a flashlight.

. . . a butterfly.

The woman was a crackpot, that was certain. *Death by a butterfly?*

He rifled under a shelf for the flashlight, but it wasn't there. Searched through a desk. Combed a cabinet.

What *if* . . .

She *did* see something, at the end, something that had caused her to pull that knife, but what? What else would she have said? Not that he could speak about such things with any certainty, but Jimmy couldn't imagine that in all the history of the world, any man ever died by a butterfly . . . unless, maybe . . . were there *poisonous* butterflies? Not here in the New Mexico desert, that was sure, but maybe elsewhere, some horrid jungle land, where every vile thing is deadly, frogs and flowers and . . . butterflies? Could a toxin-bearing fiend have found its way here to the United States, driven over by some freak storm, and even now was fluttering its wings to soar into his unsuspecting mouth?

He shook his head. *Asinine, forget it!*

Still searching, Jimmy yanked out a drawer under the cash register too hard so it broke free from its railings to spill all manner of keys and bolts and other metal things that were the loudest possible assemblage of crap to make a tremendous racket as it crashed to the floor, causing him to leap back with a heart-pounding gasp and curse.

And there was the flashlight, fallen too among the coins and steel washers. After he settled his nerves, Jimmy picked up the light, saw the lens was cracked, and switched it on. Nothing happened. He shook the flashlight hard and switched it on again. This time it flickered, flashed, stayed on.

Jimmy wiped his brow. *There wasn't Jack nor shit he should be scared of, not butterflies, not her—Jimmy Red made his own way in life.*

Once he'd been a straightforward guy, served in the Great War, 3rd Division out of North Carolina. A machine gunner, he'd helped hold back the frothing Huns at the Marne River, and when they ran out of .30-06 cartridges, he'd charged forward with two grenades and a knuckle duster trench knife. He still had the German belt buckle from the first man he'd ever gutted.

Of course, then what happened when he returned home among the banners and accolades? *Nothin'*, that's what happened, the goose egg of life, and its yolk had been on his face.

A living he could be proud of? That was a chuckle and a half: his options were to mop blood from the meatpacking floors in Chicago, or mine coal from the bleakest pits of Pennsylvania. Hell with that, he wasn't a twit. He made his own way, and if someone had to suffer for it, such was business, but—

But butterfly, butterfly, you will die by a butterfly . . .

Jimmy gritted his teeth. It wasn't that long ago he'd been laughing.

He returned to the dark outside with his flashlight, and a fresh gust of wind billowed up. Gravel scattered, something bounced off his scarred cheek. His heart skipped, and the damnedest thought crossed his mind of what a butterfly's wing must feel like brushing against a man's face: That's what he'd just felt.

The driver's door to Karla's truck was unlocked. He climbed into the cab and sat behind a steering wheel that pushed into his gut. The seatback creaked, and the truck shook from another gust. The cab smelled of woman, of cigarettes and perfume and a woman's *sweat*; even unwashed ass and armpit smelled fine, if coming from a female.

There wasn't much inside. He shined the light around, saw a half-crumpled pack of her smokes, the brand of Old Gold. A necklace of black wood beads hung from the rearview like strung-up beetles. The floor was sticky, there was ash everywhere, a sock with a hole in the toe and a scarf of calico green-and-orange were wadded on the floor behind the passenger seat.

What about an assassin, some code name of "The Butterfly"? Hell, that would make sense . . . How many enemies did he have? How many men had he fleeced? How many had he killed? Backroom card games with one too many bad hands or one too many aces? He'd been around, but he covered his tracks good, changed his name and face a dozen times, yet still, there were ways, and with his proclivities . . . well, he knew it was just a matter of time—Sure, now it made sense.

A hitman with the goddamned name of The Butterfly . . . would it be a bullet in the night that took him? A garrote around the neck? He watched the cacti and trees through the windshield, swaying in the wind, closing in on him, each a blur of a man with death in his eyes . . .

Jimmy pulled the pistol from his pocket . . . "No," he whispered to the shadows. "I ain't goin' out like that."

He kicked the cab door open hard with one snakeskin boot. The hinges groaned. The wind whistled. He leapt out, pointing the snub-nosed gun and flashlight in a circle. The signs on the gas pump and store frontage all rattled and clattered together.

He was alone.

Yet she'd said there were splendid wings . . . no hitman would be out in the desert dressed like a bumblin' fairy . . .

Jimmy took a deep breath. Holstered the gun.

And, she'd said, the real treasures are in the trailer... So what was he doing out here, fartin' around with shadows?

The black clouds swelled, blanketing the stars one by one until none remained. The night was a sea of inky gloom: *Stygian.* There was a word he'd learned long ago from some crime show on the radio—Stygian—black as the River Styx. Black as the underworld of death and damnation, black as the unblinking eyes of a stalking butterf—

A squeal ripped through the night, and Jimmy cried out, his heart rocketing to his mouth, and it took a moment to register it was just the truck making that sound, the trailer hitch shifting in the wind, or the chassis settling. He panted, paused, got his breathing under control.

He wiped a bead of cold sweat off his brow, then made his way around the truck, shining the flashlight at its side panel as he passed. The light dimmed, wavered, resumed. He read the splashy pin-striped letters: *Sweeney Circus Sideshow and Marvels.*

Like the light, Jimmy paused, considered, then kept on.

At the back of the trailer, he took the door's handle and turned it. *Locked.* He pushed the handle again, leaned into the metal door, and the sensation was solid, like pushing into a wall, almost as if—from the other side—a pressure pushed back.

This trailer is packed! Jimmy thought, feeling good again.

He walked back through the wind and chill and sand and dark to the Trading Post.

Entering, the interior lights caught him unexpectedly, blinding for a moment, all bright flashes of color at his eyes, after being outside in the dark.

Madame Karla's body still lay there, eyes frozen in shock, the palm-sized crystal ball by her ringed fingers.

He cursed and kicked her in the ribs. "Your prophecy is crap!"

Karla's body rolled over without complaint. A gold necklace spilled from under the collar of her dress.

Red and green and gold, sparkles and glitter beneath the buzzing fluorescent lights. He bent low to snatch it. The chain held a pendant, a small ruby body with green emerald wings . . . a goddamned butterfly.

He dropped the necklace as if it'd bitten him.

Could *she* be the butterfly she'd foreseen as his death? Holy Hell and Christmas, now he had to worry about her ghost, her vengeful spirit haunting his every moment for the opportunity to avenge murder . . .

"No," Jimmy said out loud to himself, out loud to *her*, so her corpse would understand his resolve. "I don't believe that at all."

He opened a closet stocked with shovels, pickaxes, and other implements used for burying dead victims in surreptitious graves of sand and rock. In their midst hung a bolt cutter. He took it in his free hand.

Armed with the cutter and flashlight, Jimmy returned outside, and it had become so dark he couldn't see where the land ended or sky began; it was all a *Stygian* blur, black but for the feeble cone of translucence given by his wavering flashlight. He'd b—

—*butterfly, butterfly,* the caress of its wings, the flash of color, the tickle as it crawls along the back of your neck. Butterfly, butterfly, a hideous thing fluttering just out of sight, waiting, waiting to strike—

Jimmy turned fast, swung the light around, turned the other way . . . nothing, nothing but nerves. His heart beat fast, fluttering, like a bu—

No! He wouldn't think it, wouldn't give in to the goddamned jitters. It was his mood, his temper, he just had to control it . . .

He moved quick to the back of the trailer without further incident, taking hard breaths through the stinging, wind-borne sand. He tried to breathe through his nose, but he was panting, dust and grit plastering the inside of his mouth. He tried to spit it all out but was not successful.

Jimmy tucked the flashlight into the crook of his arm, took each end of the bolt cutter in hand, and strained to cut the trailer's lock. It wouldn't budge. He changed position and still couldn't get it. The flashlight slipped. It dropped to the ground with a sickening crack, turning off.

Jimmy moaned, punched the metal door too hard. The pain hit, and his knuckles screamed. He cried out, cursed, gulped air. He couldn't see anything.

He went to his hands and knees feeling through the gravel, until his fingers found the flashlight. Blindly, he fumbled at the switch, but nothing. Shook it again, hard, held it to his ear, something rattled inside. He twisted the cracked lens, and the light suddenly blared on, in his eyes, in a flash of blinding radiance.

Jimmy yelped, nearly dropped the light again—he had to blink away sparkles and shifting colors.

His anger, his damned temper! He felt his heart pounding, and he forced himself to calm, to breathe slow, deep.

The wind finally died. He thanked whatever was responsible for at least that small relief.

He set the flashlight down—*gently*—on the ground, against a stone, so the light shined upward at the trailer door. Took another deep breath and gripped the bolt cutter again.

He positioned himself properly, flexed his arms, put his weight into it, and pushed the cutter blades together at the lock. With a *schunk*, the lock sheared in half and fell away.

It happened at once . . .

The trailer's door burst open, and a sudden gust of wind rushed by. There was a *whoosh*, and a monstrous unfurling, like great wings battering the air to rise up, up, high above. The clouds broke, and the moon lit all.

Jimmy's sight was filled with bursts of fire red, vibrant green, a yellow bright as summer lemons; great insectoid eyes, long pointed appendages, and immense billowing wings the length of a building, the greatest butterfly he'd ever seen, and then it dropped upon him . . .

He shrieked, loud and long.

A bolt of searing pain ripped through his chest, and Jimmy clutched there, and his high-pitched screams endured longer than he could have imagined, echoing through mountain passes, carried for miles by a foul desert wind.

His legs gave out, and he fell back to the desert floor, struggling to fill his lungs with breath, and saw, fluttering in the wind, gold-bandied letters, which read: *Madame Karla Fortuna—Psychic, Magician, and Exhibitor of Exotic Butterflies!*

A banner, a banner, a butterfly banner . . .

The strength of rage returned, cresting in an adrenaline-fueled indignation at his own cries, at the fears he'd allowed to overcome him . . . nothing but a carnival banner, crammed carelessly behind the trailer's door. He stood, unbelieving his heart hadn't burst, and swatted at the thing. It bounced up, higher into the sky, out of reach. Moonlight shimmered off a cable, tethering it to wooden signage jammed inside the trailer.

"To hell with this night," Jimmy said, to anything that would listen. He'd had enough. He could paw through the contents tomorrow, in the daylight, but now, he just needed to stow the vehicle, clean up the woman's death.

The wind began to renew, a low whistling through clenched teeth. He looked around for the flashlight but could not find it—when he'd fallen, he'd must have knocked it away . . . Inexplicably the moon dimmed. The winds gusted stronger, and he rubbed grit out of his eyes.

The banner dipped from the sky, like a kite dropping, and battered the side of his head.

Jimmy shouted, swung a fist at it again, and again it danced just out of reach with a gust of wind. He resumed his search for the flashlight, and the hovering carnival banner—at that very moment—dropped again, and its frame corner clapped the other side of Jimmy's head, knocking him to his knees. His rage was almost like a living beast, a golem of his emotions. His chest was on fire, the damned butterfly curse was going to be the death of him after all, of this he was suddenly certain.

Just walk away, he thought, and he heeded his own advice.

The banner followed, twisting, furling, unfurling.

Jimmy's heart hammered more, he shook his head at the impossibility. He began to jog from it, trying not to dwell on the idiocy of his flight. *What was happening, and how far could that tether reach?*

Thirty feet away, forty feet, the great butterfly banner pursued, and then it plunged at him, buffeting him again at the head, attempting, it seemed, to engulf him, to suffocate him in its canvas shroud. Jimmy's jog became a sprint. The banner tensed, snapped backward, away—

finally it had reached the end of its cable. Jimmy bent over, arms on his knees, gasping for breath, wary of cardiac arrest.

Then a tremendous blast of wind rolled down through the mountains, and he heard a resounding *twang* as the tether snapped. The banner shot back toward him, and Jimmy shrieked anew, fleeing blindly into the desert, the horrible frenzy of a swirling, billowing butterfly banner chasing after him. Desert sand flew into his face, nicking, pinging, while the banner whipped at his head, his neck, the sensation like stinging nettles, skin tearing, blood beginning to free.

The thought came to him, unwanted and sudden, that he should have just let the bitch go, just given Madame Karla gas, and let her be on her way, that maybe he'd pushed his luck one time too many. The thought of her reminded him of his gun. Jimmy stopped, turned, withdrew the snub-nosed pistol, and fired at the banner.

A hole punctured the canvas, and the banner fell back, its acceleration checked. It sprang at him again, he fired. Another hole punctured it, the banner drooped. Again it lifted and neared, and he fired, the sound of each blast an echo of his triumph.

The next time it came at him, Jimmy Red noticed the strangest thing, something he couldn't figure why it should matter, how it could have any bearing on the situation, but that there was a gold necklace encircling the banner, with a glittering small pendant body, rubies and emeralds, all in the shape of a butterfly, the exact necklace Madame Karla had worn.

Jimmy fired his last bullet, and it was a direct hit. The necklace shattered, and the banner fell limp, slowly fluttering to the desert floor.

The wind had stopped. That was the reason it fell, he told himself. Everything had an explanation, no need to let his heart blow its last valve. He'd put holes in the banner, so that it could not stay aloft, like perforating a parachute. He'd known paratroopers to die in such a way, their chutes in descent, peppered with flak, so the soldier would just drop, drop, drop like a flaming comet.

It'd only been the strangest of coincidences that the wind had blown that banner after him . . . Although, he'd been running *into* the wind, hadn't he . . . ? Had felt the wind on his face, the desert sand nicking, pinging his brow . . . the banner should have been blown *behind* him, away, not chasing him . . . unless something else on the tether, a cross cable or a guy line had gotten tangled around his clothing?

Jimmy patted himself down, checked his arms, his legs, found nothing of worry, except the question, *where was he now*? Where had he ended up in his panic-fueled flight?

And the thought that he'd used all his bullets . . . been tricked, perhaps, into using them all . . .

It was so dim, barren in this wasteland of a desert. He heard sounds, whispers, rustles, sighs. The moon and the stars filled the sky, and one of those stars began moving . . . not like a shooting star, streaking across the cosmos, but moving toward him, slowly, nearing, enlarging, and it wasn't a star at all, he realized. It glowed, like a firefly, although he'd never known fireflies to be in the New Mexico desert, where there are no water holes around.

And there's another one, a second firefly drifting near, its glow phosphorescent green. He turned and saw two more, three more, drifting lazily, in soft loops, a butterfly's delicate passage.

Closer they came, more in number, until Jimmy understood these were not fireflies at all, they were much too large. Each was the size of a silver dollar, but seemingly weightless, extruding quivering antennae, spindly legs, four massive, gossamer wings. *Splendid wings* . . . And something else, something unsettling—no, worse, *horrifying*—as he studied them, he saw the creatures' heads were those of humans.

One, *there!* A thin man with sunken eyes whom Jimmy had shot in the back last year. That next one, *there!* A dusky woman he'd strangled with wire because he'd coveted her car. The next, *that one!* A man with sideburns so thick it doubled the width of his face . . . Jimmy had poisoned him, had slipped arsenic into his coffee. And more . . . the sky grew thick with the beings, a memory book of what he'd done, these small shrunken ghosts, all winged, flitting in the dark. Angels have wings, and so too do the dead, the murdered whose bodies he'd hidden in the mountains, lost and never found . . .

And that realization was overshadowed by another, that he was in the dark, the complete dark, having run from the trailer, having left the flashlight there; he was in the dark, but for these ghosts that glow, that fly like butterflies. One landed on his arm, a younger man with buck teeth and round glasses. Jimmy brushed him off, the ghastly butterfly catapulting back into the dark. Jimmy felt another alight at his neck, tickling. He didn't see it, just slapped it away as one would a mosquito. Several of the creatures landed on his legs, his chest, the top of his head. One hovered before him, staring into his eyes with its own, and there the face of Madame Karla burned into his soul.

The butterflies didn't hurt, they didn't bite or scratch, but Jimmy was frantic wiping at himself, knocking them off, although when one was brushed away, it quickly returned with others. *How many men and women had he killed over the years?* He'd lost count. Finally, he pinched one of the fluttering wraiths between his fingers, trying to crush it, but the creature was spongy, resilient, like trying to crush wet cloth. The effort failed, he went back to knocking them off, while moving away, through the dark, conscious he could be going in circles, cautious not to twist an ankle.

His footfalls jarred hard in the dirt, first one, then the next, but the following footfall felt nothing. Jimmy was lifted off the ground. The sensation was of bewilderment, that something so ordinary, so assumed as to feel solid surface under his boots, did not occur.

He no longer saw the butterflies, and, for that, knew they were at his back. They'd latched onto him and were somehow pulling him up into the air. The ground dropped away, and the disorientation was so mystifying that he looked upward instead, only to see the moon grow closer, which was equally terrifying.

A glow formed around him, pulsing in waves to match the cadence of the wings' flapping. He closed his eyes, struggled, until the futility of his effort became apparent. He was caught by the butterflies, by their collective grip, and up, up, he rose, ascending toward vague clouds. The air felt cooler, tasted cleaner, and when he reopened his eyes, the view became finer, unnaturally so. Below, Red Hawk Road Stop was a child's toy in a sandbox, and the sandbox was of his own manufacture, cramped and paltry, barricaded by walls he'd erected, all of it dirty and filled with trash, with bones, with tears.

Jimmy did not have the energy remaining to scream any further, though the fright would have muted his voice anyway. Up, he flew, higher still, past night birds and mountain tops, and his breaths were furtive, searching gasps. He wondered at what it all meant. He wondered at his life then, too, as the beauty of the universe coalesced around him, quixotic chroma of blue, sage, gold, merlot, the mirroring of butterfly wings reflecting themselves, insectoid patterns, all bisected by veinous matter that overlaid one another, leading to divergences of more wings, fluttering, fluttering away the nebulas of sunsets of tomorrow; that is what Jimmy was lifted into, into oblivion.

And still higher, Jimmy was lifted, and higher, and then he was dropped.

WHEN the body of Jimmy Red was found the next day, crushed flat on the desert floor as if a meteor colliding into the Earth, the Highway Patrol did not know what to make of it. There was no great leap in deduction to solve the circumstances of Madame Karla's death, but Jimmy . . . Jimmy Red and the ninety-two corpses recovered on his land—that enormity of malfeasance required a bit more conjecture, a bit more *imagination*. Those shriveled skeletons of missing travelers seemed to have been in the process of metamorphizing as if from chrysalises, maybe some mummification ritual, investigators guessed, orchestrated by a crazed serial killer. But for that killer himself, there was no hypothesis offered as to what could have occurred during his own final moments.

The whole affair eventually got buried, and events were left to become part of the lore and legend that paves Route 66 today.

O SHADES, MY WOE

THE night wanes darker in absence of gods, darkest still in light of ill-penance. It is a darkness tinged with dreadful enchantment, a darkness of rot, a darkness men must only flee should they've any regard for the continuance of life, the preservation of soul—

Yet I flee no more.

The night is dark, yet I see things in it, things that move, that approach. For black is the sky, though mists of amethyst slither across, hiding, then revealing, occasional diamond-shaped stars, glimpses of a moon so full its bloated belly should burst, and the sad, squinty-eyed faces of pale babes that bob upon unseen waves.

Those babes mewl with the despair of abandoned kittens, their soft sweet notes as plaintive as those from a shepherd's curved gemshorn.

They come for me, and I know upon their waves I'm soon to be taken . . .

I AM a soldier in King Arthur's army, a man-at-arms crusading under the red dragon of his banner. I fought with Arthur at the fortress of Leodegran where ten thousand men died in battle, and I travelled in his retinue to far-off realms where golden unicorns rule and castles are built of glass.

I, who was born the same year as Arthur, was even present the day in Westminster when he, a boy, pulled the heir's sword from its stone-mounted anvil. O! How I dreamt it to be me raising that ancient blade in exaltation, how I thought of fate's vagaries and that I could have been anything . . .

But I contented myself, at least, to have witnessed such wonder. And when we came of age, and Arthur marched to campaign against Lot Luwddoc and his eleven armies, I joined, pledging my fealty forever to the boy-king.

And such victories were ours to be had! Death's cold hand but grazed our warriors whilst it sought our enemies like a beggar scrabbling upon lost coins. Arthur's banners raised on every defeated field high above the slain. His trumpeters called for victory so frequently that their lungs swelled and voices broke. Arthur's song was grand, his daring renowned.

And Arthur was mighty. Arthur was fair. Arthur was triumphant and wise and beloved by all of Britannia, a king who kept his peoples unknown to the strifes our land suffered whilst leaderless. Famine, disease, sedition, poverty: It is Arthur we praise for their eradication. It is Arthur we worship as heir-divine.

'Tis true he kills many, many men, but Arthur is a warrior. It is expected to slay thy enemy. 'Tis true also he fornicates with lasses in every town, but this too is expected. Tales of Arthur's lusts are heralded as exultantly as the sonnets of his battles, for when one speaks of our king's conquests, damsels and dragons may be commutable. And because of his loins' unrestraint, it was whispered he took to bed his own half-sister, Morgause.

I knew not the veracity of such musings; hearsay is as prevalent as the nits slumbering in our wool. But one does not discount idle reports either, as disquieting acts have ways to make themselves known, and not even Merlin can always shroud their secrets. Children in the shadows, talking horses, soothsayers, there is always someone—*something*—that is aware of wrongdoing. There are times even blades of grass pass along through their rustles the implications of looming peril.

It takes only tuned ears to hear their message. My raven-haired wife, Roisia, dabbles in dark magik herself (though few would have suspected such a thing), and she expressed those implications would have dire effects far-reaching even to us, though when or how she could not presage.

I worried not long at her augury, for certain events were soon dragged woefully from the mucous pits whence they stewed. *May Day*... That is when the rustles of grass grew loudest. And thereafter did Roisia glimpse what Merlin saw in his flames: That Arthur had made child with Morgause, wicked she who by seduction avenged her husband, the defeated Lot Luwddoc. Wicked she who bore most terrible enmity toward our beloved King Arthur. Wicked she who poisoned Arthur's dreams and his seed before taking flight.

Merlin foretold that this son of Arthur would himself begin the fall of Camelot, and at any cost the infant must be found. The child was born on May Day, Merlin ciphered, but the location was not known. As with all sorcerous ways, only certain shadows may be seen and not others.

King Arthur ordered all boys thus born that year on the first of May be brought before him. Mothers and fathers rejoiced that their sons were perhaps "significant" and willingly delivered their children to Arthur for blessing in providence of some great destiny foretold. It *was* destiny indeed foretold yet, alas, not in fortuity . . .

So too were there parents who mistrusted the king's decree—regardless of his trumpeted rectitude—and sought to hide their such-born sons. But Merlin's finger found them all. One-by-one we soldiers were pointed to hiding nooks beneath straw-filled beds or in small chests or behind false walls, mothers angry with fright and tears as we tore babes from their homes.

No reason was given them, no comfort provided, no word spoke further of the matter. The May Day-born sons of farmers, merchants, nobles, and beggars alike were taken and set to nurse at a secretive *hof* of clay floors and low ceiling, a shadowy relic from the days when pagan Vikings held the land. There they remained until decided upon. Roisia, through her "sight," told me the child Merlin and Arthur sought had been collected, though they could not determine which of the infants he was.

And so, two nights passed 'til I found myself on a secret mission. On Arthur's order, I and a dozen others, led by the knight, Anguselus, were ordered to the hof, to retrieve those babes.

Though weather had long been fair, that night turned unaccountably stormy, and the infants cried loud at our arrival, whether from gale or nascent foreboding, I cannot say. The soldier, Hawais, drove a covered wood cart, and his normally taciturn face evinced more dread than I've seen him show in a hundred battles. We took the babes and loaded them in stacks like fleshy logs, and at this, even mighty Symounde trembled.

The cart filled—thirty, forty—I dared not count for fear of weeping. The babies punched and kicked the air with tiny limbs and wailed in tongues none but their own mothers might cipher, calling for these very same mothers who were absent, and the children knowing not why.

Anguselus gave the command, and we departed thence for the seashore. Perhaps more enchantments filled the air as we encountered no one on that midnight road. 'Tis a strange thing, is it not, that the cries of so many infants streaming across the countryside like wafting fumes should not draw the inquiry of a righteous man? But t'was true. Though if Merlin wove a spell of secrecy o'er us, why, I ask, could he not have silenced those May babes? Or perhaps many *did* hear the wails, but sensing the malevolence of our charge, chose rightly to hide in the deepest of cellars or 'neath the thickest of blankets, praying such ill-omens never to find them. For evil such as this must always leave a linger, a residue of char and hideous smoke.

After some hours we reached a spit none could name that stabbed out into the great, frothing ocean. A small ship there awaited us, a flat-bottomed cog with single mast. Its sail was set. There was no rudder. Ierimiah, the noted jouster, whispered desperately for forgiveness, even as he took the first of the infants and laid him within the ship. If cries were knives, we should all have been sliced asunder by the child's desperate wails, pleading in dribble-specked bleats.

We worked with the haste of furies stacking the others into the boat. The wind howled malisons upon us and hastening rain drove nettles into our eyes and hands, but still we obliged our oaths of duty to Arthur. For if our king decrees this for the good of the realm, then it must be so, regardless of its despicability. And when its terrible cargo made ready, Ranulf pushed the ship into the angry, storming sea. Like mewlings of terrified kittens thrown out and drowning in a well, so too were the babes' cries—Arthur's cursed son among them—drowning under the waves of the great brine. The boat sped away, caught by the wind, and gray crests rose up like mountain slabs and fell over its bow and the mewling worsened . . .

Our orders completed, we fled. The cries fell silent as we galloped away, and I pledged to never bethink upon those events again, believing that for the greater good, the realm had been saved.

And so it was, until the dreams . . .

As when I laid in bed aside my wife and amongst the living, the dead infants haunted me . . . They promised what awaits, what befalls the butchers of bairns, and I believed all.

For the next month, on its first day, Anguselus the knight vanished from his manor. All of court wondered at his disappearance, yet no trace of him could be found. Even Merlin appeared to inquire, though he made public no venture. When his eyes met mine, he looked away.

The following month, too on its first day, another soldier was taken, Gaffere. I'd served with Gaffere at the battle of Bedegraine, and at the rout of Gwynn Collynn, and no fiercer a warrior may be found. Yet by dawn he was gone, as if a flounder snatched suddenly away by an unsparing fisherman's net.

Month by month it was so for Peregryne, and then Ranulf, and thereafter Haweis, each taken by an incremental turn of our Julian calendar. Even Ierimiah was soon lost, he whose pleas that night by the sea for forgiveness surely fell upon ears as unheeding as those who heard the crying babes.

Roisia toiled to ward off this strange bane. She wove spells like golden thread upon a loom of safeguard, and she sought council with the ageless crones underground, chanted songs of babble in the glades, pricked her finger to mine, even while a child of our own coupling took seed in her belly and ripened through the season. And still Roisia wove more, suffering malaise and bemoaning the limitations of her ensorcelled prowess. She was not Merlin, after all, nor Morgana, nor Nimueh, nor even Morgause, the least, but cruelest of them all. But finally, Roisia swore, her magik was enough to shield me, its continuance tolled by the beating of her heart.

And at the next month's start, upon a waning-moon's night, Symounde was vanished. After two fortnights Theoflis followed, and so then Maucolyn. The soldiers were taken, as passed the months, an unremitting progress of time that leads all to its terminus, soon to be gone, gone, gone . . .

After eleven months, eleven men went missing by unknown cause, and by the twelfth, only I and one more remained from that night of horror. I rode to this last soldier, Kenward, and we sought Merlin for help, but he would not hear us. We begged Arthur's audience, but he would not see us. It were as if another spell of secrecy was cast, and we were forgot by those we once served. And as a new month came, I alone stood by Kenward's side for whatever might show. Kenward, who was swarthy and hale, once had hair as raven-colored as my wife's, but of late it'd turned ashen and listless, much as the man himself.

We waited by torch in his estate, and at the bell's midnight toll they came . . .

Nere able to crawl, they showed atop the garden wall like cherub-faced goblins. They appeared when I glanced away, and the sound was of foul mewling; they were the babes we had drowned, surging to us upon an invisible current, their movements in fleeting tumbles, as if tossed to and fro amidst churning waves.

The May Day babes were naked and bloated with brine, skin like blue sponges that hold all they can and ooze excess. Their cries spoke not of vengeance, but still of fright, of pain and despair.

As that tide washed closer and closer I swung my sword—mercifully—cleaving the first child's head from its wriggling body. But its sobs did not stop, the sound instead turning only hollow, as if blowing through a chafe of wheat, even as the child's head flowed nearer, vanishing, then emerging, dipping and surfacing beneath unseen waves.

Kenward babbled ungodly oaths while cutting through one infant, then another. Suddenly he shrieked at being touched by something most frigid, causing him to abandon wits and flee. At that, the waves broke over him, while skirting me, and the dead children carried Kenward to fathoms from which there is no return.

By morn, I returned home alone, and all distanced from me but my wife, dearest Roisia, whose mother's mother danced by night in the misty bosk of the fae. And days fell away, sloughed-off skin for tomorrows, and I thought less of myself and more of my beloved, preparing to birth that following month . . . and a horrible voice filled my head: *Would my fealty have remained so resolute if our own sired were born that day of May?*

And too soon, the thirteenth month commenced. Roisia stayed with me all night, working at her spells . . .

Though I swore to smell a waft of sea salt and cold rot, the dead babes did not come. By my beloved, it worked! Roisia had saved me, and I revered her the more, and we spoke in hope for the constancy of my stayed time.

It is Arthur and Merlin who are the villains, she told me. *As oath required, I only carried out their orders, but they should be held most accountable.*

Her sight showed a day not far-distant that Arthur and Merlin will perish, their fall begat by a May Day babe—the cursed son of Arthur himself—who by wonder survived that ocean storm, while the other innocent children perished. Theirs will be tragedies all, in which no peace is ever found.

Some days passed, each a joy in itself, as worries of the drowned babes lessened while hopes for our own family thrived. And soon that day of celebration arrived, for my wife's belly set to burst, and a midwife called for. 'Tis a most painful labor, I understand, for any woman to give birth, and I did all I could to comfort Roisia whilst in her throes.

My wife's cries were brave at first, but after many hours they turned savage and racking. Her hand gripped mine with the strength of a manticore, and she writhed as her innards clenched and eased and clenched again.

The water broke from between her legs, gushing to the ground, and I unexpectedly thought of stormy ocean waves. Roisia moaned and flailed from her back, and I thought of those babes kicking the air with tiny limbs, squirming so helpless and wretched.

A soft cry rose, a bleating wail from the darkness of her womanhood even 'fore the crest of the infant's head did show. The midwife's face puzzled.

A second cry joined, frightened mewling from a great distance but drawing near. The midwife's face remade to concern, and by the third crying voice, the fourth, the chorus, she'd taken to frenzy.

I know not why we hadn't considered some wickedness, not braced for an attempt, not thought for this, but that they'd made a way to me.

The first dead babe spewed from Roisia, and she shrieked for there were more passing through, many more, splitting her womb asunder in terrible rolling waves. Bits of her splattered my tunic, precious lumps colored as wet rust and bitter wine, and incurably ravaged. Roisia's eyes found mine for a trice, then turned up, white, and she convulsed again, splitting at the seams like a burlap sack that bears too many potatoes. The children's number grew . . . Thirty, forty, I dared not count for all was in crashing fury, lunacy, screams, and chaos.

Roisia's magik was enough to shield me, its continuance tolled by the beating of her heart, and at that beating's cessation, the babes were unfettered . . . my dearest had wove so busily for me, thinking not of herself, thinking not she be menaced, and perhaps t'was true, but that she'd interfered with reparations of the damned.

Somewhere else the midwife had fallen—Fainted? Taken? I did not know, and I did not probe, for if I looked back further, I would turn unhinged.

I fled outside.

Above stayed a moon so swelled its luster was like filaments snaking down through the sky, and I reached for mercy to take hold and be risen away, but at those hopes its clinquant light thus dimmed. The night turned too dark, and the crashing waves of dead babes surged from behind, and I would flee no more . . .

Hence here I wait, O shades, knowing my words run low. I resign my fate, for who can escape the ocean that knows no shore?

And at the last I cry this grief for you, mine sad notes as those who fall lost, for such is life but we are all babes cast adrift in the great sea of nothingness, wailing for life amongst turbulent waves, until drowning beneath it all.

CARMINE LIPS AND A FADE INTO OBLIVION

AT sunset, Jack Queen opened the balcony's glass door, and a spray of fine sand came in with the breeze, sprinkling across his black derby shoes and over the carpeted floor. Once there'd been housekeeping here, but no more.

Outside, the blue waves were peaceful, gentle things rolling over the beach, and in the distance the turn of the cove rose high, up into cliffs that were rocky and mysterious and dotted with tall pines. All of it—the scenery anyway—was just as he remembered when coming here in youth.

"Melancholy much?" Ava asked, joining him.

"Over there," he said, pointing to a line of square white buildings wrapping around the shore, "I stayed for a week with friends. We rented a room that was much too small, but it was all we could afford. There was a festival, this car show and rock bands and swing dancing, all the retro nods. I could really rattle a dance hall back then."

"Well, Daddy-O, you sound like one cool cat."

He hadn't smiled in a long time, not until meeting her. Now it felt normal again. "Nothing like you, kitten."

She trailed one long finger along her bottom lip, taking a smear of carmine lipstick with it. She touched it to the tip of his nose, leaving a mark. "For you."

She was quick. But so was he. Jack moved in for a kiss, just a peck. "For you."

A daub of her carmine stayed on his lips. It tasted vaguely like the cherry on an old fashioned sundae.

Ava's giggle belonged on stage. "At this rate, you'll be wearing more cover-up than me."

"Who have I to impress, but you?"

"Lucky fella, you're a mile ahead."

He closed the glass door, drew the gold pleated drapes like the ending of a show. The room darkened.

"I feel so covert in the shadows," she said.

"I always liked my privacy."

"For later, then."

"Yes." She took his hand. She wore a ring on every other finger, each with a different gemstone: pink diamond, purple topaz, green emerald, there were more. Under the sun, her hands sparkled. "Ready?"

"As ever."

They left the hotel room together, went out the long cement landing to a flight of stairs, her five-inch heels clacking with each step. Besides the soft din of the sea, and the screech of a toppling metal signpost, there were no other sounds.

At the bottom of the stairs, through a cobblestoned path lined by overgrown lavender and wild sage, past the fountain of a dolphin that no longer worked, was a narrow turnabout in front of the lobby entrance. There were two cars on long-flattened tires, and Jack pointed to the first, a silver Jaguar Roadster with top down and the inside leather a pale cream, all of it speckled by the glittering of sand.

"That one."

Ava nodded, approving. "It suits you."

Jack escorted her to the passenger side, and said to the empty valet counter, "No need, Jeeves, I'll get the door."

Once in, she brushed back a lock of raven hair and opened a vintage Chanel clutch. Took out a compact. Looked at her reflection and flicked away a stray lash.

When Jack got in, he saw her watching through the reflection. She winked. He winked back. The clutch was still open, in her lap. It took only a passing glance to know what else it held.

"A girl can't be too careful," she said, returning the compact inside.

"Better to have and not need than to feed the worms. I think Tennyson said that."

She cocked a perfect eyebrow. "Hm?"

"Maybe not."

She slapped his shoulder. Her fingers lingered there, then trailed down his arm like falling tears.

He put an old key in the ignition that didn't fit. It didn't matter. He forced it in as far as it would go, then he sank back into the seat, dreaming of a road.

Her hand moved to the AM radio and spun the loose chrome knob, watching the little red needle fly back and forth silently across its glass face.

Jack began to sing. "*Don't let the stars get in your eyes . . .* "

"That ain't half bad," she said.

"Thanks. Choir as a kid."

"And look where it got you now."

"Serenading a doll."

"You got a way, Jackie boy."

He reached into his jacket pocket, pulled out a metal case. "Mind a smoke?"

She already had a lighter in hand, and lit one for them both. She leaned over, laid her head on his chest, and they were silent, sharing that last cigarette, gazing up at the sky that closed in around them in indigos and mauves while a moon slowly appeared as something between a shimmering pearl and a pool of champagne.

After some time, he sighed and flicked the glowing stub out the car, and it sailed end over end into eternity. "What do you know, we've arrived."

"And not a red light on the way."

He got out, went around, opened the passenger door for her. She took his arm, and they took their time moving past the same empty valet counter and into the lobby where sand skittered across the floor, and a cobweb draped away into shadows.

"The lounge here," Ava said, "I heard Dean Martin once played."

"No kidding," Jack said

"The things a girl knows. Allow me to order?"

"Surprises are the spice of life."

"More than ever."

The doors to the lounge had been fastened open, and they went inside. It was empty, but for them, with a dance floor that was intimate and painted to show the silhouette of a jazz ensemble. Tables-for-two circled around, and Jack chose one in the center, where a glass skylight arched over, and a line of chandeliers cut across.

Ava went behind the bar, mixed them each a Whiskey Smash from bottles that still lined the dusty shelves.

"We're the last two people in the world, kiddo. Make 'em strong," he said.

"We don't know that."

"The last two people around here, at least. It's too late to find anyone else."

She met him at the table and set down matching highballs. "Button those lips, baby. The subject's sore, after all."

He looked her in the eyes. "You're right. And you're beautiful."

She touched the lipstick smear on the tip of his nose. "You've still got my color."

"I'm keeping it. For luck."

"It's all coming your way then." She opened her clutch and pulled out a small plastic bottle. It was filled with colorless pills. She set it on the table in between their drinks. The end of the world, or a little sooner, otherwise . . .

He eyed it, then looked away. That smile, he couldn't help it—it came back.

She said, "Whenever you're ready."

His hand reached out to touch the plastic bottle, then changed course. He instead lifted a glass, and she did too. "Cheers to the years."

"Wish there'd be more," she said quietly.

They drank, and he took her hand, swirling one finger around her smooth palm. "A dance?"

"Thought you'd never ask."

They stood and moved to each other, and his arms went around the small of her back, and her arms draped around his neck. He nodded at the bottle on the table. "How long? I mean, once—"

"An hour, maybe two, if we're lucky. After that there'll be nothing left of us to find."

"Good thing I feel lucky tonight," and he tapped the tip of his nose.

He gave her a little twirl, and then half-stepped to the side, and she came back and stepped with him, their legs intertwining, and he nuzzled under her ear, and she held him tighter.

"All this sand," Jack said. "The dust that remains of a mountain. The Earth, our lives, everything comes to an end."

"Sing me a song, and make it sweet," she whispered.

"*Don't let the stars get in your eyes—*"

In the distance came the terrible roar, searching, nearing . . . Even as far as they were, the room trembled. The chandeliers swayed. They might have been on a ship cresting a wave.

"It's a ways off, yet," Jack said.

"An hour, maybe two," Ava replied. "If we're lucky."

"Timing, ain't it?"

"Serendipitous, at the least." She pulled him back to the table. "Better for us than the others."

She returned to the bar and poured another round, then they took the drinks and the pills, and he took her hand, and they left the lounge, the lobby, the dead silver Jaguar behind, and went back up the stairs to the room where the drapes were already pulled closed.

"I heard it's a thing to see," Jack said, "when it reaches us in the end."

"Shh, the subject is sore."

So Jack instead vowed to take off the rest of her lipstick without using his hands, and Ava giggled, and another roar came, louder and nearer, and they rode it out in each other's arms for that last hour or two, until it was all done.

THE FIRST ORDER OF WHALEYVILLE'S DIVINE BASILISK HANDLERS

I NEVER heard of basilisks 'til the night of Murrell's barn dance, but that was the night I met Rosalie, so the basilisks sorta took a back seat in my thoughts. I think it was Ronny Loom who told me, though his brother, Carter, was there too, and they're one 'n the same, being just a year apart and closer than spittin' twins.

"Poppa told me basilisks are crossing the Nolichucky River," Ronny said. "Heard Lilac and some men from Kingsport bagged half a dozen already, but more keep showing up. Lilac says they're worth more'n cougar pelts."

"That old trapper's still around?" I asked, more interested in hearing 'bout him than gabbing on new mountain game. Legend was, Lilac Zollinger had once been engaged to my great-granny Lizbeth, but Great-Grandpa Micajah dueled him for her hand and won, leaving Lilac with a bullet in the shoulder. He healed, except for his pride, which supposing got wounded the most. "Heard Lilac caught the scythe two summers ago by way of momma grizzly."

"He survived that," Carter said. "Thought everyone knew."

Me and the Looms passed under the banner for Murrell's dance and into his barn. Its double red doors were shuttered open and breathing yellow light like a hell cat, silhouetting straw-hatted farmers and their bonnet-hatted wives.

"Harv Ridout says Lilac won't sleep under a roof, but rather beds down among the trees each night so he won't soften up like us townies," Ronny said.

Carter added, "Harv Ridout says Lilac punched a wolf that was fightin' him over a cottontail."

I rolled my eyes. "Harv Ridout's got less sense—"

The sudden scream of fiddle severed my words, then the clang of guitar followed, and soon a gaggle of folks lined the varnished floor kickin' up their legs like a train of asses. I never cared much for dancing and don't know what others see in it. It's not like *kissin'* or anything, not even a little, and I should know 'cause I done both. Dancing, you're not even allowed to touch girls 'cept on their hands, or Pastor Wright'll whip your bottom scorched as Hell's eternal fury for such a sin.

That's when a girl I never seen before swung from the dance line, twirling delicate as a marigold bloom. Right away, my insides turned light and fizzy, like if ever I thought to float on moonlit mist, now would be the moment. She was tall and skinny, like me, but her hair went dark, and her eyes shone like copper pennies set in fire 'til they glowed and sizzled. She wore a dress pretty as first snow, and it clung to her in the middle and billowed out everywhere else as she moved.

Truth was, I never felt that way looking at a girl before, not even when kissing Aimee Greenwood last Harvest Day. I only kissed Aimee 'cause she started it, but I liked it too, though how it felt didn't compare a blue belle to how seeing this new girl weave and bow to each man in line did. Suddenly I felt dancing would be the greatest thing in the world, especially if with her.

"New girl in town," Ronny and Carter said together. "Heard her name is Rosalie Jacobs."

"Rosalie," I repeated, and I wondered where she came from. In Whaleyville, everyone knew everyone—even new folks—but she was a puzzler.

Murrell's barn was stuffy hot that night, and the back of my neck stuck to the shirt collar with sweat. I ran a checkered sleeve across my forehead and it came away damp and grimy, though I still felt my best in over two years, since that terrible day at the revival.

"I'm gonna ask her to dance," I vowed. But no sooner had the words been spoke did that vow fall to bitter ash when I saw Rosalie link arms with Luke Holder.

Ronny and Carter shook their heads somber as grave diggers. Luke Holder was older'n us, sized the three of us together, and meaner than a pecker full of sin. It was the cruel joke of the county that he was good looking too, with a big, perfect smile that made gals do funny things, and with eyes blue as winter quartz: cold and hard and sharp enough to cut, should you fall on 'em the wrong way.

"Hellfire," I muttered.

Rosalie and Luke swirled and dipped in the center of everyone, and Luke's hand dipped below her waist too, lower than was decent. I couldn't believe no one blinked at that, not even Pastor Wright who would've had my hide skinned and burned for offering to His Heavenly Mercy. Rosalie giggled, and I could've puked.

"Heard Missus Janey's got sweet tarts she made from honeycomb," Carter offered as consolation.

"Sounds fine," I admitted, and we went off, the sounds of music and scuffin' all around, Joe Halverson's mouth harp pickin' up speed and Holly Barber calling steps.

Must've been forty, fifty people dancing in the barn that night, and the big oak beams shook with the ruckus of stomping feet and caterwauls and everyone-but-mine's laughter. We settled on a bench of hickory and tasted the sweet wonder of Missus Janey's tarts, and I started feeling better.

"Wonder if Lilac would take us with him after some of those basilisks," Ronny mused. "Wouldn't mind to mount one for Poppa's trophy room."

I shrugged my shoulders. "What's a basilisk anyway?"

"Ain't you heard?" Carter asked. "They've been crossing the Nolichucky."

"Yeah, I heard. What of it?"

"Well, they ain't natural. Jonas Teakle called 'em the kings of snakes, but said they're not entirely serpents either, only half-so. They were called forth by the pastor at Swannanoa's church, and he's to blame they're escaping, on account he's false and their church is awful wicked and full o' sin."

"Can't be worse than ours," I said, mocking.

Ronny and Carter both threw me strange glances, and I pretended to wipe away crumbs, hiding my face. They might've said something unkind next, but then trouble occurred. Seemed Luke Holder hankered for sweet tarts, too, and he wanted Rosalie to delight in their savor alongside him.

Each was panting and flushed from dancing when they came beside us.

". . . and then I split three logs at the same time," Luke told her. "And Judge McClellan said he never seen anything like it."

"Three logs?" Rosalie repeated back, that coppery fire of her eyes seeming to burn brighter. "You'd have to be strong as an ox."

"Bet I am!" Luke answered. "And hungry as one. Wait 'til you try these tarts."

Missus Janey had stacked several dozen tarts upon a porcelain plate, and set that on a tub for folks to help themselves. You could now see the painted rose blooms and vine swirl whimsies covering the plate's face, 'cause most of the tarts had been taken off and eaten within the first hour, they tasted *that* good. In fact, only two sweet tarts remained, and Luke and Rosalie reached for them.

I can't help it, but sometimes there's a sore, vindictive part of me that resents others gettin' things I can't have. That little voice took to whispering: *It ain't fair Luke Holder gets to have the girl* and *the last of the tarts.*

My arm didn't seek council with my brain and seemed to shoot out on its own; I snatched the last two tarts from the plate and stuffed 'em both in my mouth.

"Oh no," the Loom brothers said.

"What in thunderation?" Luke yelled. "Those were our tarts!"

I tried to smartly reply how his name wasn't written on them, but my mouth was so full of the honey-baked pastries when I spoke, all that came out were chunks of sweet pie and sugar-berries spittin' into Luke's face and the front of his fringe-lined dress shirt.

"Oh no," the Loom brothers repeated.

My face flushed at the realization of what I'd done, and what I knew would be given in return; I expected the color filling my cheeks was probably as crimson as Luke's own face, though I wasn't mistaking his reddening for any type of shame. I wanted to tell him it wasn't my fault, I just act without thinking sometimes, but my mouth was sticky, and I feared what else might come out. I raised my hands to him, fingers outstretched in surrender, and they were smeared by the guilt of delicious berries. He lifted fists that could split three logs at the same time . . .

I expected Luke to be angry, and I expected I'd be hit, and I expected the Loom brothers to stand idly aside. What I didn't expect was Rosalie's reaction.

She nodded at me, like we were akin in something, and when her copper eyes glinted, I wondered what terrible secret she knew.

Then Luke's fists arrived.

NEXT morning was Sunday, and no one in Whaleyville missed attending church, regardless how poorly or humiliated they felt, or how many bruisings their face took the evening before at hands of the town lout.

Breakfast weighed heavy in my guts when we packed the rough pews of Whaleyville's First Methodist Church of God Holiness, and that was not a good thing. Never a sermon passed that I wasn't compelled to rise and sit and rise again, jostled and shoved by gibbering neighbors, forced to my knees, yanked by my collar, and threatened with eternal brimstone by frothing Pastor Wright. My innards cringed at the thought, as did my quivering knees. I hated it, just hated it, and each week I thought I might water my trousers wonderin' if the Lord would again save me.

"Receive the genuine Holy Ghost fire!" Wright shouted. "Receive, because God loathes any man who keepeth sin in his heart. Receive!"

"Receive!" Pa and Ma and my little brothers and everyone else in the congregation shouted in kind.

"Don't question His will like a puppet of Cain, fill yourself with faith! Receive the Word of God!"

Pastor Wright was fat, and I don't mean overweight like the seams of his suit coat needed loosening, but he was so over-sized he couldn't even wear a coat, and the Ladies Auxiliary had to sew special garments for him, cobblin' fabric gathered by collection plate. When Wright bellowed *The Good Word,* his chins shook back and forth like each was battling first to be saved, and his belly plummeted down and bounced back up like a supplicating heathen. Suppose gluttony wasn't so much a sin to him as it was a half-handed suggestion he could shrug off while suckin' down a couple wine-basted pheasants.

"Receive!" Wright shouted again, and we echoed it, and he rattled off a thousand Bible verses, and everyone swayed and repeated those verses by heart, and they cried tears and fell to their knees while doin' so, and a couple old ladies even fainted.

Before the revival, that would've been the culmination of our sermon, the wailing-and-gnashing-of-teeth response to satisfy any holy roller that he'd put the fear of Satan in our hearts and brought us begging for salvation.

But Wright wasn't like other pastors and, for him, our worship thus far was just stretching before a ball game.

Prior to the revival, we'd been Whaleyville's First Methodist Church, without the 'of God Holiness' tacked on its end. Walt Brackenbury was pastor then, and he was a fine enough man, tough on Sundays, but friendly thereafter. Then Creighton Wright came challenging, and he brought his tests of "true" faithfulness: *The snakes.*

For Wright, it was simple enough to uncover non-believers by way of handling rattlesnakes: After all, God would shield those who led a Holy seasoned life. The snakes knew your heart, and if you were faithful, then by Grace you'd be saved, and the rest be damned.

Pastor Brackenbury must have been a charlatan, not living a genuine godly life, for he didn't survive that first test of purity, nor did any others who clung to Brackenbury's "flaccid" style of worship. Indeed, I thought myself faithful enough, but that hubris proved me as corrupt as Cain's puppets, for the snakes bit me too, and I nearly died that day.

I'd since been terrified that my failings would prove too indecent an abomination to be weekly forgiven. I wanted to live God's life, not from fear of damnation, but from fear of the serpents. I tried, but my flaws were known . . .

"Satan throws lies in our face, and you must throw back those lies! Armor yourself with the genuine Holy Ghost fire. Receive!"

Ronny and Carter stood in front of me, and they screamed with arms lifted to touch the rafters, "Receive!"

Jenny Teakle, cousin of Jonas, started convulsing and fell to the floor flopping like a fish pulled to the bank of the Nolichucky.

"She's received!" went the joyous cry.

Old Mrs. Kittenridge, filled with arthritis, leapt in the air like a fervent hare.

"She's received!"

Mary Ruth Barton started screaming, only they weren't just shrieks, but actual words, though I couldn't understand them, sounding like a duck quacking in Latin. Her rabid tongue hung from her mouth, and she jabbered away as the others cried, "She's received!"

Four boys each carried in a snake box to Wright, and the sound of rattles clawed at my senses, louder and louder, promising to finish what they began two years prior. The beading sweat like I'd had at Murrell's barn dance returned to my forehead, only now it turned cold, even though the church already felt hot enough to cook us all. Someone shrieked and another collapsed.

"Behold the agents of God!" Wright proclaimed, pulling out a rattler that must've been seven feet long. "Blessed be their judgment, for we will cast out the non-believers!"

That snake was a monster, hideous and terrible, striped orange and black with eyes yellow as angry flames. Wright held it to his huge face and the snake bared long fangs. "Jesus shield me!"

And he kissed the thing right on its awful mouth, a deeper kiss even than I gave Aimee Greenwood last Harvest Day, tongue and all.

"Only the repentant receive benediction!" the pastor shouted. "Come forth in faith!"

And we came, Pa and Ma pulling me in a rush with the crowd to prove none of them was less holy than any others, and I shook with terror.

The serpents were passed around like taking communion, people accepting and crying in tongues, and the snakes answering back. Parents and children caressed the rattlers together as if they were precious as a mewling infant's cheek, petting the sinewy coils and glittering scales. The crowd surged like a swirling whirlpool with Wright at its center, and his rattlers hissed and judged, and one-by-one the people of Whaleyville were found righteous, unless they weren't. Three people screamed for real and fell to the floor, filled not with His heavenly spirit, but rather filled with the wicked yellow venom of the vipers.

"Open your heart to the Lord, and repent your sins," Wright said, "or the snakes will know ye!"

Pa cried out, "I coveted my neighbor John Loom's crop of bean shoots last week!" and he took a snake.

Ma admitted, "I lied when I told my sons our dead dog went to heaven, since I know animals ain't got souls!" She took the snake passed over from Pa.

I was next, and Wright shouted, "Repent!"

Horrible thoughts of the revival tent came to me, two years back when I first took a snake. I hadn't been found worthy then, and a viper's bite sickened me with wither and seizures.

Memories brought terror, and I cried tears and shouted, "I had unclean thoughts about Rosalie Jacobs last night in bed!"

The shame washed over me, the stigma and guilt of everyone knowing my deficiencies. And suddenly I saw her, halfway back in the clutches of our shrieking and chanting flock, and I averted my eyes, but not before I saw Rosalie's red lips rise in a strange, biting smile.

But the power of salvation took hold and must have leeched the sin from my heart, for my mind cleared and I immediately felt righteous. I took the rattler by its neck and its mouth hissed open and a probing, forked tongue shot at me, testing, but I stayed strong, unflinching, even when its fangs reached for my wrist . . .

O! It rattled its war cry and tried my spirit, but finally acquiesced that my faith was good, and the serpent grew harmless as a spring pond.

"Hallelujah! Hallelujah!" went the cries, and I was proven righteous as the lot.

THE congregation picnicked afterward, as the weather was fine, and folks gotta eat, so we may as well do it together since Whaleyville likes to call itself "tight-knit."

I still felt righteous, but I also knew I lied to myself a little, as part of me didn't regret at all those unclean thoughts of Rosalie . . . I only repented from fear of the snakes, which was greater than my desire of her, though that didn't cause my longing to be any lessened.

Gingham cloth was spread out, and some splintered benches and tables moved beneath giant boughed trees that were fat as Pastor Wright. The women set to laying plates and pouring drinks, and groups of men gossiped around us. I made out Herb Cranston's voice above the others.

" . . . Heard a basilisk got at Philemon Talbot's cousin in Kingsport last week, and that cousin died faster than a flying turd hits earth."

"We gotta do somethin' about it," said Holly Barber, who called the dance last night. Holly was a stout, zealous man with side whiskers that billowed under his chin like wild brambles. "Those snakes are crossin' the river."

"Ain't natural snakes, either. Hell spawn, called forth by Swannanoa's church. It's a wonder they ain't been struck down for the abomination they are."

"Snakes with the heads of chickens," Jonas Teakle added, winking at his cousin, Jenny. Jonas was always winking at her and, rumor was, he'd taken her in the husband-sense long ago and continued still, even though it wasn't allowed, them bein' cousins and all. He turned and winked the other direction at another cousin, Jimmy.

Herb replied, indignant, "We oughta teach them what the holy judgment of rattlers can do . . . "

Other men joined in, and their voices and words became indistinguishable.

"You hear that?" I asked Ronny. "They're talking about snakes with chicken heads."

"That's what we were telling you last night. Don't you listen? And the basilisks ain't chicken-headed, they're rooster-headed."

"That's perplexing."

"Heard it true from George Templeton."

"Well, I never heard of such a thing." We sat squeezed between devout Jameson Lightspeed on one side and the freckled Peckingpaw sisters on the other. I thought briefly of the three folks snake-bit today, of what they might have done worse than the rest of us, then presumed God or Wright would either save 'em or damn 'em, and join us for chicken wings and slaw afterward.

Carter said, "Lilac's been trackin' the basilisks down, but the things ain't amiable to extermination."

Ronny added, "Heard you look at one and it'll turn you straight to stone."

I couldn't even reply, that notion sounded so asinine, and I made a face that told as such.

"And if the basilisks bite you," someone added from behind, "their venom will melt the flesh off your bones."

The voice startled me, being so near. I turned, and it was none other than Rosalie Jacobs.

I puckered with humiliation. No one wants a gal to publicly discover she's the object of his midnight fantasies, and now I had to face her after professing all in church.

Ronny gulped. Carter sputtered, "A—Ain't heard that."

"I hear a lot of things," she said, "though just because it's preached, don't prove it true."

Rosalie stood over me as I sat, and her hip nudged my arm, and her hand squeezed my shoulder. The touch felt gentle and beguiling, a lush cloud to wrap me in scented billows. "That was brave," she said, "to reveal yourself like that."

"I—I'm sorry," I stammered. "I, *uh* . . . it just slipped out."

"You possess good qualities, Davey."

"You know my name?"

"Doesn't everyone know everyone around here?"

True enough. She still held my shoulder, and I saw the tips of delicate fingers splay toward my heart. Her skin was bronzed, and her nails white as daisy blades.

When I looked up to her face, all I could say was, "Where's Luke?"

Her red smile hinted that secret again from last night. "Luke has good qualities too."

Naturally, I didn't know what that meant.

Carter brought the conversation back to him. "So what're you sayin'? Basilisks ain't real?"

"Oh, they're real all right," she replied. "Like your brother said, they've got the heads of roosters. And they have little wings mid-way up the body, stubby things like a baby bat. Not good for much, except lifting the serpent halfway off the ground."

Ronny said, "I gotta see one."

"So you shall," she murmured, and he looked at her curiously.

Carter got himself excited. "I heard they're born from an egg like a chicken, only it's the rooster that lays it, not the hen. You hear that, too?"

"A male laying eggs?" I asked. "That don't make sense. Has the basilisk got the plumbing of both sexes?"

"Actually, a male from any species may lay the eggs for basilisks," Rosalie answered.

My brain twisted on that, while Rosalie gave me a look that sent all wits leaping overboard. She continued, "Though basilisks themselves are always female."

And she stared into my eyes . . .

I heard in school one time that snakes on the other side of the world—cobras—can hypnotize their prey by staring deep into their eyes, and I thought of her look as that; I was immobile, transfixed, rent open for her to peer inside my soul, judging me, as did the rattlers.

Her gaze broke and she let go of my shoulder, shrugging a signal she was done with us.

"See you later, Davey," she said, and I knew that was a promise.

Rosalie walked away, though at the same time I could've sworn I saw her walking away also from Jonas Teakle, winking at him the way he winked at his kin.

NEXT day I woke to screams coming from the neighboring farm, and not at all like the rapturous screams during Pastor Wright's sermon. Pa took his shotgun and ran out, not even wearing a shirt. His bare chest was a carpet of thick black hair, whereas my chest sprouted but few hairs, and those light and scraggly at best.

He didn't wait for me, but I got my own rifle from the oak cabinet and ran after him, as it was my friends, Ronny and Carter's family, who neighbored us.

I arrived there and saw Mrs. Loom was a terrible mess, clenching and unclenching her fists like wringing out an invisible cloth. A pile of bones lay at her feet, pooled by stinking muck that breathed steam and bubbles. She looked like she wanted to touch it, but couldn't bring herself to do so.

Carter stood in the doorframe, pale as a bed sheet. He mouthed, "Oh no, oh no."

"Where's Ronny?" I asked, and Carter's tears told me exactly where he was.

I felt to collapse.

"Goddamned snake monster got in here," Mr. Loom roared. He carried a shotgun bigger'n Pa's. "It slipped out back by the coops. We gotta get it."

He and Pa went that way, and I followed, though they didn't care if I was there or not, so taken were they by hunter's bloodlust.

"Must've crossed from over the river," Mr. Loom yelled. "Damn that hellish town!"

I followed only halfway across the long yard, Mrs. Loom's cries nervously holding me back like a leash.

Just as Pa and Mr. Loom turned out of sight around the coops, I saw it.

The basilisk seemed waiting for me, poised behind a row of hedges, for only when I was alone did it pop out from the dewy leaves. A mask of feathered crust was the creature's face, and the red comb atop its head waggled like swaying sawgrass. Indeed, I'd heard it described, but that didn't lessen my shock seeing a snake with the head of a rooster. It wasn't big, maybe the length of my arm, and half of that was just a long, ropy tail, covered in jade-green scales. Its stumpy wings flapped like crazy, only strong enough to lift the serpent's upper body, just like Rosalie said, so the creature looked like a kite that isn't quite airborne yet, its tail still dragging the ground.

I raised the rifle, but too late, its eyes caught my own! I froze, remembering what Ronny said: . . . *look at one and it'll turn you to stone.*

And it was true . . . I wasn't stone yet, but I couldn't move either, taken by the spell of its magic eyes, and I knew, just *knew*, the monster was reading me—the way Rosalie had—communicating something, or testing some quality of my spirit, and if I didn't pass, transformation of my likeness into rock would befall.

Its ancient eyes glinted at me, a wink of copper-hued acceptance, and I was released. The basilisk dropped tight to the ground, tucked in its lil' wings, and slithered back through the hedges.

I pointed my rifle under obligation and fired half-heartedly. My aim is terrible, and the bullet went wide, as I knew it would.

Pa and Mr. Loom came runnin'.

"I shot at it, but it got away."

Mr. Loom cursed and dashed toward the hedge, where I'd blasted.

I saw Pa glance, not after Mr. Loom, but the other way, enviously at a stand of golden peach trees, knowing that our own trees were withered and gave us shriveled and bitter fruit.

Pa caught my notice, sighed, and clapped me on the shoulder. "Good try, son. At least you tossed lead at it."

RONNY'S death launched the town into arms-bearing fury. By late afternoon a group of men gathered outside our church, led by Pastor Wright spittin' and frothin' and screamin' how we got to claim retribution, there being no allowance for serpents to kill folks in Whaleyville and get away with it (his own serpents being the exception, I presume).

The call went up for a party to hunt downriver next morning and kill every basilisk found, and then cross over to Swannanoa and see what needed doin' there.

Judge McClellan shouted agreement, and so too did Herb Cranston and George Templeton and all the others. Joe Halverson, who played the mouth harp, joined in, only he was smilin' all the while, though it was malicious-like, not a nice or secretive smile the way Rosalie gave to me.

"We oughta catch 'em alive and slice off their wings and tails and eyes, and send 'em still squirming back to Swannanoa's church," Joe said. He was known to break the legs of barking dogs just to watch them suffer for keeping him awake at night. Most folks felt righteous to avenge John Loom's son, but Joe Halverson was of a wrathful and vicious ilk, and he just liked cutting and torturing critters for any reason.

I felt uneasy going, but it's considered a queer thing in Whaleyville to ever decline a hunting trip. Plus Pa was big on it, and since I was friends with Ronny, everyone expected me to crave vengeance.

Though it's true Ronny was my friend, I didn't feel any obligation to avenge him; that small, resentful part of my brain reminded me neither of the Loom brothers ever defended or sought vengeance for me, even when Luke Holder practiced log splittin' techniques on my face at Murrell's barn dance.

COLD night fell, and it was all Pa could do not to wallop something, he was so excited and anxious about the basilisks, both killin' them tomorrow and double-checkin' every room to make sure they didn't slither inside tonight and get us first. Like me, he was temperamental, and I knew that small, resentful voice in my head sometimes also filled his own.

"The Looms have a stronger fence than us, and the creature *still* got through," Pa raged.

"The Looms thought they were better'n everyone else. That's what got 'em." Ma was wary of his moodiness, and weary, too, chasing after my brothers who were fighting and hollering as always.

Pa kicked over a chair, shouting at no one. "Why should their peach trees and bean shoots grow more fertile than ours?"

It all seemed too much, and I decided I'd had enough and said so. "I'm turnin' in."

"Night, Davey," they replied and went back to it.

I bedded down.

Outside, the moon was full like a pregger's belly, it glowing through my window, me pacified by its calm. I gazed upon it, letting sleep rise in slowly cresting waves, when a pebble *ticked* off the glass. The waves of sleep receded. Another pebble, another *tick.*

I went to the window and opened it, and saw fiery copper eyes lit upon a bright, pert face.

"How'd you know where I live?" I whispered.

"Doesn't everyone know everyone around here?" Rosalie replied.

True enough, I thought. *Except for you . . .*

She added, "I'm going for a stroll. Care to join?"

"Right now? At night?"

"Now is the time for all good things."

My mouth went dry. Quick as a whistle, I tossed on my trousers, shirt, and boots, and went out the window to join her.

She took my hand in her own, and it was like seizing a shooting star.

"Thought I'd head to Swannanoa," she said.

"That's fifty miles across the river! And what'd you want there anyway?"

"There's shortcuts everywhere." Her voice fell somewhere between a whisper and a sigh. "And I'll tell you what I want . . . "

The road from my home was gravel and hard earth, but already it seemed to soften under my steps and grow dim beneath rising mist.

"Like to know a secret about your town leader?" she asked.

I acknowledged that I'd love to know Pastor Wright's secrets.

"Your pastor drugs the snakes," Rosalie said, enjoying my eagerness. "The vipers he keeps are harmless, much like a growling bulldog with no claws or teeth."

"Those rattlers got teeth aplenty," I countered. "I seen 'em, I been bit by one!"

"Yes, the snakes retain fangs, but their venom glands are removed. Only parishioners that need be taught his lessons are 'bit,' and sometimes unfortunate others, just to keep the rest of the congregation honest to him. 'Rule by fear' is a common axiom to men like Creighton Wright."

The perplexity on my face must've been obvious as a cannon blast.

She continued. "It's Wright himself who *bites* people. He's got a needle hidden up his sleeve that's double-pronged to match the width of snake teeth. It's filled with rattler juice, and he sticks folks while they're clambering around him, half-frenzied and clutching snakes, so it's not noticed he's the real culprit. People can rile themselves up as much as any rampaging spirit."

I thought of Wright and how large he was, wallowing in the center of us poor, teeming sinners who were unable to see from one side of his girth to the other. He could block our sight with one hamhock arm and we'd be none the wiser while he pricked someone.

"But why?"

"Power. Ambition. The usual cravings. Wright hails from Swannanoa, though he was cast out years ago, trying to supplant certain factions. He's a dwarven man with a giant's measure of himself."

"Go on."

She did. "Your former pastor was a faithful man, kept the river strong between our sides. And he died first at Wright's hand. Now the waters of the Nolichucky are shallowed to puddles."

And so it was, for I saw the once-mighty river far beneath us, a bare and cracked thing, winding between two worlds with no less impact a boundary than a cobweb confining charging steeds. Around us, the night shone brilliant, and flecks of gold and rubies twinkled in the sky, and planets and suns moved aside as we passed.

"You possess good qualities, Davey. Attributes I find attractive."

I blushed that she'd find anything attractive in me compared to Luke Holder. I asked, "And what're those?"

"Your imperfections."

I blanched. "Imperfections, like my flaws?"

"Aren't flaws what make men beautiful?"

"I'm not beautiful."

"You are to me," she said, and my heart filled my mouth.

We arrived in Swannanoa, and what I saw seemed nothing like Whaleyville, nothing like any town I'd ever known. Tall stone buildings crumbled at their tops, like towers long ago marred in siege. The walls were slick with dark lichen, their doors and windows mere openings rough-cut in masonry that showed distant fires burning within. The town slumbered in gloom as if being peered at through shadow wisps.

And it all swept by as a moving picture in fast motion.

Rosalie continued. "I have walked among you and chosen five whose qualities I love."

At this, my heart sank that I was not alone in her favor. "So you're sweet on five of us who are flawed? Wright must be the love of your life."

"Wright is too wound up in his own beliefs. He is wicked, yes, but not . . . obedient."

Rosalie's face was still of beauty, still of midnight longings, but I felt confused, beguiled, even with her arms linked around me, and we swirling through shadow wisps, the way I first saw her swirl at the barn dance.

And the sore, vindictive voice whispered in my mind, *Life ain't been fair since that revival . . .*

We arrived at the end of roads, the bedrock of dreams, the crossroads of light and dark. There was no signage, but I knew it was the fabled church we feuded with, the one Wright laid all blights upon: Swannanoa's First Church of Ecclesiastical Holiness.

And it seemed nothing like First Methodist Church of God Holiness. Whereas our church was a steepled box built of whitewashed wood planks, here a columned façade rose above the stars, and there was no door to close people out *or in*. A pair of stone basilisks stood at each side of the entry, and their eyes followed us as we moved inside where murky gloom wafted like the rest of Swannanoa.

And inside were more basilisks, and they came slithering to our feet.

"Wright binds you through fear," Rosalie said, her voice a slippery thing, like the serpents. "Here it is only love . . . love for the First Order of Whaleyville's Divine Basilisk Handlers."

"The what?" I said, feeling myself tense nervous, fearful, surrounded.

"They love those who love them," she replied. "For basilisks are not invulnerable. Like everything, there's ways to kill them, methods that are timeless, though not oft believed. Our congregation is growing, but still small, still weak. We need men of faith to help protect us."

"Truth of it, I ain't got much faith in anything."

"I will teach you faith. I will show you what it means . . . "

And when she kissed me, a plume of fire charged through my loins, and my eyes rolled back, and my heart slammed against my ribs like an untamable beast raging at its cell. My confusion, my fears melted away, and I gasped.

Rosalie's tongue prodded, slipped between my lips, entered me. It tasted hot and sweet as Missus Janey's tarts, as supple and smooth as butter cream warmed on the hearth. It was lush forests and flowered springs and misty sunbursts. And it was not like kissing Aimee Greenwood either . . .

Rosalie's tongue was slender, delicate, and longer than imagined. Its tip split to a fork, and each end teased a place of my palate before slipping down the back of my throat. Her tongue filled my mouth, filled my airway, and still it kept sliding lower and lower like her hands as they plummeted below my belt.

My whole body went erect, and it seemed hard to relax and lie back on the stone floor when the whole of me wished to bellow in triumph and leap to the sun, but I let myself be led by the feel of Rosalie's blissful instructions, for she told me what to do without any words.

And the entire time, another little voice cried in my brain that this was wrong, this was a terrible, grievous calamity, and I must find the grace and strength to stop, *stop*! This was a different voice, unlike the mutters of resentment so often filling my head, but this new voice sounded mighty akin to the sermons of Pastor Wright, whom I hate, so I told it to shut the hell up.

Hell is exactly what this is, the voice replied, none too subtly, but by then me and Rosalie were as one, and nothing else mattered.

IT was dark when I woke in bed, having slept not at all, and dawn when I arrived at the wooded banks of the Nolichucky, dreading what must be done: I gathered with Pa and the others to hunt down the basilisks.

Twenty or so Whaleyville men were there, though Wright wasn't among us. I doubt he even knew how to hunt, and his bulk would've given him a heart attack anyway, walkin' a quarter mile in those brambles. He was all talk in more ways than one.

I knew most of the others by sight: Philemon Talbot, Joe Halverson, Jameson Lightspeed, Luke Holder, Harv Ridout, Carter and his father, and a dozen more. Only one man I didn't recognize, and he moved among us with purpose and quick words, carrying a rifle and a pack made from 'coon pelts. Though I'd never met him, I'd heard more legends concerning Lilac Zollinger than any other superstition.

He was short and stumpy with a drawn, sallow face carved by hard lines like a mining expedition hacked across it looking for precious, pretty things, of which they found none. He was the oldest man I'd ever seen but he moved like a moonlit whisper, in fleeting darts and cloaked by shadow.

"You're Lizzie's kin," he said, eyeing me while ignoring Pa. "I can tell by the hook nose and way your shoulders slump. Always told her to keep her head high, but she didn't listen."

Took me a moment to figure he was talkin' about Great-Granny Lizbeth, who was granny to Ma.

"Didn't listen either when I said Micajah would do her wrong," the old trapper continued, though his loud voice fell quiet. "That duel 'tween us, my gun misfired. Should be my blood runnin' in your veins, not his. But tell her my regards still remain."

"She died before I was born, sir."

"That don't matter," Lilac shot back. "Don't matter t'all to tell her."

I didn't know how to reply, so cleared my throat in response. Some claimed Great-Granny Lizbeth died mid-life of a lingering sadness, while others said it was no more than Micajah's drunken fists. A fortnight later, Great-Grandpa Micajah got his throat mysteriously slit while sleeping in bed, and that was that.

"Ready to bag some basilisks?" Lilac asked to no one in particular. The other men grunted and hollered and raised their rifles in the air like a group of pale savages, he their elder chief.

"Whatever you do," Lilac said, "don't look in their eyes."

He unshouldered the 'coon pelt pack and pulled out small plates of reflective glass, explaining only, "Mirrors."

Holly Barber replied, "Pastor Wright said quotin' Old Testament scripture oughta do the trick as well as anything else."

"Wright's got less sense than a filled crapper," Lilac snapped, passing out the small mirrors.

"What in Hades we need these for?" Curtis Merriweather asked. "Ain't gonna shave out here."

That got a laugh from the others who were in higher spirits than myself. Most treated the morning as a festive occasion like the annual buck tourney, wagers laid on who'd return home with the highest count.

"Use the mirrors," Lilac repeated. "Don't look in their eyes or you'll turn to stone."

CURTIS Merriweather was the first to look in their eyes and turn to stone. He let out an awful holler like a caught hen, knowing its head was about to elope at the nearest chopping block, and his flailing motions slowed, and his skin hardened to a cracked gray shell, and then Curtis froze solid. It didn't make sense at all, and yet there he was, become like the marble statue of Andrew Jackson that anchors our town proper.

Jameson Lightspeed was next to look into a basilisk's eye, and his cry sounded like a lark that's got its wing shot off, all high-pitched scrills and a fusillade of ruckus. George Templeton was a mauled bear, roaring and bellowing until he became silent.

"Don't look at their eyes!" Lilac reminded us by shouts.

Harv Ridout, like a jackass, followed Lilac's order by closing his own eyes. He stood there, rifle in hand, with eyelids clenched shut as if playing hide-and-seek, and a monstrous gold basilisk slid over, sinking its fangs into his foot. Harv screamed.

Lilac fired at the creature while it was vulnerable pumping venom into Harv, and the serpent burst in half. Its body convulsed once and collapsed, while its winged rooster-head detached from Harv's foot, flew two flaps, then dropped to the scree with a gurgling *squawk*. Harv's skeleton fell next to it in a puddle, the venom having already melted flesh from his bones.

Several of the hunters surrendered their guns right there and fled for home, and maybe they were the smart ones.

"Use the mirrors!" Lilac ordered, and he shot another serpent.

After that, the remaining men sorta fell in line, 'cause the basilisks didn't get any more. Nonetheless, I can't say Whaleyville's men did much damage either, taking pot shots here 'n there, but at least by following Lilac's lead and using the mirrors, they avoided the serpents' gaze and even turned some of the basilisks' eyes back on themselves which fossilized the beasts.

Lilac Zollinger proved a beast himself, a marauding archangel delivering bull's eye retribution through gunfire and mirror flash. He didn't miss a shot, and basilisk after basilisk froze to stone or blew to bits. It's a queer thing, gettin' in the way of a hurricane, and most of us ducked for cover, out of the line of his rampage.

And as I watched him move, victorious, indefatigable against that strange enemy, I thought of Lilac as being righteously triumphant, the sort of man we needed to lead Whaleyville, the sort of man—though gruff—who stood his ground for honor and justice and truly inspired faith. Here was a man who should never lose . . . yet in dueling for the hand of Great-Granny, he'd been jilted by a misfiring gun, and such are events that prove our fallibilities. No one can insure against all odds, no one can imagine *all* outcomes . . .

And surely Lilac did not imagine Luke Holder suddenly lifting a rifle to *him* and firing.

Lilac's forehead blossomed red, right 'tween his eyes, which bulged funny-big in surprise. It was a perfect shot and Lilac dropped like a load of grain. There wasn't anything Luke wasn't perfect at.

Carter mouthed, "Oh no," just like he did when his brother got killed. I lifted my rifle and shot Carter also in the head, but of course my bullet somehow went askew, even though I stood only two feet away. His cheek blew in, and his temple blew out, though I aimed at his forehead like Luke had, but it was good enough regardless, and Carter fell beside the old trapper.

Joe Halverson shot Holly Barber, and Jonas Teakle shot Judge McClellan, and Pa shot Mr. Loom, declaring, "I never liked John Loom anyway."

After the shootin', one other man was left over, Herb Cranston, who didn't know which hand to crap in. Luke levered in another cartridge and shot him too.

That left just five of us, and together we lowered our guns, sharing in the moment.

Though I was with Rosalie all night, it seemed I wasn't the only one she'd bedded, for if I looked close enough at the other men I could see the slight matching bulges in their stomachs—like my own—marking the beginning signs of a basilisk egg growing inside.

Five remained, the First Order of Whaleyville's Divine Basilisk Handlers: Luke Holder, vain and mean; Joe Halverson, wrathful and vicious; Jonas Teakle, lustful and incestuous; Pa, petty and envious; and me, resentful and vindictive. Our weaknesses were known by Rosalie, and our weaknesses were loved.

Later, I'd wonder exactly how those eggs were supposed to come out, but there, on the way home, all I imagined was a fine and mighty revenge coming against fat Pastor Wright and his damned rattlesnakes.

PERSONAL ACKNOWLEDGEMENTS

THANK you, dear reader, for attending this journey with me, and to all others who inspired or promoted this book, or otherwise uplift dark, supernatural, and fantastic fiction.

Great thanks also to publisher Cemetery Dance and acquiring editors Norman Prentiss, Kevin Lucia, and Dan Franklin for believing in and publishing this work.

Thanks also to the Horror Writers Association, who have been an immense resource of technical information, guidance, and insight over the years, especially my local friends in the Los Angeles chapter, who monthly vitalize me with awe and encouragement.

And lastly, most thanks, as always, go to my family for their support: Jeannette, Julian, and Devin.

Midnight cheers,

Eric
Chino Hills, California

PUBLICATION ACKNOWLEDGEMENTS

WITH great thanks to the following publishers who first printed each of the stories included within this book.

"Penny's Diner" © 2022 by Eric J. Guignard. First published in *Not One of Us* #70, April: Not One of Us Press.

"A Kingdom of Sugar Skulls and Marigolds" © 2017 by Eric J. Guignard. First published in *Haunted Nights*, edited by Ellen Datlow: Blumhouse/ Random House.

"If I Drive Before I Wake" © 2021 by Eric J. Guignard. First published in *In Darkness, Delight: Fear the Future*, edited by Andrew Lennon and Evans Light: Corpus Press.

"Bummin' to the Beat of the Road" © 2022 by Eric J. Guignard. First published in *34 Orchard #5*, April: 34 Orchard Press.

"The Telephone Game" © 2024 by Eric J. Guignard. First published in *Weird Tales* #369, July: Weird Tales, Inc.

"The Tale of Samuel Whiskers Continued; or, A London Digression" is published here for the first time. © 2025 by Eric J. Guignard.

"Drink, Drink From the Fountain of Death" © 2022 by Eric J. Guignard. First published in *Voices in the Dark*, edited by Alain Davis, Steve Dillon, and Eugene Johnson: Saturday Mornings Incorporated Press LLC.

"Ritual Sacrifice to the Great God of Skates" © 2024 by Eric J. Guignard. First published in *Cosmic Horror Monthly* #46, April: Cosmic Horror Monthly LLC.

"The Moon Over Andersonville" © 2011 by Eric J. Guignard. First published in *Flashonomics*, edited by Chris Jacobsmeyer: Shade City Press (abridged). First published in *Slices of Flesh*, edited by Stan Swanson: Dark Moon Books (unabridged).

"A Stroke of Death" © 2023 by Eric J. Guignard. First published in *Schlock! Webzine #443*, November: Schlock! Webzine.

"Ommetaphobia" © 2021 by Eric J. Guignard. First published in *Boneyard Soup Magazine #2*, April: Boneyard Soup Magazine.

"The Shimmer of Trees" © 2021 by Eric J. Guignard. First published in *Campfire Macabre*, edited by John Brhel and Joe Sullivan: Cemetery Gates Media.

"The Ascending Lights of Yu Lan" © 2020 by Eric J. Guignard. First published in *Unthinkable Tales Anthology Three*, edited by Sara Howe: Sara Howe Books.

"Two Hearts Make a Half; or, Ghosts of a Rodeo Clown" © 2021 by Eric J. Guignard. First published in *Were Tales: A Shapeshifter Anthology*, edited by S.D. Vassallo and Steven M. Long: Brigids Gate Press.

"Perchance to Dream in Voices of a Fiend: A Fanciful Epilogue to Frankenstein" © 2018 by Eric J. Guignard. First published in *Birthing Monsters: Frankenstein's Cabinet of Curiosities and Cruelties*, edited by Alex Scully and B. E. Scully: Firbolg Publishing.

"Incident at the Red Hawk Road Stop" © 2021 by Eric J. Guignard. First published in *December Tales*, edited by J.D. Horn: Curious Blue Press.

"O Shades, My Woe" © 2016 by Eric J. Guignard. First published in *Ain't Superstitious*, edited by Juliana Rew: Third Flatiron Publishing.

"Carmine Lips and a Fade into Oblivion" © 2019 by Eric J. Guignard. First published in *Cemetery Dance Online*, August: Cemetery Dance Publications.

"The First Order of Whaleyville's Divine Basilisk Handlers" © 2018 by Eric J. Guignard. First published in *The Fiends in the Furrows: An Anthology of Folk Horror*, edited by David T. Neal and Christine M. Scott: Nosetouch Press.

ALSO FROM ERIC J. GUIGNARD AND CEMETERY DANCE:

THAT WHICH GROWS WILD: 16 TALES OF DARK FICTION

That Which Grows Wild collects sixteen dark and masterful short fiction stories by award-winning author Eric J. Guignard. Equal parts of whimsy and weird, horror and heartbreak, this debut collection traverses the darker side of the fantastic through vibrant and harrowing tales that encounter monsters and regrets, hope and atonement, and the oddly changing reflection that turns back at you in the mirror.

• In "A Case Study in Natural Selection and How It Applies to Love," a teen learns about himself while contemplating the theory of Natural Selection as the world around slowly dies from rising temperature and increasing cases of spontaneous combustion.

• In "The House of the Rising Sun, Forever," a tragic voice gives warning against the cycle of opium addiction from which, even after death, there is no escape.

• In "Dreams of a Little Suicide," a down-on-his-luck dwarven man unexpectedly finds his dreams and love in Hollywood as a munchkin for filming of The Wizard of Oz, but soon those rainbow dreams begin to darken.

• In "A Journey of Great Waves," a Japanese girl encounters, years later, the ocean-borne debris of her tsunami-ravaged homeland, and the ghosts that come with it.

. . . and twelve unforgettable others. Explore within, and discover a wild range upon which grows the dark, the strange, and the profound.

Winner of the 2018 Bram Stoker Award®!

Order your copy at www.cemeterydance.com or www.amazon.com

ABOUT THE AUTHOR

ERIC J. GUIGNARD is a writer and editor of dark and speculative fiction, operating from the shadowy outskirts of Los Angeles, where he also runs the small press Dark Moon Books. He's twice won the Bram Stoker Award (the highest literary award of horror fiction), won the Shirley Jackson Award, and been a finalist for the World Fantasy Award and International Thriller Writers Award.

He has over 150 stories and non-fiction author credits appearing in publications around the world. As editor, Eric's published multiple fiction anthologies, including his most recent, *Professor Charlatan Bardot's Travel Anthology to the Most (Fictional) Haunted Buildings in the Weird, Wild World* and *A World of Horror*, each a showcase of international horror short fiction.

He currently publishes the acclaimed series of author primers created to champion modern masters of the dark and macabre, *Exploring Dark Short Fiction*. He is also publisher and acquisitions editor for the renowned *+Horror Library+* anthology series. Formerly, he was curator of the series *Haunted Library of Horror Classics* through SourceBooks with coeditor Leslie S. Klinger.

His latest books are *Last Case at a Baggage Auction*; *Doorways to the Deadeye*; and short story collections *That Which Grows Wild* and *A Graveside Gallery* (both through Cemetery Dance). His newest anthology, *Scaring and Daring*, comes out October, 2025 (HarperCollins).

Outside the glamorous world of indie fiction, Eric's a technical writer and college professor, and he stumbles home each day to a wife, children, dogs, and a terrarium filled with mischievous beetles. Visit Eric at www.ericjguignard.com; Bluesky or X (Twitter): @ericjguignard; or elsewhere via linktr.ee/eric_j._guignard.

www.ingramcontent.com/pod-product-compliance
Lightning Source LLC
Chambersburg PA
CBHW020303030826
48979CB00027B/2040/J
* 9 7 8 1 9 4 9 4 9 1 6 1 6 *